Published by Estep & Fitzgerald Books

Distributed by Ingram Content Group

ISBN-10 0-9987151-5-8   ISBN-13 978-0-9987151-5-5

Printed in the United States of America

10 9 8 7 6 5 4 3 2

ESTEP & FITZGERALD
BOOKS

Find Robbie-Ann McPherson
on Instagram @Author_RobbieAnn
Or Twitter @authorRobbieAnn
www.authorRobbieAnn.com

This book is dedicated to my parents.
I love you more than words could ever express.

TAKING LIBERTY

Table of Contents

Chapter		Page
One	*Escape*	1
Two	*The Kindness of Strangers*	21
Three	*Taking Liberty*	49
Four	*The Best Laid Plans*	71
Five	*What Happened is What Happened*	79
Six	*Mending Fences*	93
Seven	*Discovering Liberty*	105
Eight	*Raising the Roof*	131
Nine	*Silver Bells, Silver Linings*	155
Ten	*Fear Goggles*	193
Eleven	*You Are Enough*	228
Twelve	*No Whining*	267
Thirteen	*Everything Went Black*	279
Fourteen	*Liberty Lost*	288
Fifteen	*Choosing Right*	305
Sixteen	*The Kindness of Strangers, Part 2*	334
Seventeen	*Out of the Woods*	340

CHAPTER ONE
Escape

He didn't even leave the porch light on for me. Asshole.

I fumbled in the dark to slide the key in the deadbolt of our dingy beige apartment.

My shift at the Third Avenue Diner made every bone and joint ache and I could not get out of that polyester-orange Old Maid uniform fast enough. I needed the next two days off. Bad.

Brody wasn't home. He was out with his work friends, former Air Force guys like him, drowning their fears before they left for a contract job in Afghanistan. It was his first private security gig since he left the Air Force six months ago. I was scared for him, but I also couldn't wait until he left. This was life with Brody—mixed emotions, always in conflict, hot-and-cold, angry-then-sweet. I loved him but I hated loving him.

I hated myself for letting him treat me so badly, because I couldn't hate *him*. I needed him but I hated needing him. I was mad at myself for not leaving, but also mad at myself for not being able to make him happy. Everything between us was so infatuatingly good at first, way back when…I guess I kept going back there, trying to drink from that well but it had run dry long ago. He had changed.

I didn't want to be sad, I knew I would miss his arms around me at night, or I would miss his sweet smile that only showed up when he was in his apology phase. Those please-forgive-me phases had gotten shorter lately though.

I focused on the good of him leaving—I'll have six months of freedom from his insults, from his contempt and cruelty. From his constant criticism. From him yelling at me. From his twisting my words around to make me feel crazy. The constant abuse that no one but me seemed to think was really *abuse*.

When I tried to explain it to anyone else they didn't understand it. I didn't even fully understand it. And yet I felt like my insides were pulverized and my entire personality had been erased. What else would you call it? For years I actually called it love.

But then, I stayed. That was the mind-fuck of it all. I couldn't leave, even though I wanted to. Or is it that *I should* leave, and I didn't *want* to? I mean, I wasn't perfect. I didn't want him to go. How could I blame him for my own indecision, because I wouldn't or couldn't leave this shitty relationship? He wasn't awful all of the time, he had his good moments, but they got few and farther in between as time passed. Why did I still love a man who treated me so badly so much of the time?

I wasn't sure which truth was more horrifying—that I was trapped, or that I wasn't really trapped at all.

They were all out getting drunk in downtown Butte Falls—if you could call four run-down blocks in the flatlands of Central Montana a downtown. The boys would be slapping each other on the back and pretending not to be scared shitless. After all the shots and pitchers, I knew Brody would get in his huge pickup truck, which he had just bought from his friend Derrick with Derrick's old horse trailer still on the hitch, and drive home drunk.

If he made it home, I knew he would then bang around the kitchen, knock things over trying to nuke himself something to eat, turn the TV on too loud and watch some sports talk show and fall asleep on the couch with a half-eaten microwaved whatever sitting on his perfectly chiseled chest and crumbs all over the floor. If I was awake he would want me to cook him something to eat, like with pots and pans on the stove and everything, and he'd yell at me about whatever happened at whatever dive bar he was in, with whatever friends he was with. So it was always better if I pretended to be asleep. My whole life had become pretending not to really be there, just to avoid setting him off.

And yet, I stayed.

Every time he got promoted in his Air Force unit I thought he would somehow change for the better. I don't know why I always thought that kind of stuff—*when X happens things will be better*—because everything only got worse. I saw other Air Force wives and girlfriends being treated well.

Some of the military wives and girlfriends, I looked in their joyful eyes and I could tell they were genuinely happy, and they loved their family-centric lives. I envied them, but more than anything I just wondered what that was like, to be happy, and feel so loved. Safe.

But they saw us from the outside, as I saw them, and they didn't see our truth, so who knows. I wondered if the guys in his unit ever suspected about us. About me. Probably not, because Brody covered his tracks. He was two people – one to the world and one with me.

Brody was a really good-looking guy, usually the tallest guy in the room, lean, muscled and strong, pleasant and charming to everyone else, but it was like he saved up his frustrations, disappointments and self-loathing until we were alone, then he unleashed it on me. Behind closed doors, out of sight. A special brand of put-downs, rages, lies, outbursts and psychological games *just for me*. I was his emotional punching bag.

I endured the hurricanes, and convinced myself on the sunny days, which could be so intoxicatingly beautiful, that it wasn't so bad, or that the hurricanes were my fault even, and when another hurricane hit, the whole cycle began again. Our relationship wasn't a linear thing that evolved and grew; it was more like a vicious circle that just got tighter while it shrunk around my neck, choking the life out of me, so powerful on the poison of his manipulations.

And yet, I stayed.

He didn't hit me once in all that time, but he did a different kind of damage. You just couldn't see it on my body or my skin. You had to look in my eyes. See the void behind them. Five years with him hollowed me out, so not to disturb the eggshells I walked on all the time.

And yet I stayed.

"But he never *hits* you?" my co-worker Kim once said, as if I had no right to complain unless I had a mark on me.

"No," I told her. "But sometimes I wish he would, so other people would believe me that it's real," I said. So *I would believe it's real.*

"Well then just leave," she said to me, disconnecting like people do, and she went back to filling salt shakers.

I just walked away and didn't answer her. If I told her that I couldn't "just leave," I'd be telling the truth, but I'd also be wrong.

Anyway back to that night—I turned on the leaky shower as hot as I could stand it and ran the water over my sore body. At 38 years old, ten hours of carting heavy plates and pitchers of flat beer was exhausting. As I shampooed the French fry grease smell out of my hair I felt like I was cleansing my soul.

I toweled off, dried my hair and put on my flannel pajamas to keep me cozy against the chilly Montana night. If I dared turn the heat on that was cause for a screaming fight about how cold I was all the time. To Brody that was a character flaw. He screamed at me once, in his deep, booming voice on a freezing winter night to leave my puffy brown winter coat in the truck because "you should have more style than that ugly fat brown coat! It should be more important to you to look good than to be warm!"

I obediently slipped the coat off, put it in the back seat of the truck, and walked almost a quarter mile in twenty-five degree weather in a formal dress and heels to his Commander's retirement party. When we got there, everyone else was hanging their fat ugly puffer coats at the coat check.

But here's the trick that let him get away with this: it all fell back on me. It was *my decision* to leave the coat in the truck. I could have said "To hell with you, I'm taking my coat!" and just accepted the stony silence, probably followed later by hours of him berating me until two o'clock in the morning. But I chose freezing—and traded one abuse for another.

Yet I stayed... so why did I stay? Why couldn't I leave? Why *didn't* I leave? I asked myself this all the time, mostly because other people asked me this when I made the mistake of sharing my troubles. Or occasionally they witnessed our fights, but that was rare. He was careful. And he wasn't always so mean.

There's the hook—it wasn't *all bad*. Things were magical—beautiful—in the beginning, so I kept thinking there was something I did to make it go wrong, and something I could do to make it go back to that beautiful place.

At first, his dark brown eyes looked so longingly at me, my insides melted. It was an amazing, giddy, crushy feeling. For the first two months or so he treated me like I walked on water. And later, when it all soured, and I couldn't do anything right, he would show me just enough good in between the bad to keep me thinking that beautiful place was not a mirage, that if I could just be perfect enough, not break those eggshells, we could go back to that wonderful place. He would always make me think it was something I did. Something I said. Or the way I said it. Something I wore. Something I didn't wear. That it was me who changed, not him. My fault. Always *my fault*.

And then those in-betweens, when he would be so apologetic, so sweet, so loving. I would feel sorry for him, and I would break down and let him back into my heart again. No matter how much I swore off him in anger the night before, he would lay his head in my lap the next morning and tell me he was sorry and I would let him right back in.

Eventually I decided the answer to the staying vs. leaving question lay somewhere between "I don't know why," and "I don't know how." I was waiting for something to click inside of me, just push me over the edge. Or for a door to open in front of me so I could just walk through it and never look back. Or for me to not feel the inexplicable guilty pull of love for him anymore. Or for someone to let me out. Hand me the key. Leave the gate unlocked.

Or for him to do something so awful that I could *prove* the beginning was a lie, and no longer think I was just crazy and he's worth trying *one more time for*.

I had been so ground down by it all, by the slow and steady shrinking of my identity apart from him, I just couldn't find the courage in me to leave by myself. I guess that was it. I was too worn out to break free. I needed to be *set free*.

I thought I was the same old girl I'd always been, but I really wasn't. My spark had been put out by him pissing on it. My smile had been wiped off my face by his chronic nasty, stinging sarcastic comments. My pride and self-esteem had been swallowed, forced down with all the crow I had to eat just to get him to calm down after one of his rants.

As I lay in bed that night, warmed by my heated blanket, I closed my eyes and said yet another silent prayer that God would somehow show me a way out of this mess, and I fell asleep.

8

***

The ringing phone jolted me awake. It was 4 a.m.

"Hello?"

"Mags… I got popped. Come get me. My truck is at The Machine Shop. I'm at County, they said they'd let me go home if you picked me up. I got in a fight, some motherfucker—."

"Brody, stop. You got arrested? Where?"

"The Machine Shop," he said, angry I didn't get it the first time.

The Machine Shop was the worst of the two strip clubs in Butte Falls. And when I say worst, I mean think of the worst kind of sad strip club you can imagine, add a stench of cigarettes, stale beer and cheap perfume, a few layers of dirt, meth, glitter and back rooms for thirty-dollar hookers and that was The Machine Shop. The 'P' on the sign hadn't been lit since I moved there five years before, so at night it was 'The Machine Sho'.

"Where are your keys?" I said.

"I don't know. Get the spare, it's in the junk drawer," he said, and hung up.

I sat up and turned on the little Target lamp next to the bed. "Oh fucking God this is going to be fun," I said out loud. I pulled on some jeans and a sweatshirt, brushed my teeth and put on the infamous huge, fat, ugly winter coat. It was June, but as hot as it was the week before, the unpredictable Montana Rocky-Mountain Front was now under an early-summer snowfall.

Rummaging around the junk drawer I found a single Dodge key and an alarm fob, which could only be for the behemoth truck Brody bought from Derrick. With my huge satchel purse over my shoulder I started the fifteen-minute walk to The Machine Sho'.

Passing the quiet apartment complexes and turning up the residential streets lined with small, neat but shabby homes, I rued the day I moved here. What I wouldn't give to have that woman by the scruff of her neck—that woman I was five years ago, riding in the shotgun seat of Brody's old Pontiac, thinking he was my Prince Charming. My Airman, my protector, my Knight in Shining Armor.

I met him in Los Angeles, where I was living at the time. I was over 30, single, broke and with no discernable future plan, but I was free as a bird. I had a job as an accountant, a group of friends I liked, and we laughed all the time. I used to be funny. I never laughed anymore it seemed. Nothing was funny now.

Brody had come to L.A. for the weekend with some friends, from Edwards Air Force Base where he was stationed about two hours away. I was in a karaoke bar, and I sang, or butchered, the Warren Zevon song "Someone to Lay Down Beside Me," Linda Ronstadt's version, and he came up to me and drunkenly declared, "You sound like the most beautiful girl I've ever seen." When he looked right through me with those dark brown eyes, I was just done. I never stopped to think about what was, or was not, behind them.

Brody was tall, about six-feet-four, lean and strong, with thick, black wavy hair. His build was perfect—like a male prototype or something. He had a boyish handsome quality. I guess I was carried away by his charm, because I did not pay much attention to how self-absorbed he was, and how little he asked me about myself. When a man sees a woman as merely an extension of himself, an appendage or possession, her inner emotional life doesn't matter. His long-term plan was to pulverize it bit by bit anyway.

In reality, our dysfunctions were a perfect match, and somehow that poisonous, gaseous chemical reaction made us think there was intense chemistry. Or I thought that anyway. It was quite a fairytale for the first two months. I couldn't believe this perfect, sexy guy that I had such a mad crush on was so crazy about me. Me, who picked at her cuticles and was always late, and was messy and didn't really ever have her outfit quite right, and wasn't bad looking but didn't know how to maximize her beauty the way some women do. My haircut was always outside the lines, my eyeliner was always smudged and I had no retirement account. I never wore high heels. I was always in my old Frye cowboy boots.

Men like Brody usually went for those showgirl kinds of women—the ones with perfect manicures and white jeans that stayed white, hair that looked great even when they ran through the rain, and who would never wear a fat ugly puffer coat over a formal gown no matter how cold it was. They wore high heels to music festivals, makeup to the gym and they starved themselves in misguided vanity. And men like Brody respected the hell out of them for all of it. They had a shared love of vanity.

I got my first clue that we were not what I thought we were after about two months, when he suddenly started criticizing me, mostly for things he had once told me he loved about me. Where I once was "so funny and told great stories," now I was "so longwinded and boring" and I "never stop talking." Where I once was "so smart" and he "loved my analytical brain" and how it worked, now I was a "know it all" and it was "so annoying to be with someone who knows everything." I used to be "cute" with messy morning hair in my soft flannel pajamas. Now in my workout clothes I looked "like a slob" and he told me "I can't believe you go out of the house like that, with no makeup."

Just when I would reach a breaking point, ready to say "to Hell with you!" he would throw me a crumb. A glimpse of the "old Brody." "Good Brody."

He'd tell me how much he needed me. He was sorry he was a jerk sometimes. Or he would send me a text message out of nowhere that he was just thinking of me and how much he was falling in love with me. It worked like a charm, because I began to think I was somehow *earning* his love.

Over time his abuse and psychological games got worse. He would deny saying something he said, something I clearly remembered he had said, and I would start to doubt my own memory. He was a master at twisting arguments around to make me feel like I had caused them, and that my behavior was somehow exactly whatever I was accusing him of.

I remember one car ride about four years into our relationship when he was particularly tense, and obviously irritated. I asked him if he was okay.

"What do you mean, 'Am I okay?'" he said. He was very angry.

"I mean are you okay, like is something wrong? You seem tense or like something is bothering you. Did something happen at work?" I was genuinely asking him, and I really did think something was bothering him. I honestly didn't even think it had anything to do with me.

He raised his voice: "Why am I always doing something wrong with you? What am I doing that's wrong? I'm just sitting here! How am I tense? I'm just driving the car! All

I'm doing is just driving the car?! What am I doing that's angry or tense?"

I interrupted him—"Well now you're yelling at me—"

"I'm not yelling! I'm just driving the car! All I am doing is driving the car! I'm just driving the fucking car! What am I doing wrong?"

And it went on like that until we got home, where he slammed doors and screamed at me until I cried and I finally went to the bedroom and he stayed up drinking and watching TV.

By that time, he'd done so much damage over the years that I felt I was only worthy of the crumbs men like him left behind. Breadcrumbs. That was all I deserved, right? Because it was winter and I wanted to wear a coat? Or because I didn't wear makeup to the gym? Or because I asked him if he was okay? Because I occasionally had an emotion? Or a need? I stopped bringing up my needs. I forced myself to stop having them. I stopped trying to tell him anything about any bad feelings I had. I stopped telling him I had any feelings at all. I just wanted peace.

I walked up to The Machine Sho', with its muted thumping music and men milling around outside, lurking in dark shadows with enough self-awareness to know they should be ashamed to be there. My stomach was in a knot.

I found Brody's truck in the parking lot, parked far off to the side because of the horse trailer attached, and I

climbed in. It was a huge truck, and he already had piles
of papers, a pair of work boots and junk all over the back
seat. He'd had the truck for barely three weeks.

I was surprised he left so much stuff in the back. Butte
Falls was not exactly a crime-ridden town, being so small
and dependent on the Air Base for life support, but the
random murders, robberies and rapes occurred with
enough frequency to make you look over your shoulder
and lock your doors at night. There was a halfway house
for the State jail on the edge of the County and many
escapees were known to victimize the good people of
Butte Falls before skipping town. The meth-heads would
break your windows for your cup holder change.

I started the truck and drove to the southern end of town,
where the County holding center was. It was right on the
edge of the highway, across the cloverleaf from a Flying J
truck stop and a Holiday Inn. It was the last building
you'd see for a good seventy miles if you were leaving.

The cherubic-faced deputy at the front desk looked like
he'd been on the job about a half an hour out of high
school. His nametag said Taylor.

"Can I help you?" he said, trying to sound official and
polite at the same time.

"Yes, I understand you arrested Brody Thomas. I am here
to pick him up? I am his…girlfriend," I said,
apologetically.

"Okay. Please have a seat," he motioned to a grimy orange plastic and chrome bench by the front window.

I waited for a few minutes, as the deputy made whispering, muted phone calls and nodded his head a lot, which I thought was odd since he was on the phone. He looked sweet though, like the only people he would ever hurt in his life were bad guys. Guys like Brody.

I heard some commotion and looked up to see Brody in handcuffs with two deputies coming out of the lock-up.

"Hey! Mags! Where the fuck have you been?" Loud. Angry. He was still drunk, struggling to free himself from his handcuffs and the grasp of the deputies. My stomach sank.

I stood up slowly.

"This belong to you?" One of the deputies asked as he held a firm grip on Brody's arm. I just looked at them.

"Sign here, and here, and here," the other deputy said, handing me a clipboard with a pen taped to a string swinging from it.

"Sign it Mags, this is bullshit." Brody said, in a menacing voice, jerking on his handcuffs. "Wait until you hear what total bullshit this was tonight!" he said, as one Deputy rolled his eyes. I was thankful the Deputies were bigger than Brody was.

I held the pen in my hand, poised over the clipboard.

I turned to the cherubic deputy. "Just…um, just asking, but what happens if I don't sign it? If I don't accept him right now?"

Brody made an audible grunt. "Fuck? That's not funny, Mags, sign it," he said.

Deputy Taylor's eyes twinkled for a nanosecond, as if I had just double-dog dared him something spectacular: "Well…he spends the night in the drunk tank, Ma'am," he said, with great satisfaction.

I re-read the line above my name over and over "agrees to accept responsibility/custody for subject pending charges and/or arraignment…"

"FUCKING. SIGN. IT. MAGS."

The Deputy with the grip on his arm leaned into him. "Easy, Friend," he said calmly.

But Brody was not struggling with the Deputy anymore. He was frozen, staring at me, with his wide, drunken, watery, rage-filled eyes. The rest of my night flashed before me—him screaming at me the whole drive home, why didn't I sign the thing right away, how he got in the fight in the first place, what took me so long, I better take care of things while he was gone for six months, and one thing after another that was my fault, that I didn't do right, that he could blame me for so he wouldn't have to accept responsibility for his own mistakes. His own life. His own mess. His own misery. Which became my misery.

Sure he'd be gone tomorrow, but I'd have to endure a hell of a lot tonight.
I wobbled the pen in my hand.

Suddenly Brody exploded and I jumped. "What the FUCK IS YOUR PROBLEM, SIGN THE FUCKING PAPER, MAGGIE let's GO, I'm TIRED, I AM GOING OVERSEAS TOMORROW! I NEED TO GET SOME SLEEP! You stupid fucking bitch, sign the fucking PAPER!"

I startled at his volume and his rage.

"Maybe you need a night in the tank, Friend," said one Deputy. "We're full-up, or we wouldn't even give you the option."

The deputies held tight to his arms. Everyone was looking at me, anticipating, wondering what would come out of my mouth, what would I do.

I felt a strange sinkhole in my heart—not a swell of bravery, or strength or something—it was more like a total collapse. Like my solar plexus was filled with sand and someone pulled the cork out of my bellybutton.

If I couldn't get the woman that I was five years ago by the scruff of the neck, I could finally get a hold of the woman I am now. I took a deep breath, and purposefully handed the clipboard back to the deputy.

"Mags, what the fuck, SIGN IT! I need to go home, I'm LEAVING IN SIX HOURS!"

I turned to Brody. "Then, Brody," I said firmly, "you should have made better choices about six hours ago. Deputy, I decline to accept responsibility for this man."

And I turned my back and started walking. I turned my back on Brody Thomas. I turned my back on him screaming "Where the FUCK ARE YOU GOING?" as I walked away, on the noise of the struggle between him and the deputies, on the sound of the lock-up door clanging behind me. I turned my back on five years of emotional abuse, of lies, of mental cruelty and mind games. I turned my back on the last bad choice I would ever make on his behalf.

I walked swiftly through the station doors and stared straight ahead. My breathing was quick and shallow, my pupils dilated and I moved like a robot.

I got in the truck, started it up, drove to the south entrance to the highway out of town instead of north toward our apartment and I just kept driving south, eyes wide open, foot on the gas, and breathing short, shallow breaths.

I had no idea where I was headed, and I didn't even turn on the radio until I crossed the State line into Wyoming.

ROBBIE-ANN McPHERSON

****

CHAPTER TWO
The Kindness of Strangers

I needed gas and my neck and shoulders ached, so I pulled into the first gas station I saw once I crossed the State line. It was just breaking dawn and there was some strange comfort in the bright lights and old seventies music of the convenience mart as I milled around, looking for the coffee pot.

"Hon, the pot on the left is fresh, I just made it," the woman said. She was maybe late twenties, a tiny woman somewhere in her third trimester, sitting on a stool reading tabloid magazines with her awkward belly stretching her sweatshirt. She was pregnant and drinking coffee. But who was I to judge, I basically just stole my boyfriend's truck, left him in jail and walked out on my life.

"Thanks," I said, pouring the biggest cup they had. Suddenly I started crying, just crack-up, lunatic crying. I pulled a bunch of napkins out of the dispenser and the girl struggled off her stool and waddled over.

"Oh noooo, Honey, what happened? What is wrong? Why are you crying?" she rubbed my shoulder with her long fake fingernails and I wondered why she spent so much money on her fingernails, working overnights in a highway convenience mart. She pulled me toward the counter and sat me down on her stool, rubbing both my arms. Up close, she did not seem like a raggedy store clerk. She had gleaming teeth, a very expensive highlight job in her hair and a huge rock on her wedding finger.

"Oh, God, I'm sorry," I said. "I'm embarrassed. I'm just tired from driving...I just...I left...I left where I was, and I had to leave...but...I guess...I guess... I don't know where I'm going...I'm tired, I'm sorry...I don't know where I'm going..." I was speaking gibberish, wiping my eyes and slowly making the realization as I repeated it. *I don't know where I'm going.*

"You don't know where you are going?" she said slowly, like I was drunk. "Well...okay...Honey, let's just calm down then. We'll figure this out, okay we will figure this all out. You have obviously been through something, so just let's calm down, and slow down, and first thing—think about a plan here. You had to leave...someplace... and so you left. I know what that's like. As for where you are going, that's an easy one—okay, where do you want to go? The world's your oyster—what does your heart tell you?" She snapped her long fingernails right in my face. "First thing that pops in your head!"

"*Home*?" I said quietly, sniffling.

I shocked myself. Home? As in "*Home*" Home?

Spaulding Quarry, my little rural hometown in Western New York meant so many unwanted unhappy memories…it meant *Mom*. But that was the first thing that popped in my head. And for the first time in a decade, two decades, maybe more—I felt like I wanted to be there. Needed to be there.

"Well…see how easy that was?" She asked, gently tracing a strand of hair behind my ear.

"Yea," I let it sink in. Home. I would go home, and I would somehow figure everything out. Home. Why not? I couldn't go back to Los Angeles with nothing but my purse and a horse trailer. "Thank you… it's funny, I guess I was headed in that direction anyway."

"Sweetheart," she said softly, "sometimes we just need a stranger on the outside to point out the obvious, because we're too much up in our own heads, you know what I mean? The whole 'can't see the forest for the trees' thing?"

She dabbed tears off my face with a paper towel and gave me a look like "don't you feel better now?" and she hugged me for a long time. I almost started to cry again when she hugged me but I forced myself not to.

When I pulled out my credit card to pay for sixty-five dollars in gas and the coffee, to my horror it was declined.

"Oh my God," I said. I have—I have eight dollars? I'm so sorry, I—I'm—I don't know—"

"Honey," the woman said, "I'm just going to say this one is on the house."

She settled herself and looked hard into my eyes.

"I see you, do you understand? My husband and I own this little station, and a couple others. We have a really nice life. He's a sweetheart. But before him—" she trailed off and tears welled in her eyes.

"I'm just going to say to you that—well let's just say that someone once gave me a break that helped me make a big change in my life for the better, pretty much saved my life, and I am going on my gut here but I feel like I'm giving you one. I think you need this gas to get as far away from something back there as you can, and I think you need this coffee to stay awake while you're driving. So you go ahead now, and you promise me you will drive safe, okay? And all I want is for you to do pay it forward somehow, like I'm doing now, you got it, Sweetheart? Pay it forward."

I felt connected to her like I hadn't felt connected to anyone in years. I felt ashamed and relieved at the same time that she recognized her own wounds in mine.

"I got it," I said, smiling through watery eyes. "And I thank you, from the very core of my soul. Thank you."

"You are welcome, Sweetheart," she said, with so much love I almost felt it physically. "But you gotta pay it forward. Promise me. Remember that. Now get on the road and make some time. Get *home*."

I nodded, took the coffee and hurried back to the truck. In my newfound victory and basking in the glow of such a lucky break, I didn't even think about what I was going to do for the next fill up.

***

I drove for about four hours on the South Dakota two-lane, listening to a crackling AM radio station that played seventies soft rock.

I was softly singing along about the pony "Wiiiiildfire," when a loud bang made the whole truck start shaking.

I had a death grip on the vibrating steering wheel. The truck was fighting with all its two tons to go right but there was no shoulder there, just a drop off to a large ditch. Summoning some reserve of desperate superhuman strength I pulled the wobbling, chugging beast and the horse trailer towing behind it across the highway to the left and slid to a stop in a cloud of gravel dust.

I stared wide-eyed straight ahead, facing the wrong way on the two-lane shoulder alongside a long cattle fence somewhere in Nowhere, South Dakota, still gripping the steering wheel at ten and two. I knew Brody had no spare because he bragged about it all the time.

"These tires don't need a spare," he would say. "They'd drive over a bed of nails and keep on truckin'."

"Asshole," I thought.

What was I thinking? I have nothing, I'm running away like some teenager in an after-school special? Did I think I was going to actually get somewhere? Make a change? How would I explain this to Brody? To anyone? I lowered my forehead and rested it on the steering wheel.

"Fucking idiot," I said out loud. And the tears came again, leaking then gushing out of me like I was a dam that broke. I slowly climbed out of the truck, looking up and down the desolate highway, and walked around to survey the damage. The front passenger tire had blown completely out. A piece of it was hanging off the rim. I wiped my teary face on my sleeve.

My cell had no service, and all I could do was wait for someone to drive by, and hopefully stop. I propped open the hood, and sat on the tall grass against a fence post. The morning sun felt warm. It was peacefully quiet, except for a few birds chirping. I was on the edge of some massive cattle ranch, but I couldn't see any driveway or houses, so who knows how long I would sit there until some trucker, or serial killer, would happen by.

I leaned my throbbing head back and closed my eyes, and let the warm, gentle breeze gently cool the tears on my face.

Who would save me?

***

The smell woke me first—a hot, foul breath that was too voluminous to be human, accompanied by a velvety, snotty snout sweetly brushing against my cheek. It snorted and I startled, turning to face the head of a stunning shiny, white gold horse hanging over the edge of the fence. He seemed to be interested in my welfare, curious about why I was sleeping there. He nuzzled and nudged me until I stood up to pet him. He had a large scar on his nose from some long ago injury, and did not look to be from a cattle ranch but looked instead like some kind of fancy show horse. Or he once was. His eyes were soulful, and blue—I'd never seen blue eyes on a horse before.

"Hey boy," I said, petting his neck as he grabbed a mouthful of the tall grass I was sitting in. I looked at my watch. It was almost nine o'clock. I'd been asleep for an hour and a half. I hoisted my stiff limbs off the ground.

"Who do you belong to, Boy?" He had no halter, no brand. My girlhood love of horses from my grandfather's farm rushed back, and as I examined him I saw he was a finely bred horse, but he looked like he hadn't seen a fancy life in some time. He responded well to my petting him and talking to him—he was definitely socialized through some kind of training. He had some kind of injury, I could tell the way he was favoring his hind right leg.

"Can you run back to your keepers and tell them there's a lady here who needs a tire fixed?" I said to him. He was nuzzling me so much, he reminded me of my childhood cat, Lily. Lily and I were inseparable until I was eleven. My mother made me give Lily away when Lily peed on the couch at Christmas one year. Years later I surmised that Lily probably had a simple bladder infection and just needed treatment, but that was my mother—once something was broken, she threw it away. Her marriage, a job, a house, a car—once it stopped being perfect, she just left it and got a new one that was perfect, and that was the thing, until it wasn't.

The problem with me was, she couldn't just throw me out so she found ways to just leave me places—at a friend's house, even for a year at Grampa's farm while I was a baby and she was off who knows where in California, when she couldn't deal with how a baby made her life messy.

I heard a buzzing motor in the distance, coming from the woods, and the horse jerked away from me and ran off with his crooked gait toward the trees. At first I thought he was startled by the sound but I was amazed a few minutes later to see this shiny golden stallion charging back toward me, with two men on ATVs in tow. *He was leading them to me.*

They waved to me as they approached, no helmets and no shirts, obviously working what must be this huge ranch.

The horse paced back and forth in front of me until the ATVs caught up and the older man, a large weathered farmer straight out of Central Casting with his thick head of white hair and thicker belly, motioned to the young one to cut the engines and climbed off.

"Well hello there!" he bellowed, his broad shoulders supporting a strong, friendly wave. "Looks like you have some kinda highway trouble?" He pulled a dark blue handkerchief out of his back pocket and wiped the sweat off the back of his neck.

"Hello! I'm Maggie," I said, reaching over the fence to shake his massive, calloused hand. "Yes, I got a blowout on my truck. No spare," I smiled and shrugged.

"Well that, and yer facing the wrong way ya know," he said, smiling.

"Ha, well, yes, the right side, I thought I'd rather not go over that cliff into the ditch," I said, nervously wiping my face with my shirt sleeve and hoping my cheeks weren't stained with mascara.

I'd never been so happy to see a friendly face. He turned to the younger one. "Go get your mother, tell her get the truck and come up." The boy, who couldn't have been more than twelve, snapped to attention and took off on his

ATV back into the woods. The horse ran after him like a puppy. I couldn't believe how his coat shined in the sun, light he was painted gold.

"Well my name is Bud, that was my son Luke, my wife Joy will be up 'ere with the truck in about five minutes, and we'll take you back to the house, get ya fixed right up with a new tire 'n everything and get ya back on the road. Don't worry, it'll be alright. You're not the first person to break down along here, and we got all kinds of iced tea and food and you'll be on your way in no time. Sit tight and Joy will be up. Get your belongings together and climb over the fence here, our gate is a good seven miles up the road there, it's quicker if she gets you here."

I was about to say thank you, or Praise Jesus, or fall on my knees, or just pass out from gratitude but he was already starting up the ATV.

Over the loud motor he shouted "And I see you met Liberty! He told us you were here…ain't he a beaut!" and sped off into the woods.

I stood still for a second in the silence, wondering if all that was a hallucination, then ran to the truck to get my purse.

I checked the truck bed, and Brody's tool box was locked and bolted. I didn't have the key anyway. The horse trailer was empty except for a few halters and leads. I climbed into the back of the cab and pushed around the papers and Brody's smelly work boots, looking for anything I should take. Brody's Glock pistol was lying under the back seat, loaded.

"Asshole," I said out loud.

I threw it in my purse. I knew how to shoot it better than he did. I found what looked like a duffel bag that was wedged under the driver's seat. It was stuck under there, and I yanked hard enough to rip one of the handles. It was heavy and full.

I pulled it out on the front seat, and heard the truck and a honk behind me. Joy had arrived.

"Hello there stranger!" She looked like Clark Kent's mother from the old Superman comics, but younger. A lot younger than Bud. Wholesome and hearty and driving a vintage blue Ford, just like in a movie. *Maybe I am hallucinating,* I thought.

I smiled and waved, pulled my giant purse over my shoulder and turned back to unzip the duffel bag to see what was in it.

It was tightly packed with bank bands of money. Hundreds of them.

"Jesus Christ, there must be fifty thousand dollars in here," I whispered to myself, flipping through the stacks of bills with my fingertips.

Joy honked again. "You need help?" she shouted.

"Nope!" I shouted back, frantically zipping up the duffel bag. "Coming!"

I locked up the truck, and hoisted myself, my purse and the duffel bag over the fence.

"Well aren't you a lovely thing," Joy said, pausing to stare at my face with her warm, beautiful light blue eyes. They were framed by an aging but breathtaking face. She could have been a movie star, but here she was on this farm in Nowhere, South Dakota with Bud and Luke. She was probably in her 40s, close to my age, but she seemed grounded and happy, wise but youthful…peaceful.

"Ha, oh…well…" I stuttered, holding my purse and the bag tighter. I was completely preoccupied with what the hell Brody was doing with fifty thousand dollars in a duffel bag in his truck.

"That's a fine horse trailer you got there," Joy said, as she expertly turned the old truck around and we bumped and bobbed over the dirt road through the woods back to their picturesque farmhouse.

"No horse in it though?"

***

Joy drove expertly over the rutty dirt road through the woods. The sunlight flickered through tall trees as we navigated a few wandering dogs, chickens and a turkey.

"They're like family," said Joy. "We buy our meat at the store like everyone else because we can't bear to slaughter any of them," she said apologetically. Her smile was so serene.

"How long have you lived here?" I asked.

"Well the place has been in Bud's family for three generations," she said. "I've been here for about twenty-five years. I met Bud in high school."

She looked at me with a twinkle in her eye.

"He was the 4-H leader. I was 18, and…well, it was a little bit of a scandal until people got used to it."

As we came out of the woods the dirt road merged with a gravel road, and I couldn't believe what I saw—this was no farmhouse. It was a mansion. Absolutely resplendent white, with black shutters, tall pillars proudly holding up a portico over the big red double front door. The front wraparound porch was framed with beautiful white spindles, and I could see rocking chairs and porch swings. Flowers were everywhere.

There was a homey-ness to it though, not like a cold, untouchable Beverly Hills mansion. This was a place you could put your feet up on the rails and rock the swing, or show up unannounced for lunch.

"Okay! Let's get you comfortable, and we'll find a tire for that truck, and square you away! You must be hungry, so I'll get some coffee and breakfast going," Joy said, as if she couldn't wait to help me. She was like an angel, there was just something so…pure about her.

"I don't know how to thank you," I said, climbing out of the truck with my arms tight around the duffel bag. "Honestly, you are saving my life."

"Oh, nonsense," she said. "I can tell you are the kind of person who would do the exact same thing if I were in your shoes and you were wearing mine." She waved at the air as if to wave away the idea.

The house was cool inside thanks to central air conditioning, and their furniture was beautifully appointed—a lot of slipcovered sofas that you could sink into and never come out, beautiful old wooden tables, colorful hand-made rugs. It was eclectic, welcoming and very expensive, but somehow completely unpretentious.

"Betsy!" Joy hollered. "We have a guest!" She turned to me. "Bud must be out in the barn. So tell me about that horse trailer. You have a horse?"

"Oh, no," I said. "It sort of came with the truck," cutting myself off.

"Huh!" she said, confused and surprised at the same time.

"Well we—I got it used, and the trailer was included, and I couldn't unhitch it by myself. Do you need a horse trailer?" Maybe they would take it off my hands, I thought…I could save some gas money.

"No…we have plenty," she smiled. "In fact we have three too many horses. Our barn is crowded. We take in rescues, like Liberty, you know Bud can't say no to a stray," she said and winked at me.

We walked into her beautiful kitchen, right out of Country Living magazine with the hanging copper pots and the huge gas stove, sub-zero refrigerator and glass-front white cabinets.

She rustled in the refrigerator and Betsy came in, apron on. She was a college-aged girl, fresh-faced and eager for whatever Joy was about to instruct her to do.

"Maggie this is Betsy, she's my right-hand, my chef, my housekeeper, my fix-it girl. Betsy, this is Maggie, her truck broke down on the highway. Honey, will you put together a quiche and I'll get some coffee going?"

Betsy nodded eagerly and started deftly assembling a vegetable quiche. Joy buzzed around the kitchen filling coffee pots and lining up jams, pulling together a beautiful brunch spread.

"Whoa what's cookin' Good Lookin'?" Bud's voice boomed from the front hall.

He and Luke were washed up and ready to eat whatever they'd been smelling.

"Miss Maggie, I got a hold of our mechanic in town, he's gonna pick up your truck, fix the tire and bring it out here for you but it's gonna take til tomorrow to get the tire so it looks like you'll be our house guest tonight," Bud announced.

"What? But—I, you...oh...I couldn't ask you to—"

"Nonsense, it's settled." Bud had spoken. "Just say 'thank you' and that's that."

"Thank you," I said softly. "I honestly don't know how to thank you enough."

Bud and Joy smiled at me, then waved away my words again when I tried to protest.

"Where you headed?" Joy asked.

"Home," I said. "In the Western part of New York State. My mom has a little farm out there, and I'm...going to help her out for a while." Yea, that's it. I'm going to help her out for a while.

"Oh, how wonderful," said Joy, her eyes misting. "I'd give anything to see my mother again." She turned away.

"Family is the thing," Bud said definitively, glancing protectively at Joy. "If your mother needs you, you gotta go. Good for you. And no better cause than the family homestead. We have some very good friends out in New York, they do the concrete for a lot of the casinos and highways out there. Family business. How long's it been since you were home last?"

"Uh," I struggled with which brought me more shame— lying to these good people, or telling them the truth. "It's been years," I said. "Work, you know, and…well life gets…busy." And my mother and I hadn't spoken in years because she's selfish and impossible.

"Well then it's a regular reunion!" Bud said. He had a way of making anything awful seem like Christmas morning.

Joy smiled at me, as if she understood every single thing I didn't say. "Fresh starts are easy. It's the endings before them that are hard."

We sat down to eat and Joy said Grace, all of us holding hands, and I ate what had to be the best quiche I've ever tasted before or since, with fresh bagels and strawberry jam that Joy canned herself.

***

After brunch Joy suggested I go for a walk but I didn't want to leave the duffel bag. I went up to my assigned guest room, a beautiful airy floral print sanctuary with white wood trim and a giant four-poster bed. I took the bag into the bathroom, locked the door and counted out all the money on the floor. It was $49,820, in twenties and hundreds, wrapped in five-hundred dollar bundles. Holy Christ.

I shoved all the money back into the bag and stuffed it behind one of the pillows. It made me nervous to leave it but these people were obviously so wealthy $50,000 was probably what their dining room carpet cost.

I wondered how many times Brody had called my dead cell phone. I had no cell phone charger but I didn't even want to power it up and leave a trace of where I was.

He must be out of jail by now, and reported his truck stolen. I doubted the police would run an interstate alert for a used truck stolen by the AWOL girlfriend of a guy who got arrested for assault the night before. He'd be on a plane soon, headed to the Middle East. I felt a terrible pang of guilt and said a prayer for his life. I had gotten to know his fellow Airmen, and I was so in awe of their commitment to their service. It was the one decent thing about Brody.

If I'd thought that somehow Brody needed my encouragement to keep his head together I'd feel worse, but he would only say something shitty to me like "try to grow your hair out so when I get back it looks better."

In spite of the fact I'd just run out on my relationship, stolen his truck, basically left all my worldly possessions that I would most certainly never see again, left my crap job, everything about a life I'd known for the past five years, there was something about Bud and Joy and this place that made me feel so…peaceful. Serendipitous. Who knows, I was probably just in shock, absolutely out of my mind. Maybe I was dead and this was Heaven.

I decided to take Joy's advice, and walk down to the barn and look at the horses. I couldn't do anything until the truck was fixed anyway. Maybe by tomorrow I would come to my senses and go back to my shitty life.

Liberty greeted me about halfway down the path from the house. He seemed to have run of the place, maybe because he knew to come back to the barn when he was supposed to.

He walked next to me, head hung low, as if he were escorting me. It was strange, the intuition this animal seemed to have. His gleaming coat had almost a mother-of-pearl quality, it was so beautiful. I'd never seen anything like it.

"You gonna hold my hand?" I asked him, and gave him a pat on his shoulder. He shoved me with his head sweetly.

I took a path into the paddock along the fence and Liberty dutifully loped along. The grassy fields stretched on to the horizon in one direction, bordered by the forest in another. It was a peaceful, beautiful place.

I patted Liberty on his shoulder.

"So what's your story? Mine is…pathetic," I said. "A lot of bad choices and blind faith. I don't know, is blind faith my fault? Should I feel guilty about that stuff? I mean, if I really believed in something, or someone, and they let me down, is that something I should take accountability for?" I started to cry.

He snorted and yanked at a swatch of grass. I rustled his beautiful cream-colored mane, which was lovingly groomed.

Liberty stopped at a patch of long grass by the fence. I climbed up and sat on the thick white painted wood, just wiping tears and drinking in everything around me—the sweet smell of the grass, the soft breeze, the blue sky, Liberty's heavy presence next to me. He looked up at me with his almost albino-blue eyes, and chewed on a wad of grass.

"The thing is, I feel like I lost something. Or it was taken from me. Or maybe I gave it away. Or all of those…but it was in little pieces. Like losing a fortune a dollar at a time and one day you wake up broke. But I need to know where I am to blame, and where it's his fault. Part of me wants to blame it all on him, because I'd have someplace to put the anger at wasting, losing all those years, and making such a mess of everything. I really want to say it's all his fault. But I don't think it is. And that scares me more than anything."

Liberty pushed his nose into my arm, giving me a nuzzle. I scratched his ears, which he seemed to relish. I relished letting the truth out to someone who may not be able to talk back but I felt was somehow listening.

"See…at some point, the thing is, I knew that my blind faith had gone bad. And that is when, I think, it became my fault. I think from the time I knew, and I knew, Boy did I know, like within a year, that this guy was chipping away at me, and he was hurting me, and I was letting him hurt me by staying there—see that's when the blind faith became disillusion. But by then I was so broken. I was just…tired. Beat down. It's like he'd already drained my battery so much I didn't have the energy to leave. I mean is that my fault? Is it?

"And then last night when he got arrested, I don't know what happened, I just—it was like something just, not snapped, but like a light bulb went on, and I just decided that was it. That was the moment, and I was not going to allow him to do this to me anymore."

I caught my own words in my mouth. *Allow him to do this to me anymore.*

He did it, I stayed. He did it again, he caused damage, I stayed. He did it again. He caused more damage. I stayed. And on and on. Our relationship wasn't a line of time going by, it was a circle, going nowhere, slowly wearing me down to nothing. And even though I didn't deserve him hurting me, I didn't do anything that warranted his emotional abuse, the part that was in my hands was making excuses for him, and making excuses for myself, and staying.

"I should have left a long time ago, Boy," I said. "Maybe I let myself down years ago. If only I'd had someone back then to encourage me, or help me, I think I would have, but I was so alone. And people don't believe you anyway, if you don't have bruises they don't understand what it's like, the whole mind-fuck of everything. You think you are the crazy one. That's how messed up it all is. You doubt yourself. Maybe it just takes years, and that's it. Maybe this was my moment to leave and there was no better time. I should give myself credit for doing it now, right? Stop feeling sorry for myself, just focus on the future, a fresh start? Just do now what I would have done if I had left years ago, right?"

I wiped my face with my sleeves and jumped to the ground. "Okay Boy, show me this beautiful barn!" And as I turned to walk toward the path out of the paddock, Liberty kicked up a bunch of dust and ran toward the barn.

"He really was listening," I thought.

It was hardly a barn but more like a rustic, beautiful cathedral that had immaculate stalls, tile floors and reclaimed barn wood gates and stall doors. Bridles and tack hung along the wall neatly, and buckets of water assigned to each stall were neatly lined up along the posts.

Two workers were tending to the dozen horses.

As I approached each horse I could see that Bud and Joy had committed a lot to healing these animals. They were well-cared-for now, but some had scars, one had lost his eye. There were two horses tied in the center aisle, because there were not enough stalls.

Liberty stood by a water bucket and slurped. I loved the smell of horse barns; a heady combination of horse sweat, Murphy's oil soap, leather, hay, and the ever-present poop that you grow accustomed to if you spend any time with horses.

I heard Bud's unmistakable bellow behind me.

"So whaddaya think of our little shelter, huh?" he said. The horses immediately reacted to his presence, as if their master had entered the room. They all stuck their snouts out of their stalls and started snorting and getting excited.

"And how are we, Miss Danger? Good Gal," he said to a beautiful chestnut mare. Her otherwise glossy auburn coat had what looked like a burn patch on her neck. He scratched her mane and patted her neck on the opposite side of her wound. She relished it.

"She came to us from a hoarder. Unreal. The guy burned her with a heat lamp."

Bud introduced me to each horse, explaining what was so special about each one. His voice would rise and fall, from anger to pity to sweetness, as he recounted finding the horse, helping the horse heal its medical problems, and working on their psychological issues.

"Psychological?" I asked.

"Oh yea," Bud said. "It's just like you and me. You put a human in an abusive situation for a long period of time, or even a short trauma, and it messes up your head."

I let out a feeble laugh.

"Oh I get that," I said. "Yea, that makes a lot of sense... I should probably...get back up to the house soon, I'm feeling a little exhausted." I thought about the duffel bag.

"Sure," Bud said. "Just let me share with you Liberty's story. It's a good one. He came from the circus. Liberty!" Bud hollered and whistled and the horse trotted over from the doorway.

"He's what they call a Perlino Akhal Teke. Turkmenistan, you ever heard of that country? His coat is like shimmery gold, and the pearly color is rare. He was some kind of circus show horse, some Russian outfit.

"Now see here the scars?" Bud indicated the deep wide scar on Liberty's nose, and the marks on his legs, without touching them. "This ol' boy was in a train accident. He can't be ridden no more. He's a great, great horse. Maybe the smartest animal I've ever met. But he's no use to anyone because he can't be ridden and he can't stud. So they were gonna put him down once he got this bum leg

44

and hip, if you can believe that. Well Joy heard about it and she wouldn't have any of it, and she sent me over to Wyoming to get 'im and I brought 'im back up here. He's traumatized, like I said. He'll love you to pieces but he won't let you ride him. And the crazy thing is, when the train derailed, this one, he disappeared. They couldn't find him! There's blood all over the car, the ties are broken, and he's gone! He wandered in the woods for six weeks in the dead of winter. So animal control gets him, and that's how Joy heard about him. Can you imagine? Six weeks wandering in the woods, bleeding from his face and leg? Freezing? The poor guy was eating twigs and berries. We ain't even sure how he stayed alive but he did."

I looked in Liberty's eyes. They were blue, unlike most horses' brown eyes, and almost human the way they expressed emotion. He was looking back at me—*studying* me.

"Ain't those eyes something? It's the breed. We've been working with him to get that leg alright," Bud said. "When he first came to us he could barely stand and he was one minute away from the glue factory. I said no way was he lame, we can fix this, he just needs some personal attention, some very special TLC, and I gotta credit Joy, she's worked with him every day, walks with him, keeps him steady using that leg. He had a soft tissue thing in the right hip, but if he keeps up with the steady slow walks he might get over it…maybe even take a rider again, who knows."

"Wow…" I said. "You are one tough horse," I said to him, and reached out my hand. Liberty nuzzled it softly and snorted into my palm. He was looking for carrots.

"Sorry, Boy, I'll bring some next time," I said.

"He likes you," said Bud knowingly. "I can tell."

"I think…we kind of understand each other," I said. "I know a little something about surviving train wrecks, I guess."

I'd certainly been wandering in my own frozen wilderness for five years. But my scars were on the inside.

Bud shifted his weight and stretched his posture a little taller. "That's the thing about survivors," he said, looking me squarely in my eyes. "They can spot each other."

I pursed my lips into a smile and held Bud's gaze for long enough to see that he'd derailed and crashed himself at some point.

"Joy swears that Liberty lets her kiss the scar on his nose for good luck," Bud said.

I looked at Liberty. "Is that true, Boy?" I studied his eyes for a moment, and put my hand gently on the side of his head. He lowered his face slightly, as if he was leaning in to me.

"I could use a change in luck," I said to him, and gently kissed the very edge of the scar on his nose. He stood perfectly still. I patted his neck, and as I gave him a hug he sweetly shoved me a little the way horses do to people they like.

"I told ya," Bud said quietly. "He likes you."
As we walked back up to the house, Liberty loped behind us until a barn worker called him back. I found myself feeling sad to see him go, and suddenly I was really exhausted.

"Bud, would you and Joy mind if I went down for a nap for an hour or so? I think I've hit the wall," I said.

"Of course not, you go right ahead," he said. "I'll tell Joy, and I'll check in with the mechanic too, make sure everything's on schedule. We'll get ya outta here first thing tomorrow morning."

I smiled at him. "I honestly don't know how to thank you," I said quietly.

"No need," said Bud, with a wink. "I can tell you'll return the favor to somebody equal in need someday."

"Pay it forward," I said, smiling.

"Exactly," Bud said.

Maybe it was his kindness, or maybe it was the way Liberty looked deep into my soul and we understood each other, or the fact that I just blew up my whole life, or maybe I was just punch-drunk tired, but I suddenly found myself on the verge of a tsunami of tears.

I ran up the sweeping staircase to my room and shut the door behind me just in time for my body to start uncontrollably sobbing. I slumped against the door and slid slowly to the floor, quietly shaking and crying as hard as I've ever cried in my life. The reality of the past few hours sank in; I was in trouble. With money that wasn't mine, and probably wasn't even Brody's, a truck that wasn't mine, on my way to a home that wasn't mine anymore, with a mother who didn't want me there. I had no support, no plan. I left my job, my apartment, my boyfriend. *He is leaving today for six months, how could I do that to him? How could I abandon him like that?*

Each tear was a different emotion and they were all bad.

After about an hour crying on the floor, I crawled to the bed.

As I drifted off to sleep, with all the troubles spinning in my head, and all of the things I left behind, I heard Joy's words: "Fresh starts are easy. *It's the endings before them that are hard.*"

****

CHAPTER THREE
Taking Liberty

A soft knock on the door woke me up.

"Yes?" I called out. I had a terrible headache and I could feel my eyes were swollen from crying.

"Honey it's Joy, dinner will be in an hour, and Bud and I are going to have cocktails, okay? Just come on down whenever you like." Her voice was sweet and healing.

"Thank you, I'll be down in a little bit, that sounds so nice," I answered. I couldn't disguise in my voice how awful I felt.

There was a pause, I could sense she was waiting at the door for a moment.

"There is aspirin in the bathroom medicine cabinet," she said gently.

I went into the ensuite bathroom and washed my puffy face, pushed my hair around and dug through my purse for random cosmetics to patch my face into something that looked less…devastated. The towels were thick and brilliant white, hung perfectly folded. Five little yellow soaps that smelled like lemongrass were arranged in a silver soap tray. This was such a dream, to find myself here. I felt saved, in every way possible, as if I'd parachuted out of the flaming Hindenburg and floated gently down onto a giant pile of feather pillows. I swallowed three extra-strength aspirin. It was like I was in the eye of yesterday's hurricane that will be back tomorrow.

Who were these people? Angels?

Cocktails were gin and tonic on the rocks, served with sharp cheddar cheese and Ritz crackers. Bud, Joy, Luke and I sat on the beautiful wrap-around porch and watched the tree branches wave in the cool South Dakota wind. Liberty wandered slowly in the front yard, pausing by the porch as if he were listening to us. We made small talk about the weather and the cold snap in Montana.

I wanted to tell them the truth, but I was afraid they wouldn't understand. It was so hard to articulate, to explain what life was really like with him. Without a bruise or a broken bone, I must be making it all up.

Why couldn't people understand that loving someone makes you the most vulnerable you can possibly be, and they can do worse, or just as bad, as leaving a mark on your skin? It's like handing someone the keys to your most valuable possession—your psyche. Brody was so insecure, so damaged from who knows what—genetics or

his weird, creepy father and his narcissistic step mother—
that he only knew how to feel safe by making me feel
terrified.

"So Maggie, what's the first thing you're going to do
when you get home?" Joy's eyes lit up, eager to hear some
grand plans.

"Oh...well..." I struggled with wanting to vomit out the
truth, but I veered back. They were too good for the truth.
My truth, anyway. "I'll probably take a nap," I laughed
lamely. "Then maybe I'll just sit and have a nice long talk
with my mother. I haven't seen her in a long time."

Well, that was actually all true. Not so hard.

"Are you close with your mother?" Joy asked. Now it got
a little harder.

"I guess the honest answer would be no," I said
apologetically. "We've always been...different. She's her
own person, and so am I, and we...clashed...a lot growing
up, so it was tough. My dad left us when I was a baby, and
my mother had to move us in with her parents on their
farm. My mom is still there, her parents passed away, my
Grampa first fifteen years ago and my Gramma about
eight years ago. That was hard on her, I know. I was in
California then. I...couldn't come back for the funeral, so
she had to go through all that herself. I didn't go, but I
should have."

I had never heard myself say the words out loud, that *I didn't go but I should have*.

I thought for a minute about how that sounded, how the words coming out of my mouth made me sound so selfish. I was a bad daughter to her when she needed me. I remembered her calling me to tell me that Gramma was sick, and it wasn't good, and if she made it through Christmas it would be a miracle and I should come home. I didn't have the money, and neither did she, but I didn't try too hard to find it either. Gramma made it through Christmas and Mom called me three days into January to tell me she was gone. I'd never heard her sobbing so hard, even when her father died.

I loved Grampa so much. He was the only person in my life who never hurt me. He always lit up when he saw me. We shared an intense love of horses and I was the apple of his eye. When he died, I was so broken that I left for California and never went back.

I lowered my head.

"Honey," Joy said sweetly, "don't beat yourself up. You're going home to make it right. Your mom is still here. As long as she's here on this earth it's not too late." Tears were welling in her eyes, and Bud reached for her hand.

"Don't getcherself all worked up," he whispered to her. Joy shook off her memories. "Well…we all have a Cross to bear, don't we? Who's hungry? Maggie, Liberty sure has taken a shine to you. You can see that, can't you?" she smiled at Bud, and I felt like I was being fixed up on a blind date.

"He's an amazing horse," I said. "So beautiful. I used to ride when I was a little girl, at the farm. Grampa boarded horses and I'd ride them when the people weren't around. I rode English, with the helmet and the boots and the whole bit. My grandfather dressed me up like a little doll," I said. "He was a character. I really adored him. He would have adored Liberty. He loved horses with personality. He could really talk to them."

I looked at Liberty grazing by the fence. He almost had an aura, his coloring was so luminous. At a distance the scars didn't really show. *Grampa would have figured out a way to get him to take a rider,* I thought. Grampa was an absolute genius with horses.

Joy helped Betsy put the food on the table. "I am just heartbroken," Joy said. "We have to send Liberty to some sanctuary down South, and I'm just devastated about it. We don't have the room here, as you can see," she nodded toward the window.

"What happens to him there?" I asked.

"Well, we really aren't sure, are we, Bud?" Bud threw a slightly exaggerated shrug as he filled glasses with ice water from a crystal pitcher.

"We can only hope they don't—well, I'm not sure if Bud mentioned but Liberty can't be ridden anymore, and he can't stud…so…" her voice trailed off as she made room on the table for a bowl of buttered green beans.

"Oh no," I said, knowing exactly what they were shooting for, and playing right into it, because it was the craziest thing I could possibly do after running out on my life. And I felt my love for that horse swelling in my heart, like my life depended on saving him. Maybe if I saved him, someone would save me.

"Well…is he for sale? I mean I could take him to my farm, with me, or at least until you have room here or you find a better alternative. He could live happily on my mother's farm, I would love to have him there, I could send you pictures, you could visit, I have the trailer, I mean it's almost…"

"Fate?" Bud said, smiling, as he set the pitcher down. "Well…I tell you this. If I get wind you ain't taking prime care of him, I will personally—"

"Oh no Bud—you have my solemn word, he will be loved. It's my grandfather's barn, you have to know it's a beautiful horse barn. Nowhere near what you have here but he will be so happy there. And I could use the company on the drive," I smiled.

I thought of my mother's face, her expression as I pulled in the driveway, this surreally beautiful horse in tow after years of silence from me. What better way to rebuild your broken relationship with your mother than to show up unannounced with a stolen truck, a gun, fifty thousand dollars and a horse no one can ride? Come to think of it what better way to fix your life than to blow it up and start over? This was so nonsensical it made complete sense.

Joy clapped her hands together. "Okay! It's settled then. I'm so relieved. I feel good about this. Of course you will call your mother, to let her know?" Joy knew exactly what was going on with my mother, and I knew she was right.

Her blue eyes looked straight into my own, right through my pupils into my brain. It gave me chills. It was a kind look, but a knowing one.

"Um, well, I don't have the phone number, my cell is dead—and"

"Nonsense, I will look it up for you on the computer, you can use our phone. You should tell her you are coming. With Liberty, I mean." She smiled.

"That would be great," I said, guilt oozing out with each word.

"Listen, I have faith in you, Maggie. I believe in you, and I believe it was no accident that you broke down where you did. With an empty horse trailer! Could it be more serendipitous, really? This is all part of God's plan. You know that, don't you?" She winked at me and went into the kitchen.

Bud pulled out a chair at the dinner table for me to sit, and looked at me, grinning.

"Well, looks like you got yourself a horse, Young Lady," he said. He paused for a moment to look at Liberty and he chuckled to himself. "I'll be damned if the Lord don't just have it all figured out, don't He?"

I was beginning to realize there was a plan somewhere, I just didn't know I was following it until now. And I had no idea what was next.

***

My bedroom window faced the side yard, and I could see part of the horse paddock from my room. Joy had left me a pair of yoga pants and a t-shirt to sleep in, so I could wash my clothes. I couldn't imagine why they didn't ask me more questions about who I was, why I was driving alone, what was I all about. To let me sleep in their home, share a meal with them, take their precious horse...it all seemed so strange to me how much they trusted me.

Gratitude for me was a strange emotion—it was usually accompanied by guilt. I never felt worthy of charity or good deeds, because I usually felt that I'd somehow gotten myself into the predicament I was in, and this was certainly a great example of my self-sabotage. But even just petty good deeds, I think I always felt unworthy. My self-esteem was so low from years of being told I wasn't good enough to receive the things that others took for granted—kindness, goodness, warmth, especially love.

I thought about how Bud and Joy treated each other, which such respect and caring, having each other's back. I wondered what that was like. I'd never had that—not from my parents, not from a boyfriend. Not even from my friends. I had decent girl friends who stood by me, but the minute a guy came along they were gone.

Liberty was trotting across the paddock, shaking his mane in the setting sun. What a magnificent horse he was.

I wrenched open the window and rested my elbows on the sill. For all he'd been through he was such a happy horse. He couldn't be ridden anymore, yet was unafraid of humans. He didn't seem to be aware that he was no longer useful to most of them.

I pictured pulling up the long gravel driveway at Mom's farm, under the welded arch that said "Welcome to Tree Haven Farm," and putting Liberty in Grampa Bill's old red barn. The farm had six stalls and two paddocks, with twenty acres of woods behind it to ride in. The main house was a modest but sturdy old yellow-sided four-square, with original wood pocket French doors inside, beautiful tiger-wood trim all over the house and a great white-railed front porch where I used to sit with my grandmother Helen and count the cars on the distant main road as they drove by.

That house was Helen's pride and joy. The barn was Grampa Bill's world, and he would spend hours tinkering with door hinges, mucking stalls, fixing loose boards and making sure every hook and nail was perfect.

My heart started to swell with nostalgic childhood feelings I hadn't accessed in decades. I wanted to go home. I was on the right path. Whatever temporary psychotic break I had that made me flee Montana, it did me a huge favor. Like a giant hand had opened a door to a direction I didn't know I needed to go.

I figured if I drove straight through it would take me a day, with a few stops to let Liberty out to feed, walk and do his business. And some coffee stops for me. I didn't have to worry about the credit card because I had plenty of cash, wherever it came from.

The cash. I was sure Brody had put some kind of word out at least about the money. There was no way it was legal. Where would he get that much money? I could get the truck back to Montana somehow by the time Brody got back from his contract job, and I would call my job and tell them I quit. And our apartment, that was a hard one. Six months of rent and unpaid bills would not be good. I'd have to figure that one out later.

I just had to get home to New York, get back to my childhood farm, get Liberty settled, get myself settled, just sit down for a minute and have a cup of tea, take a walk in the woods maybe, smell the hay in the barn, just breathe. Let my head unscramble, and I would figure things out.

I would start fresh. My own version of starting fresh this time, not someone else's.

***

"Google," she said, smiling. Joy handed me a pretty flowered piece of paper with a name and phone number written on it.

"Pearl." My mother's name was so delicate. It conjured up a sweet woman who brought casseroles to neighbors' houses in time of need, or belonged to the Ladies Auxiliary at the church, or cut up orange slices for her children's soccer team.

These things were not my mother.

My Pearl was a petite woman, and by common standards was beautiful, with prominent cheekbones and dark brown eyes that cut right through you as they peered out of her pale Irish skin. But sweet was not in my mother's toolbox.

Pearl did what was good for Pearl, and if sweet played into that, well you got lucky. But most of the time Pearl was critical, cutting everything around her down so she could feel taller than her tiny frame. She was never fully present, with her slightly detached way of appearing like she was doing a math problem in her head or thinking of something else while you were trying to get through to her. She didn't listen to you, she only waited until you were done talking so she could say what she wanted to say.

Pearl remembered things the way she needed to remember them, in order for her to be right, or for her to be the victim. Nothing was ever Pearl's fault, but everything successful was to Pearl's credit. Unless it was a missed opportunity, then it was your fault for not listening to Pearl because she knew all along what was the right thing to do.

Pearl was an absolutely maddening person to deal with, and my father hadn't even stuck around to see me being born. I never knew him, never met him. Pearl herself took off for a year right after I was born. To "find herself" I guess. She came back when she realized she was right where she left her, apparently. Growing up I barely knew her. She was a ghost, came and went, always seemingly trying to snare some sugar daddy or who knows what. My grandparents raised me, pretty much.

After I turned eleven or so Pearl decided to stick around and suddenly be a "parent," which meant blaming me for how miserable she had made herself in life. We butted heads constantly.

When I was a teenager, Pearl and I almost came to blows over my forgetting to empty the dishwasher one night. She accused me of purposely being insubordinate, but I simply forgot—I was doing my homework and talking on the phone with my friend and I went to bed. A drunken Pearl kicked in my bedroom door, hollering about my willful disobedience, throwing a few of my records against the wall. She reeked of alcohol as she grabbed me by the wrist and pulled me out of bed. I was halfway down the stairs before I was able to get my feet under me. She dragged me to the kitchen and berated me for ten minutes as I calmly emptied the dishwasher: I was lazy, I didn't know how to comb my hair or wear makeup, no wonder I had no boyfriends, I was never going to find a man if I couldn't even iron my clothes to look decent. She was relentless, cutting and mean.

I was shaking and furious. By then I had grown a few inches taller than she was, and I'd had enough. I put away the last dish, gently closed the dishwasher, turned around and unleashed a Holy Hell of Terror on Pearl the likes of which she'd never seen. I screamed, cursed, told her she drove away my father, told her she was a bitter old drunken whore who abandoned her only child, said hateful, hurtful, painful things, told her I hated her, everyone hated her. Years of her verbal and sometimes physical abuse had built up in me and I just let it out.

Gramma and Grampa had to have heard it, but they never came downstairs, which I always thought was so strange. Back then I had not connected all the dots.

Pearl was stunned at my display, since I'd been so compliant for so long. She tried to play the victim card, the 'you should be grateful for all I've done for you' card but it didn't make me didn't feel guilty, I felt *more* angry.

"That's not gonna work this time, Mom!" I shouted. "I'm OVER this. I'm not taking your shit anymore, I'm not your emotional punching bag! You're a loser and a drunk and everyone can see you fucked up your life! *My life!* I HATE YOU!"

I went upstairs to my room, slammed the door so hard a picture fell off the wall. The next morning she acted like nothing happened. My grandparents never mentioned it. I emptied the dishwasher every single night after that, without fail, and Pearl never raged at me again. We both won.

But my words, which were designed to hurt her as deeply as possible, did just that. Other than superficial short sentences, my mother and I effectively never spoke about anything substantive again.

When my grandfather died years later, my mom and my grandmother and I were sitting at her kitchen table at the farm after the wake. I had an apartment in Buffalo about an hour away, and we were all staring down at our teacups saying nothing. It was late, and we were all tired.

"Gramma," I said, "Are you going to be okay?"

My mother didn't even look up. "She's always okay," she said flatly. "That's all she has to worry about now, herself."

"Mom!" I couldn't believe her insensitivity. My grandmother just silently got up from the table and went upstairs.

"Mom, what is wrong with you? Jesus, she just lost her husband of almost fifty years, her best friend?! Why would you make it worse for her?"

Pearl seemed to always need to make everyone around her feel worse. It was the only way she knew to feel better.

She didn't miss a beat. "Oh she will be fine. Trust me. All she knows how to do is take care of herself. She made sure his life insurance policy was up to date." My mother got up from the table and went to her room.

I was dumbfounded. My grandmother was a tough farm-raised woman, and she was no gold-digger. She devoted her entire life to my grandfather and his farm, which was always teetering on the brink of some financial crisis.

I tried to talk to my grandmother about her grief, but she seemed to shut down completely after Grampa died. I thought of the two women living in that farmhouse, with all that silent toxic energy. Within three months I was far away out in California, barely even acknowledging that I had relatives back home, let alone a painful history there. As far as I was concerned, my entire childhood, my pain and my past were boxed up, three thousand miles away, somewhere in the attic of that old farmhouse.

***

I looked at Joy. "Is there—may I have some privacy?"

"Of course," she said. "You can use Bud's office," and led me to a regal, wood-paneled study with sweeping huge windows that faced the paddock.

I settled in the big leather chair and picked up the phone. I hoped with every cell in my body that my mother wasn't home.

I dialed the number and felt my hand trembling. I thought of that day all those years ago putting away the dishes, and all the days after that of the tension between my mother and me, just thick as fog in the air between us. So much animosity had built up over the years through space and silence; imagined arguments that built on real ones. Absence did not make our hearts grow fonder. That doesn't work when two people each live in their own echo chamber of toxic memories. Angry thoughts just multiply and get louder.

"Hello." Her terse voice sent a chill up the back of my neck.

"Mom?" I said, with a strange-sounding awkward happiness.

There was a silent pause. "Margaret. What happened, is everything okay?" Her voice was flat. She knew I would only call with facts, not with feelings.

"Well—yes. I mean. Everything is okay, I guess. I just—how are you?"

"I am fine. Why are you calling?"

"Well, okay, I guess I'll just get right to it. I've left Brody, left Montana, pretty much, um, quit my job there, the whole thing, and I'm—I'd like to come home, and I'd like to stay at the farm. And I have a horse with me to put in the barn."

There was a long, stony silence on the phone. Was she going to refuse me? Her own daughter? Or was she looking for an apology, something else? No, that wasn't the Pearl I knew. An apology wasn't anything of real value to Pearl.

"I'll pay you rent and board for the horse, Mom. "

"Okay, when will you arrive then?" she said quickly. Same old Pearl.

"I'll be there day after tomorrow, Mom," I said.

"Okay then. Be careful pulling up the drive, the sign came down in the ice storm a few winters ago, and the drive is not in great shape," she said.

"Okay, I will. Thanks Mom," I said.

"Just don't hit the gate with the horse trailer on the way in, it's hanging crooked from that ice storm too," she said, and hung up.

"I will be careful not to cause any damage, Mom," I said to the dial tone.

***

The next morning I got dressed, packed up my purse and the duffel bag and went downstairs.

Bud and Joy were already on the porch with their coffee. "Good morning, Sleepyhead!" Bud said.

Joy shushed him. "We figured you needed some rest," she said.

"I'm sorry, I thought you'd wake me," I said. It was only eight o'clock.

"Eh, we get goin' around six a.m. here," Bud said. "So the truck is ready, Joy is going to take you into town and pick it up, then you come back here and we'll pack up Liberty. I'm gonna be sad to see him go. I've got a real soft spot for that ol' boy."

"I'll take good care of him," I promised. I meant it. "Um, what was the charge for the truck? I have—I'd like to pay in cash, so—"

"Well, just cover the cost of the tire, $200 will do it," Bud said. "The mechanic threw a spare he had in the back of your truck. He just had an old one laying around it turns out," Bud smiled. "Is that good for ya?" I recalled him saying they had to order the new tire, and I knew I was getting two new tires for the price of one.

"Oh, I just can't thank you enough. Really. When I get settled I will send you a giant fruit basket, or something." I had no idea how to thank these people adequately for saving my life.

Joy shushed us both. "Oh now both of you stop that, we need to get going. This is all just people taking care of each other. And Maggie you are going to give Liberty a beautiful new home so we can't ask for more than that."

Joy and I took their old truck into town, and on the way she told me about life on their farm, and how Bud made his fortune in cattle and commodities, and they were pretty much semi-retired from all that now, just enjoying life and managing their investments and two black angus ranches in Colorado that kept them flush. She said they had two sons, one had been in the military but was in law enforcement now, and Luke, who was her baby. She didn't know what she was going to do when Luke grew up. But she had a feeling he would stay on the farm. He loved the farm life, she said.

We got into town, which was more like two tiny streets of an old West movie set, and I gave the mechanic two hundred dollars. I thanked him for the spare. He nodded at Joy and said "I'd do anything for these folks, and they said to help you out."

Whatever I did to get in their good graces, I thanked my lucky stars again.

"Oh, here's your registration," he said.

My blood went cold. "What?"

"Sorry, we had to dig around in your glove box to find the wheel lock."

"Here," he handed me a pile of papers, and he pointed a grease-stained finger at the name on the registration.

It was mine. The asshole registered the truck and the insurance in my name.

I stole my own truck.

"Thanks…" I muttered, staring hard at the letters, as though they were going to suddenly rearrange into Brody's name if I didn't keep staring.

I followed Joy in my newfound truck back to the farm, wondering what else Brody had done without telling me, besides stuffing fifty thousand dollars under my car seat.

We gathered Liberty's tack and blankets, and loaded him into the trailer. He seemed fine with the trailer's confined space, which surprised me. I thought he would be scared after what happened to him, but he wasn't.

"He's good on the road," said Bud. "He can see out the sides. It's when there's no windows he has a problem. And whatever you do, don't put nothin' on his back except his blanket at night. Nothin'! I think in the accident something mighta fallen on 'im and it hurt 'im, or maybe it's that hip, who knows, but he don't like anything on his back."

"Got it," I said. "I will follow the care book to the letter." Bud handed me a two-inch thick binder full of Liberty's records and notes about his progress and treatment since his rescue.

I threw my purse and the duffel bag in the back seat, hugged Bud and Luke goodbye, and turned to Joy.

She had tears in her eyes. She was so fragile, but at the same time something about her was unbreakable. "This is a special animal," she said. "He will show you things. Talk to him. He will listen."

"I know," I smiled at her. "He already has. He kind of told me to take him with me. I think I need him more than he needs me," I said. She nodded knowingly.

"Liberty needed us for a time, and I needed him. We went on a lot of long walks together at a time when I needed that. But now he needs you, and vice versa. Take him for walks. You'll see."

She hugged me and I thanked her one last time for their kindness. I started to cry myself.

"You will never know what you've done for me," I said. "You really saved my life."

"I do know," she said. She looked at me sweetly. "And if for some reason, you ever find yourself back in Montana, look up our eldest son...he's a deputy, back in Butte Falls. Deputy Dakota Taylor." She looked into my eyes.

I thought of the cherubic faced kid on the phone at the deputy's desk. I smiled at her. They knew everything all along.

"He does mostly overnight desk duty right now, but he'll be moving up soon, I'm sure. He's a really good boy," her eyes turned a softer, more knowing shade of blue.

"Now go home, settle yourself there. You've got a head start—a *fresh* start. Godspeed and oh—kiss Liberty, for luck, remember! He loves that."

As I drove down the dusty driveway toward the Interstate, the last thing I heard was Bud's booming voice yelling "Pay it forward, now!"

****

CHAPTER FOUR
The Best Laid Plans

I could see the shape of Liberty's head in the trailer through my rear view mirror. He seemed okay, just kind of hanging out. South Dakota stretched on forever as I drove on through a light rain. The FM stations fuzzed in and out so I listened to AM stations playing a lot of weepy oldies from my seventies childhood.

Karen Carpenter's perfect alto crooned about the old melodies, sha-la-la-la, every whoa-oh-oh-whoa …and I thought of the farm. It made me feel good about getting back there.

The beautiful red barn, the old white house with the big porch and black shutters, the chicken coops and the trail into the woods that I used to ride.

My daydream of maybe restarting Grampa's horse-boarding business carried me for a good hour across the South Dakota wheat plains as I imagined a mini-version of Bud and Joy's place in Spaulding Quarry, New York on about one percent of the acreage. And the budget.

When I was in first or second grade a boy who lived a mile or so up the road used to come over after school sometimes when his mother was working. I tried to remember his name, maybe Kevin or Keith or something. He was obsessed with the two cows we had. Grampa taught him how to milk them, and Kevin-Keith whats-his-name would ask a hundred questions about the milk and how to make ice cream and what is cheese and yogurt and everything else. Grampa used to call him Egghead, which I thought didn't make sense because he was not interested in the chickens at all. Grampa said he was a great milker though.

I wondered what happened to him. He was really nice, and he had a great sense of humor. For all his love of cows though, he was terrified of the horses. His mother was divorced, and they lived in a little dingy duplex apartment they rented on our neighbor's property. She always seemed desperate and unhappy. I felt a pang of empathy for her now.

I pulled over at a rest stop somewhere just across the Minnesota border to let Liberty out for a walk, and so I could muck out the giant horseshit he'd deposited in the trailer. Who knew I would become the sudden, proud owner of a giant blue truck, a horse trailer, and a horse? I laughed to myself at the absurdity of how scared I was that I stole my own truck. With fifty thousand dollars in it.

I got a giant coffee and a bad sandwich and kept driving. With a routine of rest-stop naps, shoveling shit, drinking

coffee and eating junk food, Liberty and I found ourselves
an hour outside the farm in twenty hours.

It was just about dawn, and I was wired and exhausted
from the road but getting off the road was all I wanted to
do. I turned up "Couldn't Get it Right" by the Climax
Blues Band on another scratchy AM oldies station I'd
found, bugged my eyes open, pressed harder on the gas
pedal, and made a plan.

First, I would get Liberty settled in the barn, with all of his
tack and blankets, then I would have as much of a civil
conversation with my mother as possible, then I would
sleep. I hadn't really slept well in three days. Then I
would power up my phone. By now Brody would have
landed wherever he was headed and I'd be out of his
physical reach. I would be safe to check my messages and
start to fix this mess.

Brody. I could only imagine the cussing, violent, abusive
messages on my voicemail. There were probably dozens
of them. Especially since he knew I had his *fifty thousand
dollars*. Maybe he couldn't claim his—my—truck, but he
would certainly want to restore that money to whatever its
original purpose was.

Then the next day I'd take some of that money and go get
a suit, so I could go find a job. Maybe an accounting job
again? Bookkeeping? That was really my only skill
besides carrying four hot breakfast specials on two arms. I
was really good with numbers and books. It was a weird

thing. Grampa used to call me his Little Mathlete. He would test me on my multiplication tables, and my first job out of high school was doing the books for a bar where I was also a waitress.

Yes, that was a plan. Then I would save up as much money as I could, and maybe take in some horses as boarders for extra money. If I cut Pearl in of course she'd go for it.

After that, well, I would cross that bridge when I came to it. Or knowing Pearl, before it burned.

I exited the highway and felt a weird mix of nostalgia, sorrow and regret as I steered us along the rural roads to the farm. Fifteen years hadn't changed the landscape much.

As I approached the old gate, I saw what Mom had warned me about—the iron archway had toppled somehow, and it lay on its side against the metal gate, which was also broken and askew against the wood fence. The rusted chains and tall grass grown around it made it obvious that it had been that way for a long time.

"Well maybe we can fix that," I mumbled out loud.

I slowly rolled over the gravel and dirt driveway, but it felt like an earthquake. Ruts and craters a foot deep made it rough going and I watched the trailer nervously as Liberty snorted and stomped a few times at the bumpy ride. The driveway was lined with beautiful oak trees that stood tall

and strong, like a row of monuments among the ruins to
some bygone era.

The fields were overgrown with tall grass and the worn,
weathered fence posts were randomly down everywhere.

As I rounded the drive past the trees and saw the barn and
the house, a sinkhole opened up in my chest and I stopped
the truck.

"Holy fuck," I whispered aloud. My mouth hung slack
jawed.

I got out of the truck slowly and surveyed my
grandfather's barn. His pride and joy. The great doors
were hanging crooked off the hinges, their faded and
peeling paint announcing years of neglect. The roof
sagged in the middle, dotted with missing shingles and
discolored patches. There was overgrown grass
everywhere—weeds and wildflowers randomly popping
up through bald spots in the middle of the driveway.

The house had lost three shutters, and was in very bad
need of a power washing or repainting or both. A few
porch spindles were missing, so the once gleaming farm
porch looked like an old homeless man's teeth. Two gray
tabby cats lazed on the steps.

Fallen twigs were all around, and the deep ruts carved in
the mud made walking an ankle-twisting nightmare.

"Maggie?" Pearl came out of the beat-up screen door to the front steps. I looked up and she raised her hand in a half wave. Pearl looked so small, frail almost, and her hair was now white.

"Hi Mom," I said flatly. I wanted to say "WHAT THE FUCK MOM?" but I didn't think that was the best way to start off.

I walked up to the steps and gave her a polite hug, which she returned stiffly. I could smell coffee inside. Her black eyes, framed by a now-hardened, wrinkled face, stared past me.

"That the horse?"

Yea," I said. "I see the barn—the roof—is it safe?"

"Well we had an ice storm, and you know since Gramma died money has been really tight, so I can't make any repairs except essentials. Plumbing, electrical, the septic tank, that kind of thing. The roof is okay, for now," she sounded like she was challenging me.

"Okay, well I'm going to get Liberty out of the trailer and settled and then you and I can talk, how does that sound?"

She eyed me and shrugged. "Fine," she said and turned back into the house. "Coffee's on," she said with her back to me.

I took a deep breath. I didn't remember my mother being so frail. And so...*old.*

I brought Liberty out of the trailer and tied him outside with feed and water. He seemed fine with his new surroundings, even if I wasn't.

The barn inside was even worse than the outside. Bats had taken residence in the rafters and there was bat shit everywhere.

"Literally, bats in her belfry," I said out loud.

There were two stalls in the back of the barn that were covered overhead and bat shit free, so I cleaned them out—the barn had become a repository for old rusted tools, two rusted out lawn mowers, dozens of moldy horse blankets, four old weed whackers, rolled up electrical extension cords, piles of rags and the odd boot or glove.

I swept the floors and hung Liberty's tack on the hooks my Grampa had so meticulously installed decades ago. If the rest of the barn was a disaster, at least that one stall was nice. I worried about the bats and diseases but I had no choice at this point. I couldn't leave Liberty in the trailer all night.

The paddock and the training corral fences were broken in too many places, so I put Liberty in the cleanest stall for the time being.

"I will fix this shit all up, don't worry," I said. Hopefully one of those lawnmowers worked.

Inside, Mom was sitting at the kitchen table sipping her coffee. The interior hadn't changed so much. The furniture was the same, just more worn. The hardwood floors were shabby but not too bad, and I didn't even want to think about the roof on the house.

I brought in my duffel bag and my purse, and found my old room walls to be pretty much as they were fifteen years ago, although all my possessions were gone. It was a shrine to my grandmother's sewing now, and full of giant Tupperware tubs of her belongings. Apparently my mother hadn't gotten rid of any of her clothes or costume jewelry or anything else. "Just her money, right Pearl?" I mumbled.

In the upstairs bathroom I turned on the faucet to wash my face and the plumbing made the most awful sound before a spurt of brown water came out. Then clear water came out.

"Shit, that's not good," I looked at my tired reflection in the mirror. "Congratulations, Maggie. You got yourself out of the frying pan, and dove right in the fire."

****

CHAPTER FIVE
What Happened Is What Happened

I went downstairs and poured a cup of coffee from my grandmother's old percolator pot. God it was good coffee. I missed her. She'd have hugged me for a long time, and smiled with her red lipstick and said *"Let's have some tea and toast…"*

"So…Mom, how are you?"

She set down the newspaper she was reading. "I'm fine. What is this all about? You have no luggage? A horse? What the hell is going on here?"

"Well…I left Brody, I left Montana, in fact…I'm sort of…rebuilding, I guess? Starting fresh? The horse is a rescue. His name is Liberty." I tried to read her dark eyes for any emotion, but all I could see was judgment.

"Rescue? You're rescuing horses now?" Her tone was slightly mocking, something I was used to from her. I bristled. I needed her now. And I hated that I needed her now.

"Well, it's temporary," I lied. "Look, Mom, all this is temporary. I just need to stay here for a few months until I can get a job, get back on my feet. Like I said I'll pay you rent and board for Liberty. And…I can see the farm needs some work—"

"Ugh. This place. The taxes alone are killing me. They ate up all Gramma's inheritance money. The roof on the barn, one more bad winter is going to knock it down. The plumbing, electrical, the grounds are overgrown," she said.

She held up her hands. Her fingers were beginning to twist at the knuckles.

"See this? I am in so much pain, all the time. Arthritis. I can't do much, I just can't, so I just watch it all wither away, I just sit here and it withers away, it falls apart around me. I put it on the market last year but the only offer wouldn't even cover the second mortgage on the place."

I'd seen my mother pull the victim card, but I'd never actually seen her be a victim. She wasn't crying, but this was real.

"How much do you owe, Mom?" I braced myself.

"Well when Gramma died all she had left was about eight thousand dollars, that was it. And we had to replace the septic tank—"

"Eight thousand? Where did all her money go? How much, Mom."

"Fifty-five thousand," she said.

"Hmmm." My head was spinning. "And the taxes. Mom? How much in arrears?"

She lowered her head. I couldn't believe this was Pearl. My Pearl. Lowering her head?

"Twelve thousand."

I sat back in my chair. "A septic tank isn't fifty thousand dollars. And this place hasn't been repaired in who knows how long. Where did the money go?"

She sat quietly for a moment, staring down at her misshapen fingers.

"Mom. Where did the money go."

She barely whispered. "There was a man—"

My shoulders dropped.

"Not me!" she protested. "It was Gramma! He used to come around after Grampa died. Gramma was very sad for a long time, and this guy comes around. She loved him, he would do odd jobs around, and she would make him lunch. He would drive her into town. He wanted to start this business, some kind of landscaping thing, and he convinced her to take out extra money. She gave him almost thirty thousand dollars. He took off, she never heard from him again. That was right before she died."

"You never mentioned this guy?" I said. I couldn't believe she let my grandmother do this.

"Mom did you not see this guy was some kind of grifter? What were you thinking?"

"What was I thinking? I was thinking he made her happy! I had no idea she was going to give him thirty thousand dollars! I thought she took out the mortgage for twenty-five thousand to cover the septic tank and electrical. I had no idea what she did! He drove her to the bank! Please, it's not like you cared. You know what? You didn't even come home when she was sick! You broke her heart when you didn't come home when she was sick. You didn't even come home when she died! But now you come here out of nowhere, with some goddamned horse and start judging me and you have no idea what has happened here!" she got up from the table and started to walk away.

"Mom—wait. You're right. I'm sorry."

I saw Joy's sparkling eyes in my mind, and thought of her words, that it wasn't too late to make things right.

"You're right. I should have been here. I was wrong to not come home, and I'm so sorry about that. I want to know what happened. I want to know what happened to the farm and to you."

"What happened? What happened IS what happened!" she choked on her words and for the first time in my entire life, I saw Pearl cry. Real tears. Not fake dramatic tears to manipulate someone, but real tears.

"Mom, I'm sorry. Really. Please—" I reached out to hug her but she pushed me away and started to go up the stairs, lifting her limbs slowly. Was she really in that much pain? She gripped the rail with her left hand and shook off her emotions.

I tried to process the gigantic pile of shit I was standing in.

"Mom," I said softly, "I came here to make a fresh start. That means with you too." She ignored me, but at that moment, we both realized why my coming home was so timely, and so difficult, for both of us.

We both needed each other. And we both hated it.

***

I woke up the next morning from what felt like a coma, tied Liberty outside in the fresh fall air I and went into town to go shopping and go to the bank.

Spaulding Quarry's downtown was quaint, touristy, dotted with fancy street lamps. The central gazebo was surrounded by a mix of high-end boutiques catering to the wealthy people that had million-dollar summer homes on the lake, and old-timey everyday shops that were clearly for the poorer people who cleaned those homes and mowed their lawns. There was a giant outlet mall about twenty minutes up the highway, and a big casino resort on the Indian reservation about an hour away. A few big-box retailers had moved in along the highway exits, but the town was still charming and small. It hadn't been overrun by strip malls yet.

At the bank I opened an account in my name and deposited three thousand dollars in it, explaining to the bank manager that I was a waitress long ago in Montana and saved up my tips to move home. I decided I would pay Mom's tax bill on a payment plan through the account, and I'd deposit enough to pay the tax bill each time so hopefully no red flags would go up about where the money came from.

At Target I picked up a few things like a hairbrush, underwear, a sweatshirt that said ironically "I heart me" and a pair of jeans, work boots and some deodorant that would help me feel like I wasn't a fugitive any more. I also got a phone charger. I stared at it in my hand for a good long minute before I threw it in my cart. I went to Handy's Hardware and bought enough supplies to fix a few things around the barn and fix the fence on the small paddock, and I asked around about a handyman, and the bat problem. The hardware guy said to call the university, they had a bat research program and maybe they would help.

I stopped at the grocery store and got some food for lunch, and when I got back Mom was awkwardly sweeping off the front porch.

"Should you be doing that?" I called to her as I unloaded the truck.

"Oh it helps to move around a little," she said.

"I brought lunch," I said. "And I'm going to get to that small paddock and fix a few things around here. Can we talk about some stuff, Mom?"

She stopped sweeping long enough to nod at me suspiciously.

Over tuna sandwiches I told her I wanted to pay off the farm taxes on a payment plan, that I had some savings I could use. That would alleviate the immediate danger of us losing the place. I explained that if we fixed up the barn and paddock we could board horses and take in a little cash, maybe fix up the farm enough to eventually sell it at a good price to cover the mortgage, or if she wanted to stay, to pay it off with the boarding income.

I told her we should look into selling off some acreage on the edge of the property too, and maybe talk to a financial planner one day, to make sure she was okay for the future. I laid out the plan in simple terms, and downplayed it all like I was trying to get a squirrel to eat out of my hand. Pearl spooked easily if she felt like you were trying to control her. I wasn't, but that's how she would take it if I was too forceful.

"So…just think it over, Mom. I don't want you to lose this farm. And I'm grateful to you that you took me and Liberty in. I want to help is all," I said.

She eyed me warily.

"I'll go along with the first part of the plan for now," she said sharply. "But I'll pay you back for the taxes when the farm sells or I die, whichever is first. I have a life insurance policy that will almost cover it. But you pay me $500 a month for rent now, minus expenses for repairs, you give me receipts, and $100 for boarding Liberty," she stood up suddenly to take her plate to the sink.

That's the Pearl I know. Don't show your poker face. Don't show your face at all. She will never say "thank you" or even "you're welcome," because that would mean telling me she felt something.

***

I took Liberty on a tether to the paddock to walk the fence and see how badly it was damaged. There were a few spots where the rails had just fallen out of the post holes, and a few rails were missing. The grass was badly overgrown, but if any of those weed whackers worked I could do all this work myself over the next few days. Liberty accompanied me like the gentleman he was, occasionally stopping to yank a clump of tall grass out of the ground for a snack.

"I think we can make this work, yea? Just fix the rails, maybe use some of the rails from the large paddock for now? Get you settled in this paddock and then figure the rest out?" I patted his muscular shoulders. He was such a stunning animal, even with the scars. Bud and Joy had left me a bottle of mane oil with Liberty's belongings, and I hoped I could maintain its sheen like they had.

I repaired a few broken hinges in the barn, fed Liberty and went back into the house. Mom was freshly showered and she was vacuuming.

"I made some iced tea!" she shouted above the whir, without looking up.

Interesting, I thought. When I arrived the house looked like it hadn't been vacuumed in months.

***

After the ceremonial brown water spurt in my bathroom upstairs I washed up, and checked my phone. It was fully charged.

With a deep breath, I pressed the button down and the phone buzzed to life.

As it beeped through its booting up process I felt sick to my stomach. It had been two days now, and Brody was long gone on a plane to the Middle East, but he had to have known somehow that I ran off with his truck—my truck—and the fifty thousand dollars that was stuffed under the driver's seat.

It was down a little now, I mean I was actually *spending* this money. Was it drug money? Brody was never into drugs. He was too vain to do drugs. Was it someone else's money? I had no worry spending Brody's money. He stole my soul, he stole my self-esteem, he stole my happiness, he stole five years of my life. He owed me a lot more than fifty thousand dollars. But the thought of my spending someone else's money put a lump in my throat.

The phone blinked on and I saw that I had six messages. Five from the diner, and one from Kim, my coworker. That was it? No other messages? Nothing from Brody. Well, was he going to yell at me for stealing my own truck? I laughed to myself how proud he was that he paid cash for it. He probably put it in my name because he couldn't get it insured otherwise.

The phone had been dead almost four days now. It felt like weeks since I walked out of the sheriffs' station but it was only four days ago.

I would have missed two shifts by now. I braced myself.

"Hi, Maggie, this is Paul at work. Just wondering where you are, hope you're not sick, wondering if you're coming in today. Thanks."

"Yea, hi Maggie, this is Paul. I hope everything is okay, it's not like you not to show up so…please call when you get a chance. Thanks."

"Hey Maggie, didn't hear from you yesterday and you're not here now again, so I'm going to go ahead and cover your shift today and tomorrow. I'm not sure what to think. I called the hospital, nothing, so…just call when you get this."

"Hi Maggie, Paul again, just trying to reach you."

"Hey Mags it's Kim, where have you been? Paul is like, either she's dead or she ran away. My money is on ran away…we all know Brody's gone …call me so I know you're alive, please."

"Hi Maggie, this is Paul. I'm afraid I have to let you go, and terminate you immediately, as of now. I'm sorry to do this in a voice mail but three shifts with no phone call or notification, I just can't have that. I'm sorry. Please return your uniform and nametag as soon as possible. Thank you."

I breathed a sigh of relief. I never had to go back there. I never had to bang the side of the coffee machine to get it to start working. I never had to carry four burning hot plates on my two arms. I never had to endure grabby drunks on an overnight shift again. I never had to wear that stained, plasticky polyester uniform. Smell that rancid grease smell. Count out *nickels and dimes* in my tips.

89

I thought about the day Paul hired me. He was a paunchy, sweaty balding man, with an aura of defeat about him, who just wanted someone to cover the damn shift already. I hadn't been completely worn to a fine powder yet, so I probably looked like a positive, fine prospect that day I walked in and begged for a job.

And here, I left him with the one thing he hated most—a stiff on a shift. My mother's voice snapped me out of my guilt.

"Maggie! Maggie, can you come down here, I need to talk to you about the paddock and the front gate! And this article I found this morning."

***

Pearl and I sat on the front porch, cold iced tea in our hands, and surveyed the worn front yard. The farm's glory years were still visible if you really looked for them; but weeds and the aftermath of death had pretty much taken over.

"Maggie, this plan for the horses, to board them—the barn roof needs work. See the sagging part there? We had a bad ice storm about six years ago and the damage was pretty bad. But I read this in the paper this morning. Look at this."

The roof looked like I felt—as if it had just let out a really big sigh. I read the article she handed me. A woman in the next county over had just been arrested for hoarding twenty-three horses. They were malnourished, some had to be euthanized.

"The authorities are going to be looking for places to take these animals in, and they are going to pay, the County will pay. If we fix up the barn we can take five of them," Pearl said. "Then we can heal them up, get them re-homed, and we will be in business," she clapped her hands together twice.

"But if we want to do this boarding thing we need to fix that roof, and we need to fix the big paddock," Pearl said flatly. She stared straight ahead. "And the front gate. Nobody wants to board their horses at a place where the gate is broke down and rusted out."

She was right. The fallen arched sign rested on the ground, in profound announcement to the world that things at this farm were no longer going so well. It may as well have said "Abandon all hope, ye who enter here."

"I think you're right, Mom," I said. A flicker of a giddy smile flashed across her face. I hadn't seen her smile since I'd arrived. "I think the small paddock is fine, I can fix that fence myself. But the big paddock, well, that we are going to need a lot of help with. What exactly do you propose here? And the sign up front—that's going to require a welder. And money."

Pearl frowned. "Yes, I know. But you said, you said...you have some saved up? And I was thinking. I do have a little bit, I was keeping it for an emergency, hospital, something like that, but if we can do this right, we can make that back in no time. Winter is coming and they will need places to put those poor horses."

"Mom, this is all a great idea, but I have to just ask one question, just a practical thing—"

She frowned again.

"Mom, I can't take care of six horses alone. I will need some help. And you—well —you hate horses, Mom."

She focused on the front gate in the distance again. "I've endured a lot of things I hate," she said. "I can learn to love it if I have to. I wasn't your grandfather's daughter without learning a few things, you know," she said as she went into the house and let the screen door slam behind her.

There was the Pearl I knew. But also a Pearl I'd never seen before.

****

CHAPTER SIX
Mending Fences

For the next six weeks the farm was a beehive of activity. Pearl and I didn't have time to get along or not get along with each other because we were both zeroed in on the same thing—getting the farm back to where it once was, or at least where it had to be.

I called the POWER2PAWS animal rights group and talked to them about the horses seized from the hoarder woman's farm. I explained that if they could send me volunteers to help me clean up the barn, then we could house five of the horses that had been seized. I asked for five able-bodied people and to my shock *twenty-two* showed up—younger ones, old ones, big ones, little ones, all donning red shirts and ready to get dirty. They were "between jobs" or retired or who knows what, and I was grateful for how hard they worked.

Six of them were little old ladies, so I put them on weed-whacker duty. I told them curb appeal was very important and they were like Ninja warriors with those things.

Two guys, both coincidentally named Ken, whom I dubbed The Kens, were assigned the roof. One was a retired carpenter and the other a recently college-graduated hopeful architect who just lost his barista job. I paired them together and asked them to use their cell phone cameras and their two brains to assess the roof damage, but please without getting themselves or anyone else killed. I made the sign of the Cross as they ascended the ladder.

Others who could lift heavy fence posts and wield power tools helped me fix the small paddock perimeter and carry all the junk out of the barn so the bat researchers from the university could get rid of the bats.

That was unreal, like a Hitchcock movie. An army of hazmat-suited, bespectacled researchers went inside the barn with bat traps and humanely trapped dozens of them, while hundreds of other freaked-out bats flapped out to escape over our heads. Then the researchers had some kind of crazy solution spray, a vacuum and a fire hose to clean out the bat shit.

The university asked if we minded if a local TV news crew did a story on the whole thing, and I said fine, as long as they mentioned it would be *clean* after, they would say the "Tree Haven Farm" a few times, and did not mention me or my name, or show my truck.

Pearl got a few phone calls about boarding horses after it aired, and she kept the names and numbers. She really had a way with the news crews. They loved her coffee.

At night, I went to work on the downstairs den, painting and fixing it up as an office for us to use. Pearl cleaned out an old filing cabinet and I salvaged our old dining room table from the basement, sanded and painted it white to use for a desk.

Pearl took to fixing lunch and snacks for all the volunteers, a daily process I watched with my mouth agape. She would smile like June Cleaver and set up a lovely buffet of sandwiches and iced tea on the porch. Then she'd set up full coffee service in the afternoons with a little ceramic cream and sugar set. This was definitely a Pearl I'd never even met, let alone not seen before. It was like a pod replaced her in the middle of the night.

One of the POWER2PAWS volunteers, a thirty-something woman named Tara, seemed to always arrive early and stay late, and she took great interest in Liberty and making sure the barn would be ready in time to take in the five horses.

I asked all the volunteers one day at lunch if they knew of any welders and I almost fell over when Tara, a beautiful olive-skinned brunette and the girliest girly-girl you've ever seen, raised her hand.

"I can weld," she said, as if anyone could.

After explaining that her father, who was a Seneca Nation Native American second-generation welding master, owned his own rebar company and all of his children

learned how to weld during their summer jobs working for
Dad, I sent Tara off to get a quote from her father's
company to make the *Welcome to Tree Haven Farm* arch
stand once again.

As the weather cooled, we moved our lunches inside, and
the initial half-hour breaks stretched into hour breaks with
a little more conversation among everyone. It was like
group therapy. I found myself listening more than I spoke,
and realizing how many of these people had been through
hardships like I had. Maybe different details, but some
kind of life storm that knocked the wind out of their lungs
and made them gun shy to go for any more brass rings for
a while.

The Kens were developing a real father-son relationship,
which turned out well because the younger Ken's father
was something of a shit, a guy who wanted Ken, Jr. to
follow in Sr.'s dusty old attorney footsteps instead of
studying architecture. And when Young Ken couldn't find
a job in architecture, and could only earn a living saying
"would you like an extra espresso shot with that?" his
father would not stop grinding him about it. The ultimate
humiliation came when Young Ken went to work one
morning and the coffee shop was closed. The owner ran
off and left his employees hanging. And Young Ken had
to move back into Dusty Old Dad's house.

"My dad was like, 'Son, you make foolish choices, you
get foolish results.' But if I'm just working toward doing
what I am good at, and what I really want to do, how is
that foolish?" Young Ken looked down at his worn

sneakers. "I'll find an architect job, it will just take time," he said.

But Old Ken, obviously the blue-collar foil to Young Ken's silver-spoon sob story, spoke up.

"Eh listen—my old man was a carpenter. He wanted me to be a carpenter. And that's exactly what I was. A carpenter. For forty fuckin' years. And the Old Bastard still hated me. Fuck 'im!" And everyone laughed, including Young Ken, and Old Ken messed up Young Ken's hair a little, and then everyone got back to work.

Tara came back with a quote for five hundred and fifty dollars for the sign, which seemed low to me but I learned from Bud and Joy not to look a gift horse in the mouth, literally. The only catch was it would take four weeks, because they had to take it back to their shop, work on it around their other current jobs, and return to install it.

"Perfect," I said.

The farm was now beginning to resemble the Tree Haven I once knew; the Old Bitty Ninja Weed-whackers had cleaned up the tall grass around the house and the barn. The bats were gone, except for the occasional wayward Dracula lost and looking for what used to be his little Transylvania.

The small paddock fences were fixed and Liberty was lolling around out there, happy as he was at Bud and Joy's place. Some of the volunteers were painting the rails a beautiful white. Liberty loved all the activity and the volunteers loved him. They were warned about being gentle with him, but they were all accustomed to wounded four-legged creatures. They all kissed his nose for luck.

One of the volunteers, an older, small Guatemalan man named Cataldo, was retired from the nearby racing track, and he offered to do some of Liberty's stall-mucking and grooming.

Cataldo had been a groomer for thirty years at the track, and in his broken English he told me he understood horses better than he understood people. He had a wonderful way with grooming around Liberty's scars, and he knew how to use the mane oil that Bud had sent along.

"That's why I do this volunteer. Horses, they just want kindness, and they give kindness," he said. "If the horse is in pain, the horse don't hurt people, the horse just leave, or hide. 'Leave me alone, I am in pain,' he say. But people in pain, they want to hurt another person. They want everyone else to be in pain," he said as he gently brushed Liberty's pearly flank.

Cataldo showed me how to use the mane oil, and he told me to take Liberty for long walks. "He like to walk with people," he said. "His leg and his hip, he need the walking."

"I know," I said. "Someone else told me that. I've been so busy trying to get the farm ready. I haven't been taking walks with him like I should."

"All those woods," he said, as if I were missing a great blessing. "Winter is coming," Cataldo said. "Gonna be a bad one, I can tell because my left knee is stiff. Start soon, the walking," he said, rubbing the mane oil into Liberty's tail hair with his fingers.

I looked at Cataldo's hands. They were rough, hard-working hands, and his whole being was a humble person who would probably never hurt a fly. I wondered what his story was, where his family was, if he was married. I was about to ask him when I heard Pearl calling my name.

"Maggie! Phone call for you!"

"Excuse me, Cataldo," I said. "Thank you for the advice," and I smiled at him. He just nodded, all business.

I grabbed the old yellow wall phone in the kitchen. 'Hello, this is Maggie," I said.

"Hello, this is Frank Pederson from Pederson Gravel & Stone. We understand you were looking for help with a quarter-mile drive, dirt and gravel, pretty bad shape, with ruts and several deep pot holes? Is tomorrow morning at seven a good time for someone to come out and take a look for an estimate?"

"I'm sorry, I didn't call—are you…who called you?" I wasn't sure what kind of scam this was.

The voice on the other end laughed a little. "Let me back up here. My name is Frank Pederson. I own Pederson Gravel & Stone, we're a gravel, stone and concrete outfit about thirty minutes from you. A little bird told me you may need help with your driveway. Is that true?"

I thought for a moment.

"Mr. Pederson, may I ask you a question?"

"Sure, go ahead."

"Do you know a rancher named Bud, and his wife Joy, from South Dakota?"

There was a slight pause, and I could almost hear him smiling. "Well as it turns out, yes, my son served in the Air Force with their son. I also am partners with Bud in a cattle ranch in Colorado," he said.

"Mr. Pederson," I said officially, "any friend of Bud of Joy's is a friend of mine, and if you want to come out and assess my driveway tomorrow, or today, or in the middle of the night, I will have a nice hot cup of coffee waiting for you and your crew."

He laughed. "Well I won't be there, I've got to get out to a concrete job at the new casino upstate, but my crew will be there tomorrow, seven o'clock a.m., okay? They'll ask for you."

"Perfect," I said. "Mr. Pederson?"

"Yes?"

I cleared my throat. "Thank you."

"Oh, no worries, Maggie. Just, you know…paying it forward," and he hung up.

"Who was that?" Pearl asked.

"Another fucking miracle," I said, wiping a tear from my cheek.

***

I stood bleary-eyed the next morning, sipping Pearl's percolated coffee on the porch at six fifty-two a.m. and right on time a monster truck came bobbing down the choppy driveway. Pearl had taken it upon herself to make sure there was coffee brewed every morning at six thirty a.m. And I needed it bad. The volunteers arrived at seven, but one or two would always come early. The farm was becoming something of a social club for all of us.

Two large men with clipboards got out and once introductions and coffee pours were over we talked about the driveway.

"Lotta pits and holes but overall it just needs some leveling and filling," the taller guy said. Pederson would do the driveway for the cost of materials, which was unbelievably generous, and the two guys told me that Frank told them if that was still beyond my reach that it would be free. I said no, we'd figure out something once the estimate came in.

The taller one noticed the roof on the barn.

"Wow. That's not going to make it much longer, is it?"

"Yea, that's my next problem," I said. "You know anyone who does barn roofs? Cheap? Free?" I laughed feebly.

"Well I know a guy who does roofs, period," he said. "Since I know you're a friend of Frank's…I'll have him call you. His name is Hank."

"Wow, thank you so much, that'd be great…I just cannot say enough about how kind Bud and Joy have been to recommend you guys," I said. "And any help we can get with this roof before the winter would be great."

"Sure," said the taller one as he looked at the shorter one. "We've met Bud and Joy Taylor once or twice over the years. They came through on a jet to a football game in New York City the one year, it was wild, they used to pick up Frank and his wife and they would all go down there. 'Course a lot changed after they lost the baby," he said.

"Oh no, Frank and his wife lost a baby? Oh my God that's so sad," I said.

"No, no," said the taller one, "it was Bud and Joy. The baby was a few months old. It was about two, three years ago, Joy had named her Miracle and everything, it was just the saddest thing you could imagine. Joy's younger than Bud but she's late in the child bearing years, you know. Poor little angel just died in her sleep, SIDS they call it. Joy was just knocked out for a while about it, Bud too, and then they started collecting all the stray horses and everything. I guess she's okay now but for a while there Frank was a little worried about her. Frank's wife Jeannie went out there the one time and Joy was getting better, once she really got into rescuing the horses. I guess she kind of channeled her energy, you know? It was like healing the horses helped her heal herself."

The short one suddenly furrowed his brow. "How do you know Bud and Joy?"

"Oh," I stammered, letting the puzzle pieces of what I'd just heard fall into place. "I…stayed with them on the way here from Montana. I…took Liberty off their hands. That horse—my horse—was one of their rescues," I trailed off.

"He's a beauty," said the short one. "Looks like he showed at one time maybe."

"Yea, he was a circus horse, if you can believe that…he was in a train accident and nobody can ride him anymore, but he's amazing. He's got the eyes of a wise old man or something…Joy used to…" I caught myself. "Joy used to just adore him, and I took him because they didn't have enough room out there."

"Well—" I said, "you guys better get going and I have so much work to do." "Thanks again, I just can't tell you how much I appreciate it."

"Oh—" the taller one stopped as he got into his truck. "Frank said to tell you to not forget and pay it forward."

I nodded and smiled. "I won't forget. I promise."

Liberty was in the small paddock, standing on a patch of mowed grass. Slowly but surely we were getting that whole paddock into shape. I grabbed a halter and lead from the barn and called him over to the fence.

"Come on Boy," I said as I gently slipped the halter over his ears. "Let's go for a walk."

****

CHAPTER SEVEN
Discovering Liberty

A fall wind was blowing the leaves around but I had my Big Fat Ugly Coat on to keep me warm.

Liberty and I started off on the trail into the woods behind the house. It was overgrown but still walkable as long as there was no snow or rain.

His massive head bobbed next to me as he lumbered along. I pushed the bare branches out of the way.

"So…is this like therapy?" I said. "Like I tell you my troubles? Do you magically start talking like Mr. Ed when there's no one else around, huh Boy?"

The sky was October gray, and looked bleak through the tree tops.

"I haven't heard a thing from Montana," I said. "Nothing. It's kind of odd. No messages from Brody, nothing from the landlord. I don't want to know. It's like a box I closed up, put in the attic and set something heavy on the top of.

"Things are going okay here, though right? I mean you're happy, aren't you?" I scratched his neck. "You seem healthy. The vet says you are doing well. The farm is slowly coming together. Even Mom is coming out of her shell a little, taking off her armor piece by piece. Yesterday she actually was talking to Tara about planting some perennials and I saw her really smile. Like a genuine smile. So that's cool."

"I can't believe what happened to Bud and Joy, and their little Baby Miracle. That must have been absolutely crushing for them. I mean they're such amazing people, and giving, and loving and all that and to have something taken from them like that…I don't get why bad things happen to good people. I mean why them? Why anyone, right? Why did you get stuck in that train accident? Look at these scars, I can't imagine how scary that was for you. I read about these New Age things, like we choose the life we lead before we're born or something, and I think who would choose losing a child or a train accident, or me with the childhood I've had and what Brody did to me?

"I don't know if I believe in all that stuff. I believe in something out there, for sure—too much freaky stuff has happened just since I left Montana—I mean Bud and Joy were like angels dropped from the sky—but maybe it's all about the choices we make here and now. Maybe that's what is important."

A squirrel rustled across a branch above us.

"Look at me, getting all deep and existential on our first walk," I said. Our walks became our morning ritual, and I found myself storing up things to tell this blue-eyed horse who never talked back, but I swear understood every word.

***

Pederson Gravel & Stone were almost finished smoothing over the bumpy driveway, and Tara came in late one morning, running breathless from her car up to the porch.

"The sign is finished! It's finished! So they can come to install it but they want to wait until the driveway is done!" Her enthusiasm made me almost cry, I was so grateful for it. It struck me how this group of misfits needed the farm almost as much as Pearl and I did; they needed a place to belong and to feel needed themselves.

The few of us who were standing around sipping Pearl's magical coffee whooped and applauded.

Tara, Liberty and I walked up the driveway to talk to the gravel guys and the shorter one said sometime in November would be good.

We decided to raise the sign at high noon one day, and to make it a little celebration for all the volunteers. Somehow it seemed symbolic, like The Tree Haven Farm would rise again, or something. A symbol for all of us, that some tide was turning in all of our lives.

Cataldo was the last to leave that day, and I sent him off with some leftovers for his dinner. Pearl was in the office, eating a chicken salad sandwich and glued to her laptop Googling perennials and landscaping ideas for around the front porch. She had a different energy, a positive one.

"Mom, what's this pile of shoeboxes here?" She had six old worn boxes sitting on the table, with some crinkled old brown paper bags stacked on top.

"Oh, those are old photos," she said, never taking her eyes off Google. "I found them in the attic and I thought maybe when the winter settles in I could make a project out of putting them in albums."

"Can I look at them?" I asked.

"Sure, but they haven't really been sorted out yet."

I took a box and sat on the couch in the living room. I thumbed through dozens of thick, old black and white photographs, maybe from the early nineteen fifties, stiff and faded with curled white borders.

I recognized my Grampa and Gramma immediately, arm-in-arm standing in front of the farm porch. They were smiling, young and vibrant. My Gramma had red lipstick and some kind of fancy suit with a lapel brooch. It looked like they were going to Easter service or something.

There were several from this same day, what I figured out was my mother's Christening. Everyone in suits and dresses at a dinner table set for twelve. There was a picture of my mother, as a tiny baby in her little white dress.

I made myself a sandwich and for the next two hours I poured through photos of my mother; sitting on a tricycle, posing with a birthday cake, riding a pony somewhere at a petting zoo, always with a big grin on her face. My grandmother was radiant, my grandfather laughing and smiling. I could almost hear his baritone voice. I didn't remember them this happy. They were so young.

"Wow Mom, Gramma sure took a lot of baby photos of you," I said. Pearl didn't answer.

As I shuffled through the stacks I came to a series with my mother, when she was about five or six years old, holding another baby—and pictures of my Gramma holding the baby, My Grampa holding the baby, and all four of them together in what looked like a portrait.

It was a baby boy, and there was an entire box full of baby photos of him with my mother from what looked like one summer vacation.

"Hey Mom?" I called out. "Who is this baby boy?" I got up to ask her but she wasn't in the office anymore. She had gone upstairs to bed.

***

With the bats gone, the barn cleaned out and the driveway almost finished, we were closer to actually taking in the horses. I called Hank the Roof Guy in the morning and he agreed to come out that day and look at the barn roof.

I was completely unprepared for Hank.

A 'Hank' to me is a guy who may have a little butt-crack showing with his tool-belt hanging low, or a beer belly finely rounded by years of sitting on a bar stool at the local watering hole. Hank is not the dreamboat who drove up our less-lumpy driveway on that day.

"Hi, nice to meet you, I'm Hank," he said, and the rest was a blur.

He was tall, slender but strong, with long lean legs, and the bluest, sweetest eyes I'd ever seen. They were vivid blue, almost as if they were lit from inside his head. It was hard to focus on what he was saying because if he happened to smile, his toothy grin made my knees feel wobbly. Hank was boyish but gentlemanly, old fashioned in his manners and some kind of throwback to a bygone era in a way; an Old Soul, as they say. I had about five years and ten thousand bitter miles on him.

"Listen," he said. "I'm not going to lie, that roof is in bad shape. You need two new beams and I would like our architect to look at this rotted wood over here. I don't like how it looks to me. The supports...they don't feel right," he said, touching his flat, strong very un-beer belly. He was like the Roof Whisperer. It was adorable.

"Okay," I managed to say. "Whatever you think, you come highly recommended. What kind of costs do you think we are looking at here?"

"Hard to say," he said. "You have some kind of boarding business here? I noticed a few years ago the Tree Haven sign came down."

"Well, hopefully one day," I said. "For now I am very fortunate to have all these volunteers, and we are just trying to get the farm in good enough shape to take in some rescues. We are sort of starting over here after some…challenges. Once we are in the black then we can take in boarders, do lessons, the whole bit. No pun intended," I smiled.

Hank nodded, looking like wheels were turning in his head. "Uh-huh…Okay, well let me get the architect over here and I'll give you an estimate. Can he come by today?"

"Sure," I said, surprised it was so soon.

Hank went back to his truck, hopefully oblivious to me watching his long legs stride comfortably across our front yard, and he made a few phone calls. Liberty loped up to the side of his truck, nosing around, and I could see Hank petting him out of the open driver window. Liberty tried to stick his head inside the cab, and I laughed as Hank fed him an apple from his lunch.

"I see you made a friend. So what's the news?" I said.

"Great horse…well he can get here in two hours. Mind if I hang around til then?"

"Um, no," I said mildly, while my insides flipped around.

"Would you like some of Pearl's famous percolated coffee?" I asked, like it was hundred year-old Scotch.

"Wow," he said sweetly. "That would be great. I have my laptop here, I can show you some roof options." He seemed totally unaware of how ridiculously handsome he was.

"Follow me," I said, instantly regretting another chance to walk behind him.

***

"Here you go," I said, pouring him a cup fresh from the stove. Pearl was in the den office, peering over her laptop into the kitchen at us.

"Pearl, this is Hank, the Roof Guy," I said. She nodded.

"Pleased to meet you, Ma'am," Hank said. It was like he was raised in Mayberry.

"So Hank," I tried to sound upbeat and daisy-fresh, not like my sarcastic, bitter, bruised and broken self. "How do you like the roofing business?"

"Well, it's my family trade," he said modestly, "but I sort of…took to it. It sounds corny I know, but I love the work. There is something about roofing that just…I don't know, it's really satisfying to me. Building something that lasts I guess. Driving by a building and going 'I built that,' if that makes sense," he said. "There's something noble in providing shelter—" he stopped talking.

"I sound like an idiot," he said bashfully.

"No, no that does make sense," I said. "I used to be an accountant, I'm really good with numbers, and I would figure things out like where a loss was or where there was a mistake, and just seeing the perfect totals match, like there is no gray area with numbers, it's a five and a five or a six and a six, you know? If they don't match you know it's not right. I loved it. Numbers and me, we just click," I said. I was good at numbers. *I was good at something.* I hadn't acknowledged my accounting skills in forever.

"You said 'used to be,'" he said. "You don't do it anymore?"

"Well," I drew a long breath. "I worked at a firm in California years ago, and then I moved again…to another state, and I changed jobs. You know how it is. I was a waitress for a while."

"No, what do you mean?" he asked, but not in a suspicious way. "Like you didn't like doing it so you stopped, or you wanted to waitress for a while? Where out of state?"

"Well I just…" I looked into my empty coffee cup. "Would you like another cup?" I asked him as I got up. He nodded and stood to hand me his cup.

My mind rolled over a bunch of white-washed stories and I landed on just fuck it and tell the truth.

"Well—I met a guy in L.A., and I moved with him to Montana, and I tried to find an accounting job there, and I had one for a while but I got laid off, so I ended up waitressing for the past four years. I just moved home here from Montana." I felt a weight fall off my shoulders. "The guy and I…broke up, and I am here, starting over. Starting everything over. Everything. From nothing."

I poured him another coffee, handed it to him, and searched his blue eyes for judgment.

He smiled instead. "Well I just finalized a divorce last year, so here's to fresh starts," he said and clinked our coffee cups.

I could not imagine what woman would divorce those sparkling eyes.

"You know what they say," I said, trying not to feel so giddy because he was single, "Fresh starts are easy. It's the endings before them that are hard."

"I like that," he said, and I swore he stared into my eyes for a second too long.

"So let's talk about your roof," and he opened up his laptop. I sat close enough to him at the kitchen table to inhale whiffs of his cologne. He had a program that showed different designs, colors, shingles and options with different price points. All of them were too much money but I let Hank show me Every. Single. One.

***

The architect bumped down the driveway in his fancy Audi over the remaining potholes, and I was glad it wasn't the driveway we had three weeks before.

He got out of his car, and stared up at the roof with his hands on his hips. He wore a cashmere sweater tied around his shoulders, and pleated pants. I hadn't seen a man in pleated silk pants since I lived in Los Angeles. His sunglasses were little round mirrors.

He dramatically swiped them off to get a better look at our bad roof. Yes it was a bad roof. We knew.

"Is this your architect?" I pointed out the window, one eyebrow raised. Hank nodded.

"Just trust me," he said. "He's the best."

Hank went out on the porch and called out to him. "Charles!" Charles turned toward him and smiled warmly.

We made introductions and the three of us went into the barn. Charles shone his flashlight up in to the rafters, and along the supports.

"Oh yea," he said with a thick East Coast snark. "This is brutal. One more winter, this thing is going to drop," he said. "You want to board horses in here?! You need a total tear-off, brand new roof. No question."

"A tear-off? We can't do a tear-off right now. We just don't have any funds for that. What can we do just to get us through this winter, have it safe for the horses, up to code and everything? Is there anything?"

Charles hemmed and hawed, and asked for a ladder. "I gotta see up close, these two supports are bothering me." The same supports that bothered Hank. And The Kens.

Without hesitation Charles climbed the ladder in his silk pleated pants, shining his flashlight here and there, and mumbling "hmmm" and "oh yea, okay" every so often.

"I can get you up to code and through the winter where it's not going to come down on you, but snow weight will put a hole in it for sure. I'm going to say about eight thousand now, fifteen next year for the tear off. Am I right Hank?"

Hank shrugged and nodded. "Yea, give or take a little," he said, "I wanted your opinion on those two supports. They bothered me too."

Charles looked down from the ladder. "Your gut told you, right, Henry?" Charles flashed his dashing matinee idol smile at me. "This guy is spooky," he said as he sashayed down the ladder like Gene Kelly in "Singin' in the Rain."

I exhaled and slumped my shoulders. Between the taxes and all the expenses that was too much. I couldn't do it. The money just wasn't there.

Tears welled in my eyes. "I can't do that, Guys. I can't, I'm sorry. I'm sorry to have wasted your time. I wasted everyone's time." I looked around at the volunteers busy working on their projects. A hole opened up in my chest, and I lowered my voice. "This whole thing is off."

I thought of how happy Pearl had been, how she'd even begun to fix up the house, making lunches, opening up to Tara, planting her perennials. Pearl was at the nursery to pick up tulip bulbs for Christ's sake. My heart caved in.

Charles looked at Hank, then at me, puzzled as though he didn't realize he just killed everything. "I'm sorry," he said. "I—I didn't mean to be the Grim Reaper, I just—"

Hank held up his hand. "Let's not get ahead of ourselves. Charles, why don't you head on out and write it up anyway. Maybe we can work out something, and we will need the work order fast with the winter coming." Charles looked confused but Hank just waved him off. "Just go write it up," Hank said.

"No, Hank," I said firmly," I appreciate that but WE. DON'T. HAVE. MONEY. I don't know what I was thinking about this. It was a bad plan and I dragged all these people into it. I just hoped, I don't know, I thought—I didn't think—"

Hank looked at me steadily, this time fully aware of what his gaze could do to a woman, and smiled. "That coffee was really good. May I have another cup?"

"Sure," I said, completely disarmed.

***

Pearl and Cataldo came back from the nursery with bulbs, some winter trees and a few tools. Cataldo unloaded the truck and I asked Pearl to come into the house to talk about the barn roof. She frowned.

"It's bad news, isn't it?" she said, her fierce brown eyes accusing me of ruining a good thing.

Hank threw his smile her way. "Well we need to work out a few things is all," he said smoothly.
Even Pearl wasn't immune to Hank and his Old Timey charm. She thawed a little when he held the door for her, and when he remarked on her delicious coffee suddenly

Pearl was fussing with her hair and suggesting she make lunch for a group meeting about the barn.

He winked at me and followed Pearl into the house. Over the last of the chicken salad I explained the roof problems to Pearl, Cataldo, The Kens and all the volunteers. Hank said he'd seen worse, much worse, and that as long as we could shore up the sagging parts by winter we should be okay. Then next spring we could work on a total tear-off.

It was an optimistic meeting but I still couldn't figure out how the hell I was going to pay for all this. The fifty thousand dollars had to go for the mortgage and taxes, and expenses. The roof was just too much.

The staff left one by one, and Hank lingered in the kitchen, helping Pearl clean up the lunch meal. I think I heard her actually giggle at one point. It was as though he saw past her angry eyes and her tough expression, and just brushed them away like a lock of her hair. He treated her like she was a fresh, delicate wild flower he'd just found. It wasn't phony though; he was just…*nice.*
"Well, I better get rolling," he announced. "Thank you, Pearl, for what has to be the best chicken salad in New York."

Pearl waved him away and rolled her eyes, but she was actually blushing.

"And Maggie I will get back to you as soon as I can about costs and things like that," he said.

"Thanks so much," I said. "This is all we've got, and if we can clear this hurdle I think we'll be okay. We just need to get through this winter with horses in the barn."

"Consider it done," he said. "And Maggie—" he looked into my eyes, and it scared me, like he was going to see right into the wounded parts of me, and he smiled the most comforting smile. "Don't worry," he said with a shrug.

"Okay," I said. And I almost didn't.

As Hank's truck buzzed down the driveway in a cloud of dust, Pearl watched me on the porch, watching him.

"No ring," she said.

"I know," I said. "He's divorced. He told me today."

"Did he, now?" Pearl stifled a smile and went inside.

**

I woke up in a panic from one of those stress dreams where you can't get somewhere, like you're in an airport and you missed your flight or you're in high school and you forgot to go to a class all semester. This time, I dreamt I was lost in the woods behind the farm, and no matter which way I tried to go I ended up in circles. I couldn't yell, I had no voice, and I was freezing cold.

It was only three a.m. but I couldn't get back to sleep so I figured I'd just get up, and see if I could figure something out about paying for that barn roof.

I smelled Pearl's distinctive coffee as I came down the stairs and found her sitting at the dining table, with stacks of old photographs piled everywhere. She peered at me over her reading glasses.

"What are you doing up, Margaret?"

"Eh, I couldn't sleep, Mom. What are you doing up?" A bottle of Irish whisky stood on the table next to her coffee cup.

"Oh, I started going through these and they are all out of order and mixed up so I thought I'd sort through them," she said wistfully. "Days of wine and roses, or something."

"You want a warmer?" I asked as I poured a coffee for myself.

"Yes, thank you. But leave some room," she said. I smiled. I left room in my cup too.

She poured a shot of whisky in her cup and hovered the bottle unsteadily over my cup, her eyebrows raised.

"Yes please," I said, wondering where this was all going. Pearl seemed way ahead of me.

"You know," she said, "I wish someone had told me when I was young that life doesn't turn out how you plan it. No matter what we do, or try to do, or want to do, some decision or someone else's decision causes a left turn somewhere and boom! You're way out of line with where you thought you'd end up. Off track. What's the old line, 'the best laid plans of mice and men' or something? Hah…make all the plans you want…Life just comes in like a bull in a china shop and says I'll show you. I'll shatter your fine platter just like that!"

She tried to snap but her gnarled middle finger couldn't do it. "Shatter your platter….I'm a poet and didn't know it," she mumbled with a lame chuckle.

"Mom," I said with a smile, "I get that. More than you could possibly know. How about that? You and I agree one hundred percent on something."

I put my hand on her arm. She looked at me, her black eyes softening.

"We all have plans, Maggie. But every choice we make is like turning left or right and if we make too many wrong turns we go in a totally different direction. Or backwards. And even if we do everything right, do everything we are supposed to do, some bastard puts up a detour, a road block, and we go off course anyway. Sometimes we have no choice which way to go. And sometimes, we just…stop."

She stared past me, lost somewhere in some long-ago detour she took.

I looked at the photos next to her cup. She had two of the photos with the mystery summer vacation baby I'd found.

"Mom, who is that baby in those photos that summer with you and Grampa and Gramma?"

Pearl took a deep breath. "That," she announced flatly, "was your uncle. Your Uncle Johnny. He lived exactly four months and three days. Broke Gramma's heart. Grampa's too, but Gramma was never, ever the same after that. A big piece of her died with him."

I was dumbfounded. I had never heard of my mother having a brother.

"What? No one ever talked about him? What happened to him? Mom, I never knew about this?"

"He had a terrible condition, a brain thing, today he'd probably survive but back then they didn't know what it was. He couldn't really function so well. The doctors said he would live maybe a week or two but he lived those four months and three days. Gramma used to say his eyes went blank, and the next day he was gone. He was the sweetest, happiest little baby. He never cried. Not once," she trailed off.

"Oh Mom, Jesus, I never knew any of this. I can't believe Gramma kept that inside her whole life. I can't believe you did?"

"Of course you didn't know. There are all kinds of things we carry in our hearts," she said. "Not all of us put it all out there. Some things are so awful, they do so much damage, we just lock it up and put it away. The problem is, when you lock up things like that, it's like putting a bear in a tiny closet. The bear will tear up that closet trying to get out. Shred it. Just tear it up from the inside," she said, pointing to her heart. "It doesn't stay quiet, doesn't…die…it grows…doesn't…ever…stop."

Her eyelids were getting heavy.

"Mom," I said, gently getting her to her feet, "let's get you up to bed."

I slowly shuffled her to the stairs. "Can you go up, one by one, Mom?"

"Yea," she said quietly, wincing as she put weight on each creaky knee.

"Maggie, thank you," she whispered, as I sat her on the bed and pulled her shoes off. I covered her frail body with Gramma's old red, white and blue quilt.

"Ha, for what, Mom? Helping you to bed after too much Irish whisky?"

"No. For coming home," she said.

***

The next morning I took Liberty for our daily walk. I poured a travel mug of coffee, put on The Fat Ugly Coat, and walked the wooded trail behind the paddock. Winter was definitely approaching. I thought a lot about my Uncle Johnny, and what that must have been like for my mother, to have a baby brother who died when she was so young. I wondered why my grandmother chose to keep it in, like a shameful secret all these years.

I wondered what Brody was doing in the Middle East, and if I was in trouble with the lease on our apartment. I never heard from the landlord, so I just let it go. Brody did all the paperwork so I assumed he had given them my phone number too. And I assumed at some point they would come after me. I'd been gone nearly three months now and I hadn't heard a peep from anyone in Montana. Which was fine with me.

As Liberty and I plodded along the leaf-covered trail, stepping over fallen branches and overgrowth, I talked out loud about everything. I talked about Johnny, and how that must have affected every minute of every day of my grandmother's life. What was it like for her to see me as a baby? Did I remind her of her little lost boy? Did Grampa tell her to suck it up and get over it? He was that way about most trials and tribulations. They were suddenly these strangers to me now. Like Gramma and Grampa took off these masks and revealed different people underneath.

I wondered why I decided, all those years ago, to leave my family like I did.

Why I decided it was okay not to come home to visit my grandmother when I knew she was dying. Why I let my mother deal with her grief by herself, knowing that what happened to the farm was exactly what would happen.

My rationalization was money, but the truth was I felt like if I didn't come home to see it in front of my face, it just didn't happen. Instead of being something that affected me, it was just something I heard about.

I didn't have to see Gramma wasting away, in pain, struggling to speak or eat or move. All the things that are so heartbreaking to see someone you love going through. And in the aftermath, if I never came to help Pearl through her grief, then I never had to acknowledge my own. I rationalized that away by pretending to feel like she deserved it for being such a selfish, awful mother while I was growing up. But if that was true, then what did I—the selfish, awful daughter—deserve now?

My walks with Liberty did in fact become my therapy; him listening, and the nature around us offering me comfort, or challenging me with sounds, silences, and rustling breezes.

My years with Brody began to unravel in my head too, and the funny thing was, the more I remembered each lie, each argument, each instance of his exerting his dominance and rage, using me as his emotional dumping ground, I began to see clearly how sick he was. How what he was doing to me was not love, and how so early on, my mistaking those first good months for being the real him was when I gave him the power. That very first time when he exploded, when he screamed at me suddenly over the phone about how I interrupted him when he was talking, that was the turning point, when I handed him the reins to my life. We talked often on the phone because we had a long distance relationship, but that was the first time he screamed at me.

"Don't fucking interrupt me when I am talking!" he shouted. "Don't you understand that I hate talking on the phone? And when I make time for you like this, we should be talking about important things, or having phone sex?" he yelled. "I mean other guys, their girlfriends send them sexy pictures, they have phone sex all the time, I never get that from you, all you do is want to complain about how hard your job is. I have enough to worry about, I don't need to hear you whining about how hard it is to push papers around. If you don't like your job, quit and get another one," he said. I could tell he'd been drinking before I called him, and it was settling in.

I remember at the time I was so shocked at his cold-hearted response to my telling him that I didn't get a promotion I'd been gunning for, I just shut down, and I was so infatuated with him, or more the idea of him, that I accepted his criticism as advice, and I internalized it.

"You're right, I'm sorry. I didn't mean to interrupt you, and I didn't mean to make our conversation about work. We can have sexytalk if you want," I said, feeling as pathetic as it sounded. It was hard at that time, I was in L.A., he was at Edwards Air Force Base three hours away and we were new, long distance, and I was so desperate to keep him. I was desperate to be perfect and good, and to never do anything to bring out the mean side of him again. That night he roared on and on about his work, how important he was to the Air Force and how hard it was to be him. My feelings, my life and my needs were nowhere to be found in his diatribe. And I recall thinking that I was being a good girlfriend, being supportive, and doing the right thing by ignoring my own feelings, telling them they were not important and they should sit down and shut up.

But as I walked in the woods, all these years later, with Liberty at my side, I saw it so differently.

Why didn't I say "Who the hell do you think you are to talk to me like that? You're an asshole, goodbye!" Why didn't I leave then, so early on, when the stakes were low, and I hadn't thrown away years of my life to be with him? Now that the smoke cleared I saw him for the emotional child he was, but back then, all I could see was me deciding it was my fault, that I had been a bad girlfriend to make Wonderful Brody go away so suddenly. But it wasn't Wonderful Brody that vanished, it was *Fake Brody*.

A revelation of shame mixed with relief washed over me. I realized that in those early days, I had so much more power than I gave myself credit for. The only thing that trapped me in that relationship back in the beginning was me. And that was comforting and shameful at the same time.

But what about the later years? What trapped me then? I used every excuse I could come up with—money, security, fear, exhaustion. Money? I left a city with a lot more job prospects to follow him to a tiny town with nothing, and I ended up a waitress, living in poverty, and he spent my money like it was his money, but if I spent any of my money he acted like it was his money. Security? He made me more fearful and insecure than anything else in my life. Exhaustion? It was so much work to keep him calm and happy, and no matter how much work I did to make everything exactly how he wanted it, he would still find something to explode about and the cycle would work itself through, wringing me out like a dirty mop.

And yet I stayed.

Five years I put myself through such bullshit. I know I did not deserve it, all the lies he told me, denying other women I could sense but not prove. Manipulating my emotions. I knew it wasn't my fault. I knew in my mind that I didn't do the terrible things he said I did and I wasn't the horrible person he told me I was. I knew he had no right to treat me the way he did.

But if my mind knew all this, why didn't I leave during all those years? Why did my heart always believe in Fake Brody, and win the argument with "*If I could just be more perfect, he will love me again, and it will be like it was*?"

What made me walk out of that Sheriff's station that night, just so suddenly? Was it seeing him held back in handcuffs? Realizing that in that moment I had a tiny window, buoyed by a bunch of deputies strong-arming him? Was I suddenly empowered?

Holding those truck keys to freedom while he was shackled, I just finally *decided.* I did what I should have done five years earlier, when he first showed who he really was. I chose *me.*

I cried a lot on those walks in the woods, for a lot of reasons. And when I really thought about that first fight with Brody, I cried harder because I realized the person I had to forgive in order to let go of that whole relationship wasn't him. It was me.

****

CHAPTER EIGHT
Raising the Roof

A few tiny November snowflakes were flying around as the volunteer crew gathered for morning coffee. Pearl had taken to baking corn muffins for everyone periodically, and since Hank was due to come around later that day with Charles she had quite a spread. I felt so proud of her for some reason; like it was good to see her taking a risk at being happy. She also noticed the lip gloss I was wearing, because I hadn't bothered to wear any before.

Our crew had thinned a little with the end of the nice weather, but Tara, Cataldo, The Kens and our loyal Old Bitties were still with us. The Old Bitties had moved indoors now, helping Pearl with her photo project, and there was some talk of knitting or something. Pearl had never knitted anything a day in her life, but whatever kept the women around to socialize with her was a good thing.

Cataldo was incredible with Liberty, and he knew more about horses than I could imagine. Liberty's mane and coat looked even better than it did at Bud's and I didn't think that was possible. I looked forward to the day when I could pay Cataldo to work with our boarded horses. I hoped he was legal, but I was a little afraid to ask.

"Hello?!" Hank knocked on the front door and Pearl practically scrambled out of her seat. I'd never seen her move so fast.

"Hank, Charles, come in!" she said, like she was Liz Taylor welcoming them into her parlor. "We have muffins and coffee."

"Well hello, Pearl," Hank said, and took her hand gently to kiss her on the cheek. "I cannot wait for a cup of your fantastic coffee," he said. I think she might have actually floated into the kitchen.

Charles swept in with his camel-hair coat and cashmere scarf, heading straight for the muffins. "Delish! I'm starving," he said, and I realized his affectations weren't just theatrical, they were gay, which explained the pleated pants and scarves, cashmere and the matinee idol looks. It made him endearing to me, and I suddenly loved that he climbed into the dirty rafters that day in his fancy outfit without a second thought.

Hank was carrying three giant binders with him, and he set them down on the coffee table. "You and I need to talk later," he said.

I smiled.

"Sure," I said, feeling the sweet rush in my chest as his blue eyes connected with mine.

Hank clapped his hands and got everyone's attention.

"Okay Folks, I'm just going to announce this at once, to Pearl and Maggie and everyone. We start work on the roof tomorrow morning. Trucks and workers arrive. We are going to fix the two support beams, and do a little repair work to get this barn through the winter, it's going to take two weeks to finish, so three weeks from now you will have horses in the barn!"

Everyone applauded, and Pearl and I stared at each other, mouths agape.

"Great, right?!" Hank looked at me, waiting for my applause.

"Hank, that's—" All I could think was how the hell were we going to pay for this.

"Now Maggie's too shy to brag but here's what we worked out—she's going to help me out with my books," he pointed to the three binders on the coffee table, "And in a barter kind of thing, we're gonna fix your roof. How about that, genius, right?"

Pearl smiled knowingly at Hank, as the group chattered their *yays* and approval. I could only stand there with my eyebrows arched.

"Maggie's doing me a really big favor here, so it's the least I can do," Hank said, and he beamed a grin at me that would have knocked me out if I hadn't been so frozen in shock. "You said you were an accountant once, right Maggie?" He winked.

"Yes," I said, smiling back at him and swallowing the lump in my throat. "A long time ago."

"Well, good, because I have some serious problems with these books, and somebody's got to fix them," he frowned, but his blue eyes were not sad at all.

Pearl sent them on their way with muffins and coffee in to-go cups, giggling and telling them she would make them a wonderful dinner when they were finished.

***

Later that day, at high noon, a freezing wind whipped around the small group gathered at the entrance of our driveway. I held Liberty on a tether and he stood proud in his red winter blanket. A smattering of whoops and applause made their way around as a small crane lifted the "Tree Haven Farm" arch upright. The Kens took pictures of a beaming Catalo pointing up at the sign.

Tara's father's welding crew positioned the sign into the concrete bases on either side of the driveway, and as they lowered it into place, I saw Pearl's lip quiver a little. I put my arm around her, and she stiffened like I knew she would, but I kept my arm there anyway.

"Speech!! Speech!" Hank shouted as he clapped. "Miss Pearl we would like to hear a few words!"

Pearl smiled at him and waved him off. "Okay, okay." As the wind kicked up, she held her coat around her neck and shouted with her small voice.

"I want to thank you all for this. Thank you to Tara and her father's rebar business—look at that beautiful sign! And all of you volunteers, I cannot describe what you have brought to our farm here, you brought us back to life. We would not be here without you. So it is my promise to you that we will always be here for you. Thank you for being here. And thank you to my daughter Margaret, for coming home."

I did something I had never done in my entire life. I hugged my mother in front of people. She gave me a stiff hug back but it was good enough.

As everyone applauded I let the wind whip away the tears in my eyes. I did not expect my mother's public acknowledgement of gratitude to mean so much to me.

But it did.

***

The next morning Hank's guys were like bees buzzing all over the barn, attacking the roof. We were finally caught up on the taxes and the mortgage. The small paddock was finished and the large paddock fence would be good by the first heavy snowfall. The horse rescue was scheduled to deliver the first of the horses in three weeks.

Tree Haven Farm was rising again.

Hank stalked his crew like a kindly prison guard, making sure every detail was perfect. They were used to him, and they knew their work was good, so they nodded and rolled their eyes as he checked and double-checked measurements and levels, safety goggles and scaffolds.

I was surprised he was on the farm so much, considering his company had huge commercial jobs along the highway, and much better paying jobs in the wealthy parts of town.

"Please, Maggie, the boy has a crush on you," Pearl said as she handed me a coffee tray to take out to the crew. She bought take-out cups so they could enjoy her coffee while they were working. Hank wouldn't let them bring their muddy work boots into the house.

"Oh Mom, whatever. He's just being nice to us," I said. "He feels sorry for us."

"Pity is not what is behind those blue eyes when he looks at you," Pearl said wisely. Secretly I was dying for her to be right.

I took the tray out to the crew and I loved that Pearl had little sugar cubes and cream for them. Watching burly roofers use the little sugar cube tongs and pour the flowery ceramic creamer was priceless. It was so good to see her taking pride and joy in her surroundings, finding purpose. I thought about how I'd found her, surrounded by dust and bitterness, and how she found me—defeated and scared like a wounded animal. I was shocked we hadn't had one blowout since I'd come home. I made a mental note to figure out why that was on one of my walks with Liberty.

Hank showed me the progress on the roof, and how replacing the two beams would shore up everything for the winter, and patching a few places would get us through until the spring.

"A bad storm might do some damage but it's not going to come down," he said. "It would take a helluva gale force blizzard to do that."

"So…Hank, speaking of damage, I took a look at your books," I said to him. "They are all perfect. Not a thing wrong. Debits, credits, everything to the penny is perfect."

"Really?" He looked away. "Hmmm, because I was sure there was something…maybe you better look again. You gotta earn this roof you know," he flashed his sweet grin and walked away.

I could have sat there all day just replaying that grin in my mind, but I shook myself out my stupor and took Cataldo into town to get tack and supplies for the incoming horses.

***

The tack store was small, but they had everything, and it was quality gear because of all the wealthy horse owners along the lake. Cataldo and I picked up a dozen halters and leads, feed buckets, blankets and brushes. There was not much of the cash left, but as long as we had some boarders by the next month we would be okay.

Gary, the guy who owned the tack shop, wanted to know what it was all for, and I explained our rescue boarding business that we hoped one day would become like it once was years ago when my Grampa ran it. Gary knew Cataldo from the track and he asked Cataldo how it was working for me. I cringed, knowing I hadn't been able to pay him yet.

"It's very good," Cataldo said. "It's a great farm, and her horse is the smartest animal I see in many years. Maggie and Miss Pearl are great bosses," he said.

I smiled at Gary. "We'll be back," I said. "A lot!"

"Thanks Cataldo," I said when we got outside.

"It's true," he said. "I know when you can, you will pay me what I am worth. I work now for free, but I know you will honor my work. This way, I think this way," and he pointed ahead.

"Forward," I said, nodding my head slowly. "Yea, pay it forward. I promise you, Cataldo. I will not let you down."

I prayed I could keep my word.

I owed a lot of people a lot of forwards.

***

The days got shorter and shorter with the coming winter, and Thanksgiving found Pearl and I feeding five of the volunteers, who it turned out had no family in the area. Or no family they would rather be with, anyway.

The younger Ken, three of the Old Bitties and Cataldo came to the farm for Pearl's Rockwellian spread. Pearl outdid herself; I almost questioned how much she spent on the meal but I didn't want to flatten the spring in her step.

We were all carrying dishes in a caravan to the table when the doorbell rang.

Pearl set a piping hot bowl of mashed potatoes on the sideboard. "Maggie, why don't you get the door? Whoever it is, we have plenty."

Still wearing the oven mitts I used to carry a hot casserole dish, I opened the door and I could feel my eyes pop, my mouth widen into a smile.

"Hi," Hank said. He was carrying a bottle of wine, and a tin-foil covered bowl.

"Hi," I said, holding up a red mitt. I was happy but so confused. "What are you doing here?"

Hank's eyes blinked hurt and confusion for a nanosecond. Pearl shouted from the dining room. "Who is it, Maggie?"

"It's Hank, Mom," I said. I took the bowl in my giant red mitts and he followed me into the house.

"Oh lovely!" she said. "We were expecting you!"

"I brought you some wine, and yams," Hank said as he took off his coat. He wore a pressed shirt and a little more cologne than usual. "My mom used to make these yams, she taught me the recipe, I love them, so…"

"That's wonderful, Hank," said Pearl, smiling warmly at him. "Cataldo, why don't you lead us in a Thanksgiving prayer?" She took my hand on my left, and Hank took my hand on my right. His palms were slightly rough, a roofer's hands, but they were still gentle and soft. His fingers slowly wrapped around mine.

Cataldo cleared his throat.

"Heavenly Father, we thank you for this food, and this friends, to share this day of love. I thank you for Miss Pearl for cooking this meal and to Miss Maggie for bringing me here to the farm. We are grateful today for very much. Amen."

Cataldo looked to Pearl and she nodded her approval. "That was lovely, Cataldo."

Everyone dug into the mashed potatoes, gravy, stuffing, turkey, Hank's yams, the Old Bitties' green beans and onion casserole, a boneless ham, rolls and butter, and globs of cranberry sauce.

We talked about the progress on the farm, the barn roof, and the welded sign. Cataldo was very excited about the rescues coming soon, and other boarders. He lamented the look in the eyes of many of the horses at the track; they were captive, he said. Not all of them liked it, and you could tell which horses were miserable. He suspected that some of them would turn up.

As one bottle of wine turned into two, and Hank opened up the bottle he brought, the conversation became a little louder, a little more animated.

He poured a round and made a toast. "To Pearl," he said, winking at her. "The chef. Amazing meal, Pearl," he said. She shook her head and smiled.

"My family used to do this thing," Hank said, "every Thanksgiving we'd go round the table and say the one thing we were most thankful for that year. Gotta be one thing. I'll start. I am thankful for the dry summer we had this last year. Work was really busy because of it, so we made a bunch of money," he paused so everyone could cheer and raise their glasses, "and being busy really helped me through some tough stuff here," he said, pointing to his chest. "You know, I just threw myself into my work, that kind of thing, and it was really good for me to just keep moving forward. So…that's mine. Ken, you go next. What's yours?"

Young Ken wiped his mouth with his napkin.

"Well, I guess I am thankful for this. You people. Maggie, you and Pearl. And Old Ken, who is with his family in Ohio right now."

He looked down at his lap. "I didn't expect to be learning so much from Old Ken, I didn't expect to be... I didn't expect to feel...I didn't expect to make friends. But you are all my friends, even though like Barb you're like fifty years older than me but you're my friend, you know?" Barb shrugged, bemused at the back-handed compliment.

"And Pearl you're always there, always with coffee and muffins or whatever, always, always. You're like clockwork. It's so comforting. I never had that growing up, I just came home, no one was home, my parents were at work, I nuked some stuff in the microwave and watched TV. I don't know, I can't explain it, you're just...*solid*. So anyway I'm grateful for this, right now." He fidgeted with his fork stem and wouldn't look up.

Pearl, solid? The Pearl I knew when I was a little girl used to take off at a moment's notice or fly off the handle, and I never ate a full meal at a table with her unless my Gramma made it. And even then she wasn't really present. Pearl's idea of family dinner was me making myself a sandwich while she was out somewhere drinking.

I looked over at Pearl. Her worn face was beaming. Her long-gone youthful beauty was shining through the years and miles that had stolen it. She looked like she'd won the lottery.

"Well, Ken, we love having you," she said. I did not know who this woman was. Or who she was becoming.

Hank had been quietly watching the two of them. "That's beautiful, Ken," he said. "Yea this whole farm has kind of a …stray-cat thing going on, doesn't it? Barb, why don't you go next?"

"Well I'm so damned old I'm not sure I can get the words out," she said, teasing Ken. Everyone laughed. The Old Bitties gave their thanks, Barb for being brave enough to get out of the house finally after her husband passed away last March, and Polly had gotten over a hip replacement, and Fran's son recovered from his heart attack.

Cataldo said he was thankful that his daughter in Guatemala recovered from an appendix operation. He said when he worked at the track he sent money to her every month, and as soon as he started working again he couldn't wait to send her more.

I looked at his brown eyes, so humble and sweet, with a thousand years of wisdom behind them. I thought of all those people who went to the track, gambling thousands of dollars into the wind, and for Cataldo, sending fifty dollars to his daughter made him a hero.

Hank turned to me. "Okay Maggie, your turn."

So many things spun around my head, it was like a dryer full of clothes and I just had to open the door in the middle of the cycle and see what fell out.

"Well. It's been quite a year," I began. "I have to think about this for a minute."

I thought about running out on Brody, what was I thankful for there? A moment of temporary insanity? The woman in the gas station, I wouldn't have gotten to Liberty without her. Liberty finding me, Bud and Joy, and my mother taking us in. I had so much to be grateful for. Hank fixing our roof for basically nothing, because he knew damn well his books were perfect. All the volunteers, without whom we wouldn't have gotten this far. Tara and her father's welders getting that sign back up. Finding fifty thousand dollars under the seat in Brody's truck?

"Maggie, don't tell me you have nothing to be thankful for?" Pearl said.

"No Mom," I said, as the tears started to roll down my face. "I have *everything* to be thankful for. There have been so many life-changing things that I wouldn't be here without. I can't even begin to try to parse it all out. But I will start with…you, Mom. I am thankful that you took us in. Liberty and me. Thank you for that. And I want to say that I'm so grateful for all of you. I'm sorry, I don't know why I'm crying." But I did. I knew exactly why I was crying.

Hank handed me his napkin, and I dabbed my face. "I'm sorry everyone. Really, I'm just overwhelmed with everything I guess," I said, laughing feebly.

Hank raised his glass. "A toast," he said royally. "To us. No better people ever lived." Everyone shouted "Cheers!" and clinked their glasses.

It was the happiest moment I'd had in years. And I felt the gratitude flow through my veins like some kind of painkiller, just washing away so much regret and dulling the worry and anger over time lost. I dared to feel hopeful in that moment, that everything was going to be okay. But in the back of my mind I knew there had to be some kind of storm clouds beyond the horizon.

***

I stood at one side of the open barn door, and Hank stood at the other, each of us holding a giant red ribbon. Pearl stood between us, holding a pair of pinking shears in her arthritic hands. Liberty stood behind her, cloaked in his fancy tartan blanket. It was lightly snowing, but our little bundled up group didn't mind much. With a "One, two three!" Pearl cut the ribbon and Tree Haven Farm was officially open for business. I swear it seemed like Liberty held his head up high like he knew what was going on, like so much of this was for him. *Because of him.*

That afternoon the first trailer loaded with two miniature ponies arrived, and Cataldo set them up in a stall like they were the King's horses. He had never worked with miniature ponies before, but he had their files, a stack of printouts from Google research, and his natural intuition.

"They need to be together," he said. They are herd animals." He noticed one had a bad hoof, and he consulted for a long time with the veterinarian about how to care for her.

That night, I went upstairs to my room and pulled out the box where I kept the gun and the duffel bag cash. I counted it all out on my bed. I'd burned through all but nine thousand dollars.

"I just want to know one thing," Pearl's angry voice startled me from the doorway. "Is that some kind of drug money?"

"Oh God, no Mom," I said. "Well…I don't think so." She sat on the bed, eyeing the stacks of money, then eyeing me.

"Margaret. Where did this money come from? And the gun?"

I sighed. It was time.

"Okay Mom."

"When I left Montana, I didn't exactly *plan* to leave. I sort of—took off. And I sort of—took off in Brody's truck, which turned out to be my truck anyway."

She looked at me, confused. "He put the whole thing in my name and didn't tell me. The gun is Brody's. And all this money—there was a lot more but this is what I've been paying the taxes with—it was under the seat in a duffel bag. It might be Brody's. I honestly don't know whose money it is. And I should have called the police, or given it back, but Mom, he was…he was so abusive and I—"

"He hit you?" She asked flatly. She didn't seem surprised.

"No, he never raised his hand to me. It was more…mental. Emotional."

I braced myself for the eye rolling, the judgment: *well it couldn't have been that bad… why didn't you just leave sooner…*

But instead she just nodded her head. "Go on," she said calmly.

I cleared my throat.

"Well, in the beginning it was really great, with the lovey-dovey stuff and he was so…in love with me. Like I walked on water. But when I moved to Montana with him, when we moved in together, he changed. Suddenly I was the worst person he ever met, and he told me, every day, in subtle ways, little digs at first, then just full-blown insults. And I would start crying and he would get really angry and either leave to go drinking or just shut me out to watch TV. Then he would apologize and be nice, and draw me back in again.

"I started to doubt yourself, because it must have been something *I did* to make him so angry. It was like he put a mask on, and suddenly the loving, romantic guy I knew who thought I was so amazing, was irritated by every single thing I did and said. I felt like I'd driven him away because this one time I wore my ugly coat when it was winter—"

"Margaret," Pearl's eyebrows raised.

"He didn't put a mask *on* and suddenly become cruel when you moved to Montana. He took one *off.*"

I stared at her.

"Men like him—they prey on women like you. They need a good-hearted woman to suck the life out of. They are users. They need someone to blame all their bad decisions on. You were a scapegoat for all his failures. He pretended to be Prince Charming for as long as it takes to hook you, and then he ripped the mask off, and chopped you to pieces. He didn't want to hate himself, so he hated *you*," she said.

I was dumbfounded by her insight.

"And when men like that have used you up," she continued, "they drop you on the side of the road like a fast food wrapper. You are no use anymore. And they quickly find a new one to suck the life out of. I bet you dollars to donuts he was a cheater too," she said.

"I never found anything concrete, but I suspected a lot and I found all kinds of strange emails and texts and things he would explain away or make me feel crazy about. He was very guarded about his phone. His phone was some big secret. And if I texted him from work at night he never texted back."

I started to connect dots and I realized how little I really knew about how he spent his time when I was on my night shifts. And I recalled how much he encouraged me to take those night shifts.

"What a stupid, stupid fool I was," I said, as a few tears rolled down my face.

Pearl put her hand on my arm. "Margaret," she said sternly. "You were not a fool. You were a good woman. That is all. And you were taken advantage of by a real operator. The important thing is you left. You escaped. You got out," she said as tears welled up in her eyes.

"Mom how do you understand any of this? I mean, you and I have not always…been…on the same page…but I have not been able to get anyone to understand this and I have felt so…alone—" I choked on the word and let out a sob.

Pearl took a sharp breath. "Margaret," she said calmly, blinking away her own tears, "I've never told you about your father. And why I really went away. But you and I...apparently the acorn did not fall so far from the tree."

I felt like a giant cymbal had crashed in my face.

"What?" I said, in a tiny voice.

"Your father. He was a piece of work," she said. "Regular Don Juan. He was a salesman—timeshares in Mexico of all things—traveling back and forth from Buffalo to Boston, and I was working a diner off the exit. One thing led to another and I ran off with him for a bit, and I fell for all his flowers and poetry and...bullshit. Oh was he smitten with me! He poured it on thicker than raw maple sap and I lapped it up, fell for it all. Talk about a fool. He made me feel like I was the most beautiful thing on earth, and even now I am ashamed of how much I wanted to believe all the great things he told me about myself. That's part of their game, you know...you are so ashamed that you bought into their lies, because their lies were about how great *they thought you were.*

Well, I got pregnant with you, and that was it. He changed like Jekyll and Hyde. He went kind of crazy and tried to kill me, kill my unborn baby. Beat me within an inch of my life. Grampa was ready to do the guy in. It was a big drama and then I found out the real truth. Talk about a mask. *He was married.* He had a family in Syracuse. Two kids, the dog, the station wagon, the whole thing. He was a lie, we were a lie. So, to save my baby, and me, I told him I was moving away, I told him I would get rid of the baby if he gave me five thousand dollars, and I took his money and disappeared. I had you of course, and stashed you with Grampa and Gramma, and…well, yes I went nuts for a while trying to find myself after that whole thing. But when try to find yourself by running away you lose yourself even more. I only found…more trouble," she said with a regretful smile.

I was dumbfounded. My mother was a total stranger. My father was now less of a stranger. All the lies I'd been told as a child, and all the assumptions I'd made about my mother driving away the people she loved changed color in my mind. She had walked a million miles in the shoes I was now wearing. And suddenly I saw her as a human being, not an ogre who had ruined my childhood. She had tried to save it.

"Mom, Jesus, I don't even know what to say except why didn't you tell me when I was old enough to understand? Why did you let me believe all these years that my father was some kind of saint that you drove away?"

"Is that what you believed?" She recoiled in horror. "If I'd known that was your take on the whole thing I would have told you!"

"I just thought… you gave up on me," she said. "I thought everyone did. I couldn't imagine the things you must have told people about what kind of mother you had. Margaret …" her voice faded.

"Now that I am old, and things have gone so far down the road to ruin, I see in hindsight where I went wrong. I also see where I was right though. And I know I should have done things differently later on, but I think you might understand a little of where I was way back then and why I thought that disappearing from your life was the best thing I could do for me, but more for you.

"Look where you are. How many people have you tried to explain his 'abuse without bruises' to? And try explaining way back then, when you're pregnant by a guy who is married with two other kids, how he said some mean things so, oh, he's some kind of terrible monster? Back then, the woman was the one who wore the Scarlet Letter, not the man. I'd have been strung up if I'd gone public. And I guess I felt like my own crazy years after that did me in. I was just…searching for a while there, desperate to find someone again who would tell me the things he told me in the beginning, so I would know those weren't lies too. And once you truly believe bad things about yourself, it's so hard to believe good things after that. They just don't sink in. So I drank, I ran, I floundered. I screwed up…. I really screwed up. But I didn't think telling you the truth would bring anything good to the situation. I did the right thing, Margaret. I just did it badly."

She waived her hands. "But let's look at the bright side! We can wipe our tears with twenties," she said, picking up a bill and wiping my face with it.

I smiled and reached to put my arms around her.

For the first time I could ever remember, Pearl didn't stiffen. She hugged me back.

***

Walking with Liberty the next morning, the woods looked beautiful in the morning light, with the bare branches gilded in white snow.

My Fat Ugly Coat felt good wrapped around my body, and I had a travel mug of hot coffee. Liberty wore his thick winter blanket. I carried carrots in my pocket and he would nudge my hip every so often, reminding me he wanted a treat.

Digesting what my mother had told me was like one of those snakes trying to digest a giant woodchuck. It just sat in my gut. I had two half siblings somewhere. My father was not only accessible, living somewhere I could probably track him down, he was also a complete asshole, apparently. But the strangest part was seeing my mother for the first time as this three dimensional woman, like me, who was once in an impossible situation even worse than mine, and she just did what she could based on her resources.

I thought of my not coming home after Gramma's diagnosis, or after she died, and how hard that must have been for Pearl. The guilt pangs screamed in my head and I felt the shame swell in my chest. It was physically painful. I understood so much now about Pearl's hardness, and her focus on survival. Her shutting out of everything emotional and loving, because those things had betrayed her. They had promised her love in return for her giving love and trust, and one by one the people in her life had either gouged out and stolen her heart and soul, died, or just left.

"You know, Boy, I owe her an apology," I said to Liberty. "I really need to own up to where I went wrong for her. We've come a long way in these past few months, Pearl and I, but I think I owe her a real explanation myself for why I didn't come home then." I handed him a carrot. "There is so much that gets lost in silence. Years, just lost to two people in their separate dark rooms, not seeing the full picture."

A thought brushed against my guilt, that she had yet to apologize to me. But one of us had to lay down our arms first, and if that had to be me, so be it.

****

CHAPTER NINE
Silver Bells, Silver Linings

Christmas season was in full swing, and Pearl had decked out the house like a Norman Rockwell painting. She and the Old Bitties had crafted a wreath for the front door, and fashioned every imaginable knick knack in red and green with a snow man or Santa on it to stick in various nooks around the furniture.

I loved seeing her so alive, and making friends with these women. They chattered away about curtains and felt and hot glue guns. Nothing deep—and no one brought up their painful pasts, which was just as well for Pearl. And probably the rest of them. The occasional fun memory of a long-gone vacation was about as far as they'd go. These women had all endured something painful and managed to soldier on past it, and were all learning to cope with it in the sunset of their lives—alone.

Barb was a cat foster mother for a local rescue group, and she brought my mother a kitten to "meet," she said. Pearl gave the fuzzy cat the side-eye, but when Barb placed him in Pearl's lap, and the little guy curled up and fell sound asleep purring, Pearl's ice-cold heart melted.

"I'll name him Johnny," she said. She glanced at me and looked away.

"That's perfect, Mom," I said.

The little guy imprinted himself on Pearl and followed her everywhere; he insisted on sleeping in her room, if he couldn't find her he meowed until she appeared again. Pearl's veneer started to crack, and I caught her smiling and nuzzling him.

"Mom I'm going into town to get some Christmas lights for the porch," I called to her. "Do we need anything?"

"Yes, please get milk!" she hollered from the kitchen.

I drove the big truck along the snowy country roads into the village. There was a Target on the border of town, and I wanted to get some gift cards for all the volunteers. I had offered Cataldo five hundred dollars a week salary, and he almost cried. We were getting some money from a grant and from the County for two rescue horses we'd temporarily taken in, and some for the miniature ponies. A woman called about boarding her horse but she wouldn't start until March.

Still, we were scraping by and between Pearl's Social Security, Brody's cash, and the rescues, we were going to make it at least until the spring. If nothing else went wrong.

***

Target was a mob scene of shoppers making messes of carefully folded clothes, knocking over displays and a cacophony of motion-sensor Christmas decorations barking out carols and dancing in jerky movements as people passed by.

I picked out some Christmas lights and went to the beauty aisle for shampoo.

The print on the dandruff shampoo bottle was tiny and as I struggled to read what kind of dandruff it helped cure, a voice behind me said "Hello Maggie."

I whirled around to see Hank, in all his handsome glory, smiling down at me from under a knit cap.

"Hi!" I said, trying to lower the telltale bright blue bottle and shove it back on the shelf. "What brings you to this insanity today?"

He smiled and pointed to his overflowing cart, with tubes of wrapping sticking out in all directions. "Oh, I needed some stuff, last minute, you know. I'm a guy. You?"

"I'm getting some gift cards for the volunteers," I said. "And some Christmas lights for the front porch."

Hank's perfect blue eyes lit up. "Do you need some help putting them up?"

My heart felt like an old, dead machine that just got a shot of oil and the wheels started turning again.

I nodded slowly. "Yes…I…think I do. Can you come by today?"

"Sure," he said. "I'll be over about one." He pushed his cart gently past me. "Tell Pearl to fire up some of that coffee," he said over his shoulder.

"Okay," I said, feeling like any moment now an anvil was going to fall on my head because there was no way a guy that great was interested in me. It had to be a trick, or a ruse. I wondered what Hank was like once his mask came off, and the rusted works in my chest slowed to a halt again, and I pushed my cart forward.

After I grabbed the dandruff shampoo.

***

Pearl and I were outside on the porch when Hank pulled up in his truck. I was pretending I wasn't going to use a staple gun to put up the lights, and she was telling me the lights better not burn the place to the ground.

"Mom, these are LED lights, they don't get hot. They don't make those lights like that anymore," I said.

"Hi Ladies," Hank called. Pearl waved like a little girl.

"Well hello, Hank! I'll get your coffee!" She ran inside to pour a cup from the pot she'd brewed just for him.

"I brought these, so you don't have to use a staple gun," he said, showing me some plastic clips. I laughed to myself.

"Great!" I said. Hank assumed ladder duty and I fed him the string of lights, as we lined the porch roof and posts with the colored bulbs. Pearl shuffled outside with two steaming mugs of coffee and he climbed down a few rungs to take a sip.

"The BEST coffee, EVER," he said dramatically. I'm taking this with me," and he climbed the ladder with the cup.

We finished just as a heavy snow began to fall. "Okay, Pearl, hit it!" Hank shouted. Pearl turned on the lights and a beautiful glow filled the porch.

"Wow," I said. "The old homestead looks so...homey."

"Merry Christmas, Ladies," Hank said, putting his arm around my shoulders.

"Let's go inside," I said nervously. "It's cold out here."

***

I woke up three hours later on the couch, snuggled next to a quietly snoring Hank in front of the glowing fireplace.

"What is an Alpine?" I had asked him earlier when he mentioned drinking one.

"Oh, you're in for a treat," he said, and he ran out to his truck, returning with a bottle in a long thin paper bag.

"Rumple Minze one hundred proof peppermint. You put it in hot chocolate, and that's an Alpine. Peppermint hot cocoa that'll knock you off your feet. I make great Alpines." Indeed he did, because after two, he had to help Pearl upstairs to bed, and after three, he and I passed out on the sofa.

We had a great talk before the Alpines kicked in though; I learned a little more about him, his divorce, and why he didn't really gallivant around town like so many divorced men.

"The way I see it," he said solemnly, "it was so painful—the whole process felt like such a failure to me. Like I'd done this prideful, love-declaring exercise in front of the whole world, and then it just sank, in front of the whole world. And I am not about to go around like some horny teenager showing everyone how insecure I am. I see men my age dating women in their twenties and I just shake my head because if it's really love, okay, but I know for them it's not. It's about proving to the world—and yourself—that you are still viable to young women. You're virility is intact. But I don't see my partner as

some extension of my arm, or some measure of my worth like an expensive sports car tells the world I'm wealthy and important." His voice softened, and he stared at the marshmallows floating in his 'I heart Xmas' mug. "I want a best friend, someone in the fox hole with me so to speak, who understands how to let me be the man but if need be, she can hold her own too, or help me when I need it."
"Geez," I said. "That's some mature outlook. You're like a unicorn among men."

He laughed. "Eh… it's a lot of therapy." I was shocked at how easily he admitted it.

"Really?" I said.

"Oh yea," he said. "Therapy really helped me get through it all and keep a level head. I didn't get stuck in the past, or stuck on anger or regret or any of that. I'm a big believer now in therapy. I'm not ashamed to say it. You think I should be ashamed?"

"Oh no," I said. "I just never went, I don't know much about it."

"Well," he said, "if you ever want to go, let me know, I'll ask mine to recommend someone for you."

"You still go?" I asked.

"Yea, once every two weeks," he said. "It keeps me focused forward, on healthy stuff. On me when I should be focused on me, and on others when I should be focused on others. It's like someone giving you an emotional toolbox, only they have to give it to you one tool at a time because you won't understand how all the tools fit together until you've learned how to use each one."

"Hmmm," I said, as I was getting sleepy, leaning a little on his shoulder. "I could use some tools…so much to fix. Starting with the big fence in the paddock…the roof…"

***

The chill woke me later, as the fire in the fireplace dimmed to embers. Hank's arm was around my shoulders, and I didn't dare move. He was asleep, his head knocked back on the couch and he snored lightly. But he managed to still be handsome and somehow gentlemanly.

His blue eyes opened and he turned his face to mine. In the low light he looked fifteen years younger. I was praying I did too. At least maybe about ten thousand miles less than the hard-road mileage I felt like I had on me.

Without saying a word he leaned to kiss me and I pulled away.

"No?" he said, looking hurt and shocked at the same time.

"No—I mean yes—I mean… I probably should explain some things to you, before you decide to get involved with me. And then you can decide based on knowing all the facts." A serious look washed over his face. I hated it.

"Okay," he said, sitting up. "Shoot."

"I left Montana…suddenly," I began. "I was in a very bad relationship. Well—it wasn't bad at first, but it became very bad over time. And it did—*he did*—damage. Here," I put my hand on my heart. "And here," I said, pointing to my forehead. "He was cruel, and he made me think I was going crazy. He would say things and then deny he said them. I would catch him with evidence that he was unfaithful to me and he would just deny, deny, deny until I was so unsure of what was real and was not. He insulted me, he made fun of me, he told me that other people told him I was boring, annoying, all kinds of terrible things. He compared me to other women, other wives or girlfriends, even his ex-girlfriend, and said I should do this, do that, be more like them. Things he loved about me in the beginning he began to nitpick about and criticize, and he chipped away at my self-esteem little by little. He picked fights over nothing—if I heard 'you ruined the whole night!' one more time over the stupidest thing…I would try to calm him down and say I didn't understand why this escalated so much into such drama but he would repeat '*you* do this to me! This is *your* fault!' over and over again."

I looked in Hank's eyes. His gaze was steady and he was alert. He was listening. Not judging.

"I questioned myself every day, why did I still love him? Nothing I did was right. And things he said didn't make sense when you put them together with his actions. He was gradually driving me insane and sucking the life out of me.

"He told me *I was the one* who drove him to become this frustrated, angry person. So I tried to be perfectly, exactly what he wanted. But it wasn't enough. There was so much shaming...

"In between, he would throw me these breadcrumbs... these little bitty bits and pieces and I was so starving for anything loving and good from him that I gobbled them up and couldn't wait for another one. I just became this hollowed-out shell of a person."

"So...why am I telling you all this...well, because one day, about five months ago, he got arrested in a bar and instead of picking him up from the jail I just took off. I ran away. I escaped. I did the most irresponsible, cowardly thing, and I came here. On the way, I got a flat in South Dakota and ended up taking Liberty from the people who helped me fix the flat, Bud and Joy. It was one of the strangest nights of my life but those people were living angels to me. Somehow, experiencing their kindness like that, and taking this horse, this crazy thing I did for no other reason than to love him and be loved back by him— I just found the tiny grain of hope I needed to really, finally, escape.

"And now I am here, basically a fugitive from my old life. I have nothing, I arrived here with the clothes on my back, some money, Liberty, and that truck out there.

"So…before you really kiss me, I just wanted you to know who I really am…if I really am honest, like three Alpines later honest, I have to say that a part of me still feels as low as he said I was. That I'm as worthless and unlovable and that I deserved every cruel bit of treatment I got. "So, there. It's all out there now. You can make an informed decision."

I looked down. My heart was pounding and I had never felt so completely open, like one of those summer party tents with no walls—exposed on all sides, anchored to nothing.

Hank's eyes scanned the ceiling, searching for words somewhere in the pebbly shadows of the popcorn plaster. He cleared his throat.

"From what you describe," he said quietly, taking my hands in his hands, "you were in an emotionally abusive relationship. The thing he did where he says something and then denies saying it—that is called gaslighting. It is a manipulation and it's designed to keep you off kilter, make you doubt yourself. The part where things don't make sense to you, they don't line up – that's cognitive dissonance. The constantly comparing you to other people, especially exes or other women—that is called triangulation. That is to use another person to make you jealous or feel inferior. The beginning, where everything is so wonderful—that is called lovebombing. They do that so you think they are your soul mate. If he made himself appear to be a perfect match to you, with music, movies, things like that, that is also a manipulation called mirroring. And when they stop all that, and turn nasty on you, that is called the discard."

He took a long slow breath. "These people are almost sociopaths, they really don't have normal emotional functions. They think they do, but they don't have the conscious feelings we do, like understanding that it is wrong to mess with someone's head like that. For them, it's all about whatever they need emotionally at the moment. If they need to beat you up verbally, fine. If they need to cuddle, fine. If they need to cheat on you, fine. Sometimes their needs line up with yours and sometimes they don't. The one consistent thing is that it's all about them, all the time." He sighed.

I was shocked, there were names for this, and categories? This was a thing?

"Hank, how do you know all this?" I asked.

He looked into my eyes and smiled proudly. "Therapy," he said. Then he smirked. "And my divorce attorney."

I laughed weakly.

"…Your ex-wife?" I was a little ashamed at how happy I was that he might understand the invisible hell I went through.

"She was," he said. "I've worked very hard to put her, and that relationship, and the damage done, behind me. So when I tell you I understand what you are saying to me, I understand it more than you know."

I smiled and gently squeezed his hands. "I am torn—I want to ask you a million questions about this, but I also…kind of never want to bring it up with you again. Like I want to draw a line deep in the sand, here and now, and step over it, and leave all this stuff behind it."

"You have some healing to do," he said. "I'm not going to lie. The mind games take some time to unravel. But I'm all for putting a lid on it, at least for a while until…after I kiss you?"

He smiled, and this time when his blue eyes held my gaze, I kissed him. And he kissed me back with the warmest kiss, sweet but manly and strong, reaching right down through my chest, vibrating my bones with some strange magical feeling that I think was…joy?

Hank held me for a while, running his hand up and down my back and not saying anything. I was absolutely peaced out, just enjoying how safe I felt enveloped in his warmth. Thoughts of Brody and how I'd felt so safe with him at first too crept in, but I pushed them away.

"I'd better head out," Hank whispered in my ear. My heart sank.

"Okay," I said. "I have an early day around here tomorrow too." I walked him to the door and he held me and kissed me one more time.

"See," he said, "that was a completely informed decision."

I felt silly for making it sound so dramatic.

"Thank you for sharing all that with me," he said. "I like the honesty. So…I'd like to take you to dinner this weekend. Like a date. Could we do that?"

"I'd love that," I said. My heart buoyed up in my chest. "We'll talk tomorrow?"

He smiled and nodded. "Goodnight, Maggie."

I shut the door behind him, put out the rest of the fire and went upstairs to bed.

I'd forgotten how lush it felt to be giddy about something good. When my bar was set at "Thank God it isn't worse" for so long, a kiss like that was a seismic shift.

***

Winter was setting in, covering the farm in a thick layer of snow. We hired Old Ken to plow the driveway, and I eyed the barn roof as the snow piled on.

We now had four miniature horses, and two cows from a young family that had thought they would try the whole "homestead" living thing. When they realized it involved cleaning a lot of cow shit and actually doing a lot of work, they bailed on the animals and ran back to their trendy rented loft in the city. We inherited a bunch of chickens from them too, which Pearl loved for the never-ending eggs. Liberty was like the foreman, wandering the farm and checking in here and there, keeping the chickens in line and being a big brother to the miniature ponies. His hip problem was all but invisible now, and his gallop was strong.

Cataldo worked with the vet and the blacksmith to figure out a way to shoe Liberty's right foot so it relieved some of the pain in his gait.

The cows were a little dirty and malnourished but otherwise healthy, and Cataldo learned pretty quickly how to nurture and milk them. All the volunteers were thrilled to learn how to milk a cow, and Pearl and I smiled at each other at their wide-eyed excitement as they filled buckets with the warm milk.

There is kind of a trick to it, and as Grampa used to say "you gotta respect the cow, how would you like your dick or your tit to be yanked and jerked once a day by somebody who doesn't know what they're doing?" He loved knocking people off their guard with a little profanity.

Hank called and we set a date for Saturday night at eight o'clock. He would pick me up. It felt so old fashioned, just like him. He asked to take me to dinner, and maybe a movie later if we were so inclined.

I hung up the old yellow wall phone on the kitchen wall and Pearl looked at me.

"Well?" she said.

"I have a date," I said.

She smiled and nodded. Then she looked at my tattered jeans and my "I heart me" sweatshirt and frowned.

"Yea…I should go shopping," I said.

"I'll go with you," she said hopefully.

***

Pearl and I walked along the all but deserted snowy village streets of Spaulding Quarry. Most of the summer homes were closed up for the season, but a few people still came in on the weekends to ski at the small resort nearby.

The Plaid Shoppe stayed open until after the Spaulding Quarry Club New Year's Eve Party, so we went in and looked for something a thirty-eight-year-old woman would wear on a first dinner date with a dreamy old-fashioned guy who happened to be younger and probably chasing women off his lawn every night with a broom since the ink dried on his divorce papers.

"It's got to be…stunning," I mumbled out loud to myself. I swished the dresses to the left on their hangers one by one, trying to picture myself answering the door and Hank thinking "Wow."

"Yea…," I said out loud. "It has to be 'Wow.'"

Lainey, an apple-shaped woman in her late sixties with perfectly arched eyebrows and upswept platinum blonde hair, had owned the store for thirty years. She brought over three maroon, matronly-shaped dresses that were clearly not "Wow."

"I need something…a little more…festive? Or…sexy maybe?" I sounded apologetic about trying to be sexy.

Lainey cocked her head and furrowed one brow, eyeing my sweatshirt. "Hmmm. Yes, I have something." She disappeared in the back.

Pearl was in the corner trying on hats. I watched her for a minute, admiring herself in the mirror with a feathered fancy hat on, imagining herself at some dinner party. "Mom, that's a great hat," I called to her.

"Isn't it? It's funny, I have a dress, a very old dress, that would go with this exactly…" she trailed off, lost in her reflection. She looked younger somehow, as if decades of dead weight had lifted off her shoulders.

Lainey came out of the back holding up a dress with two hands like it was the Shroud of Turin. "This. This is the dress," she said flatly. "You're what, a six-eight?"

"Yes," I said, marveling at her Old-World accuracy.

"Try this." She held up a black velvet dress, fairly simple in its cut, but with a beautiful red velvet ribbon around the collar, and a delicate black sequined detail embroidered on it. It was stunning.

I tried the dress on. It fit like a glove, like some Cinderella fairy dusted garment made just for my hips, my waist, my bust and shoulders.

I stepped out of the dressing room and Pearl audibly gasped. "That's the one," she said. "You look…beautiful, Margaret."

Lainey just nodded, her job done, her mission accomplished. "I'll write it up," she said. "It's an abandoned alteration. You can have it for a hundred bucks."

"Seriously?" I said.

"Seriously," she said, without looking up from her old school carbon-copy tear-off receipt contraption.

"Thank you," I said to Lainey. I leaned in and lowered my voice so Pearl couldn't hear me: "Can you please also write up that hat she's got over there?"

Lainey peered over her glasses. "That hat's a hundred twenty-five," she said, looking at me scoldingly.

"It's okay," I said. "It's a gift for her, just please wrap it and hold it for Christmas."

She shrugged and continued writing.

On the ride home, with the dress, a new pair of black pumps in the back seat and the hat stashed secretly at Lainey's, Pearl fiddled with the radio until she found Christmas music.

She sang softly with the song as she stared out the window. "City sidewalks, busy sidewalks…dressed in holiday style…"

She knew all the words. I'd never in my life heard her sing before.

***

I stared at my reflection in the bathroom mirror. My wet hair was combed back, and my bare face stared back at me, daring me to point out its many flaws.

There was a tiredness about me—a worn look that wasn't exactly old, but more like *spent.* The corners of my mouth turned down a little, as if I had been frowning for so many years that my expression was permanently etched that way. My eyes were dull. If you looked deep in them, you saw a murky fog obscuring the path to my psyche. I was very resistant to giving anyone the keys to my heart and soul ever again.

As I covered my face in makeup, painting on a vibrant, open personality, dabbing sparkly shadow on my eyes to draw attention away from their jaded stare, hiding the truth of my reluctance to really feel vulnerable again with another thick coat of black mascara, I started to regret saying yes to this date.

What if he's doing what Brody did? What if he is just putting on a dog and pony show, and the reason he knows all about the love bomb and the gaslighting and all that stuff is because *he did it to her?*

As I dried my hair I became angrier recalling how easy it was for Brody to fool me with all the platitudes and bullshit. What kind of an idiot am I? Am I that shallow that I fell for all the ego stroking, and then he went in for the kill? I deserved to get pummeled by him. I deserved to get creamed like I did, for being so stupid and vain as to fall for all that shit.

Why would a guy that good-looking go for me? Why was this guy taking me out? Why did he really help us with the roof? Was this all just a bunch of *lovebombing* and bullshit, and I was going to walk right into another trap? And in a few months Hank would start criticizing me or say, *"Well, I did help you with your roof, and you never fully paid me back."*

And then I'd say "But we had an agreement," and he'd say *"No we didn't, I never said that."* And then he would make me feel crazy. And it would be the same shit all over again. And no one would believe me because he was so nice all over town. And he would start to suck up all my energy with whatever he had going on—*his* business, *his* needs, *his* way, *his* activities. I didn't really know anything about him. I'd never seen his home, or how he lived. I was going to go out with this guy? And trust him?

And Pearl—she was pushing him on me, who knows what her motives were.

I slid the dress over my head, and awkwardly zipped it up in the back. It looked stunning. I stepped my feet into the new shoes, and it had been so long since I'd walked in heels I had to take a few steps to find my balance.

Pearl knocked on the door to my room. "Well? Can I see?"

"Come on in," I answered quietly.

"Oh Margaret. You look beautiful," she said. "I brought you this little handbag, it was Gramma's. You can't go on a date with that giant awful slouchy thing you carry." She handed me a beautiful glittery black vintage clutch, big enough for a wallet and lipstick and my cell phone.

She motioned for me to take a slow spin and I did. "Good Lord you always did have Gramma's gorgeous figure. If he doesn't fall in love with you tonight, then there's something wrong with him."

A spark of terror struck my heart. "It's just a date, Mom, just a date. Dinner and a movie. Period. I hardly know the guy," I said as I dug in my giant purse for my wallet.

Pearl shrugged. "When is he supposed to pick you up?"

"In about ten minutes," I said. "Why?"

"Because he rolled up the driveway about five minutes ago, with his lights off, and he's sitting outside freezing in his truck, probably waiting to be exactly on time," she said, with a wry smile.

She went downstairs and I sat on my bed, staring down at my new shoes. What the hell was I doing? Letting the fox back in the henhouse? I was just getting to a place where I didn't hurt anymore and I was just starting to un-believe all the bad things Brody said I was—boring, unstylish, uncool, uninteresting, unattractive unless I was wearing the right clothes, shoes or makeup, and Brody's very favorite phrase: "you aren't *special,* you know."

How long would it be until Hank started saying nasty things like that to me?

I could hear a knock on the door, and Pearl and Hank's muffled voices greeting each other. "Margaret! Hank is here!" she called to me.

"I'll be right down!" I called, like I was Joan Crawford.

I stepped down the stairs in my high heels with exaggerated kicks like some Ziegfeld Follies girl because I was afraid to trip and fall, not because I had that much style.

Hank stood at the bottom of the stairs, holding a bouquet of flowers. He was dressed in jeans, winter boots and a flannel shirt. I was mortified.

He looked up at me and his jaw slacked open. "Wow," he said. "You are going to be the best dressed woman at the hot dog cart."

His comment struck me like an arrow right in my heart, and I slumped to the step midway down the staircase and burst into tears. I was humiliated.

"Wha—no! I meant, I mean you look beautiful, it was a joke," he stammered, handing the flowers to Pearl and running to me. He sat next to me on the step, and put his arm around me. "I'm so sorry, that came out wrong. We weren't going to a hot dog stand. I just—I never dress up, I didn't think you would go to all the trouble—I wasn't—this is my fault. Please don't cry, I can't stand to see you cry, I'm sorry—"

My face was in my hands and I just sobbed. The more I sobbed, the more humiliated I was, and the more humiliated I was, the more I sobbed. When I looked up, I saw Pearl's face contorted into a question mark. She circled her face with her index finger as if to say "your makeup has melted all over you" and pointed upstairs for me to go clean myself up.

Hank was rubbing my back and desperately trying to assure me that he did not mean to insult me, he had never seen anything so beautiful coming down the stairs, blah blah blah but all I heard was Brody, making fun of me for overdressing and thinking somehow I was going on a fancy date. How typical of me, to be *so uncool and not know.* Like I wore a giant rabbit costume to a business party.

Hank finally knelt on the steps below me, put his hands on my make-up smeared face, and said kindly, "What do I have to do to convince you? How can I get you to accept my apology?"

I stopped crying. I searched my heart. I searched my brain. I had no answer.

He tried to wipe the smeary black tears off my face.

He pleaded. "You blew me away in that dress. You caught me off guard. I know I said something really stupid. I'm so sorry," he said. He looked at me sweetly. "Maggie, what is this really about?"

Pearl handed me some tissues and went to the kitchen to put the flowers in a vase, and give us some privacy.

I wiped the snot from my nose, and I figured this was probably the end of The Hank and Maggie Story so what the hell, let's tell him the truth.

"I'm sorry I overdressed," I said. "I'm not good at this stuff, like knowing the hip thing to do or wear or the place to be. I just kind of go, and do, and see, and I'm a curious person, and I like to have fun and just enjoy the moment, and I don't really think about the 'cool' rules or that kind of stuff. I never have. So there's that."

Hank laughed. "I don't care if you wear that dress cleaning the house," he said. "You look fantastic. You look sexy and stunning and I would take you anywhere in it. Including the hot dog cart," he said, trying to laugh a little.

I shrugged and smiled. "But there's this: How do I know?"

"Know what?" he asked.

"How do I know… you're not *him?*"

"Ahh," he said, his whole face relaxing into understanding. "Projection."

He sat back up on the step next to me. "Well…you don't. But here's my take…you are projecting your ex, and his abuse, onto me, expecting me to do the same thing, or be the same way," he said matter-of-factly. Then he tapped his forehead. "Therapy."

"Maggie, the truth is, you can't know. You don't. Your radar is all screwed up, because this guy screwed it up. He put a magnet on your compass. He manipulated you and worst of all, he lied to you. He robbed you of the chance to make a real choice about giving him your heart. You made your choice based on a lie. If he had told you upfront that he was actually a sociopath, with only selfish motives, and that he would use you up, cheat on you, and when he was done with you he would throw you out like a piece of trash, would you have given him your heart?"

I looked at him like he was crazy. "Of course not!"

"Well then he had to lie, and be a phony, and put on an act, didn't he? And you fell for it, because you are a true, caring human being. These people don't prey on others like them. Their schtick doesn't work on their own kind. They need people like you to feed off of. It's like vampires—they aren't going after other vampires because they need the human blood. They are emotional vampires.

"So…how do you know I'm not a phony…again, you don't. But here's a clue: I'm not going to ask you to give me anything you aren't ready to give me. And I am going to tell you flat out, that you should hold back your heart until enough time has passed to kick my tires, examine my motives, dig through my history, whatever it takes for you to really believe that not only am I not him, I am *nothing like him*. I can't guarantee that if we keep on seeing each other and we blossom into something that I won't be a dunderheaded guy and hurt you. But I can guarantee that it will never be because I am using you as an emotional dumping ground so I don't have to own my own bullshit, and I can guarantee you that I will always make it right. And as much as I can humanly make it happen, my words will line up with my actions. That I promise you. But don't take my word for it. Sit on the fence until you're sure. Wait and see."

"Wow," I said softly. "You *have* been to a lot of therapy," and I started laughing. He started laughing too. "Yes, yes I have...I have the bills to prove it," he said, and put his strong arms around me.

"It might be something for you to think about too, Maggie. It helps to have a professional unravel all this stuff. It can get you back to your real self, not the shadow self you created to cope with his cruelty, and all the guilt you felt for wanting to leave, and...not leaving," he held me tight as he spoke those last words.

"I did feel guilty...all the time, about everything," I whispered into his chest. "But why didn't I leave sooner? And why do I still feel guilty now? Why?" I started to cry again but he pulled my face up with his fingertips under my chin.

"You feel guilty because he *blamed* everything on you. He manipulated every situation so you thought every bad thing was your fault. Including the weather. But you know what? No. We are not doing this now—your feelings are valid, and I know what a mind-fuck it all is. It took me three years to really leave my ex-wife after I actually made the decision in my head.

"But you and I, we are not going to do *this* now. We're not going to let *them* into *our* space. You have plenty of time to unravel that stuff, and you will do it, in the right place, with the right person—a professional. I'm here for you, but I'm not going to carry his bullshit around in my pockets and neither are you. You and I, right now, we have a date to go on. Come on."

He stood up, took my hand, and pulled me up off the stairs. "Where's your coat?" he said.

Oh no. My coat, I thought. The Fat Ugly Coat. I frowned and pointed to it, hanging on the coat rack in all its fat ugly brown glory.

He lifted it off the hook like it was a sable, stood behind me and slid my arms into the sleeves. "Here you go," he said. "Now zip up, its cold out there and you are wearing one sexy short dress under there," he said. "I'm going out to warm up the truck, I'll be right back."

I smiled. "I should go upstairs and fix my face," I said quietly, wiping my eyes.

"Nope, no time," he said, and took my tear-stained, black and gray water-colored canvas of a face gently in both his hands.

"*You are enough*," he whispered, and kissed me gently, slowly, deeply, so much so that I felt my knees go a little weak.

We stood outside in the snow at the hot dog cart outside the theater, me in my Fat Ugly Coat with the ugly hood pulled up, my make-up stained face peering out of the faux-fur trim, and him in his wool flap hunting cap and ski coat, laughing as we ate all-beef specials with everything, including onions. We had just seen a terrible slasher movie in a theater full of teenagers, who stared at my tarnished makeup job wondering what my story was. I just laughed and acted like I had no idea what they were looking at. We fed each other popcorn and screamed at the scary parts and yelled at the screen like everybody else in the theater.

He kept randomly kissing me all night and loudly asking anyone who would listen, "Isn't she beautiful? Isn't she?" and then he'd gaze, all exaggerated in love at my raccoon eyes and kiss me again. No one was in on the joke but us.

He took me home, walked me inside and gave me another knee-buckling kiss goodnight, and asked if I was free the following Friday night. I said yes. He asked if I would wear that dress again. I said yes, but only if we were going to the hot dog cart again. He asked if I could do my makeup exactly like that again. I said no, my crying days were over.

We had the hot dog kid take a picture of us with Hank's cell phone. I looked hideous. Hank had mustard on his grinning face and some smeared on his coat, with his arm proudly around my shoulders. My eyes had not sparkled like that in years.

***

I woke up the next morning just before dawn. I'd forgotten that beautiful feeling, when you wake up from a deep sleep and instead of remembering that your life is terrible upon waking, you remember that this magical thing happened last night, and it was real, and it's still real. It flows through your veins like heroin and a smile stretches across your face. Your heart feels like it's drinking cool water after being in the desert for years.

The house was chilly, so I put on jeans and a heavy sweater for my morning walk with Liberty. I didn't dare attempt Pearl's percolator, but a big mug of tea would keep me warm during the walk. With The Fat Ugly Coat wrapped around me, and a scarf tucked around my neck, I quietly closed the front door behind me.

Cataldo's car was in the driveway already, and I found him in the barn, brushing Liberty's gilded coat to warm him up.

"Good morning," I said.

"Good morning," he said without stopping his work, "I know it's cold today, I think he needs warming before your walk."

"Thank you so much," I said. "I came down to do that very thing. How are you today?"

"Good, good, I'm good," he said, quickening his short, circular strokes. I sat on a hay stack and sipped my tea.

"Cataldo, would you like to come on my walk with me today? I could use the company."

"Uh, sure, sure, okay," he said, putting the brush away and swinging Liberty's blanket over his back. We started to walk out of the barn and I noticed Cataldo only had on the sweatshirt he always wore.

"Do you want to get your coat?" I asked him.

"I—I forgot my coat," he said. He didn't forget anything.

"Hmmm. Okay, well, let's go inside and see if my grampa has an old coat you can borrow?" I looked up at the house and the kitchen light was on. "And we'll get you a cup of coffee too."

We went in and Pearl's coffee smelled like salvation to me. "Well good morning, Cataldo," she said. "Can I pour you some coffee?"

"Pearl, could you make that two cups to go, Cataldo is going to walk with Liberty and me this morning."

"Oh, yes," she said, giving Cataldo the reverence he deserved. I dumped out my tea.

"Also Cataldo left his coat at home, Pearl, so we need one of Grampa's old coats? Where are they?"

"Oh…" Pearl frowned. "Grampa's coats are long gone," she said. "But…come with me."

***

Upstairs in the guestroom, Cataldo put on my grandmother's old mink fur like it was Cary Grant's cashmere gentleman's coat. He held his arms out in front of him, and nodded his head in approval like he was admiring the fine stitching.

My grandmother Helen was a tall woman, and the hem skimmed the top of short Cataldo's feet. His broad shoulders barely fit inside the coat. Cataldo was such a serious man, so committed to his work, and I knew so little about him, I was afraid to burst out laughing.

He looked uneasily at my mother and me, and I realized he must be thinking that if he laughed it would be rude in light of such a nice gesture, to be wearing Pearl's dead mother's heirloom coat and then burst out laughing.

"Do you have a hat?" he said, covering his ears. "Pearl handed him a blue knit pom-pom Buffalo Sabres hockey team hat from a plastic tub of old winter wear. He pulled it over his ears. He walked solemnly over to the full-length mirror and studied himself, pivoting left and right.

The three of us stood stone-faced, staring at Cataldo's misshapen reflection, with his feet sticking out of the bottom of the coat and his blue head with the yellow pom-pom hat poking out of the top.

Cataldo cleared his throat. "I think the hat really ties it all together," he deadpanned.

We collapsed into painful, breathless laughter.
Pearl had tears coming out of her eyes, and Cataldo was roaring a throaty, "OH-HO-HO-HO!" laugh that echoed all over the house. He smiled so wide for the first time I could see he had a handsome grin.

I took a picture with my cell phone and Cataldo bent his elbow over his shoulder like a pinup. I could barely steady the phone, I was laughing so hard.

Pearl was bent over, trying to catch her breath, waving her arms. "I've never—if my mother—I wish—I can't—" was all she could get out.

"Hello?" We heard a shout from downstairs. "Roof guy! Anybody home?" Hank called out.

"We're upstairs," I called back between laughing seizures.

"Come on up!"

Hank stood in the doorway for a moment.

He looked at Cataldo, frowned, and deadpanned, "Cataldo, your shoes are all wrong."

***

With a proper plaid wool man's coat from the back of Hank's truck that I knew Hank would "forget" to collect, Cataldo and Liberty and I took our coffees and set off on our walk. The ground was covered with about an inch of light snow, and the skies were a bleak, bright gray. There were no leaves left on the trees, but back in the dense woods that bordered the large paddock you could still lose the trail in the thick underbrush.

Liberty loped along behind us as we walked, and Cataldo held his tether loosely in his left hand, sipping his coffee with his right.

"Do you have a big family?" I asked him.

"Yea, back home," he said. "I try to bring them here but only two, my sisters, can come. My wife and my three daughters stay with her father."

"It's hard, right? Being away from them?" I felt so relieved we were able to pay him. For now, anyway.

"Oh yes," he said. "But I am grateful for the work, and I send money home. My girls go to school better with me here."

I thought about his sacrifice, for his girls to have a better life, he allowed himself to have a worse one. He *chose* to live a difficult life because it made theirs better. Every choice he made was not for him, but for them. I thought about my own self-centered choices, and my heart sank remembering again not coming home for my grandmother's funeral. I thought about leaving Brody without saying goodbye, with no explanation after five years. Even coming home, although I ended up helping Pearl, was a selfish choice.

"Cataldo, can I ask you a personal question?"

He glanced at me, a little uneasy. "Sure."

"What are your dreams?

He looked confused. "You mean like when I sleep?"

"No, like when you are awake," I said, smiling. "Like when you were a boy, what did you dream about for your life?"

He stared at his worn boots crunching in the snow as he walked.

"Well," he said matter-of-factly, "Here is the thing. There are boy dreams and there are man dreams, and there is reality. When I was a boy, I dream of being a rock star, or a TV star, to have all the girls love me, to have the money. Silly dreams. When I get a little older I dream of being a jockey, racing horses and winning the trophy. I get a job at a track and start learning what I can, I see I am very good with horses. I understand the mind of the horse," he held up his coffee cup to his temple and pointed a finger at his head.

"But, then I meet Sophia, and we have the girls, and I have to work fields too and more jobs to pay for bills. And then one day, I was riding a horse around the track, training for a jockey job and I fell. I hurt myself, I break my right hip, and I cannot ride no more, not for racing. So there is reality. But life don't stop, don't end, and I don't give up, because I have Sophia and my girls, so I say riding cannot be important now. What else is important now? And nothing matters more than my girls and their life now. I can't make that dream come true anymore, so I dream a new dream. I dream I make enough money to send my girls to school in America. And when they come, Sophia will come. And when that happens, I will have everything I love."

"Wow," I said. "I had no idea you were a jockey, or were close to becoming one. I'm sorry it didn't happen."

"No, it's okay," he said. "If God push me this way instead, I was going in the wrong way then. I had the wrong dream. My father, May God Rest his soul, used to say,

'Dreams don't *come* true, we *make them true*.' And if
something happen to stop a dream dead like that, that's
God telling you to find a different dream, this dream is not
for you. One is better for you somewhere. If God show
you a new path, it's a sign."

I marveled at Cataldo's ability to see the silver lining. I
thought of my failures, my bad choices, and I thought
differently of the events of that night in Montana those
months ago, as God pushing me into a new dream, asking
me to stand at a new fork in the road and make a different
choice. Literally and figuratively, maybe I just walked out
on a dead dream, and here was a new one forming around
me and I hadn't even noticed it.

"Cataldo, your father must have been a wise man. And
you are a wonderful person, and I am very lucky to know
you," I said.

"Thank you, Miss Maggie. I feel the same of you and
Miss Pearl. You are good people. You rescue a horse even
who doesn't ride. You respect what he say he can't do,"
Cataldo said, looking back at Liberty's bobbing head.

"I hadn't thought of it that way," I said. "That it's a matter
of respecting what Liberty can't do. I was thinking in time
we would try to get him to ride again, that he just needed
to feel safe and heal."

"Maybe. But I think he never rides anyone again," Cataldo
said solemnly. "I feel something happened a long time

ago, and he decided, he made a choice and he say I'm never letting anyone there again."

"I can relate to that," I said. We stopped for a moment at the fork in the trail. I patted Liberty's muscular neck.

"We should head back," I said to Cataldo. "Once we go past the fork it gets a little rough in those woods."

"You just decided, huh Boy?" I said to Liberty as I took his lead and turned him around. His blue eyes peered out underneath long white lashes. I adjusted his blanket a little, and I rested my head on his broad shoulder for a moment. I understood completely deciding not to let anyone climb on your back and kick you, jerk a bit in your mouth and tell you what to do and where to go, against your will, ever again.

****

CHAPTER TEN
Fear Goggles

Hank and I went into town to get some supplies for the animals and place an order for boards at the hardware store. We figured we would be gone most of the afternoon, and the volunteers were all leaving early to avoid a white out predicted that night. The winter weather was always tough in our area, which locals called the "Snow Belt."

I asked Hank to stop at the grocery store so we could pick up a few things for Pearl, and we headed home in the early stages of what looked like a pretty bad blizzard.

Hank's heavy four-wheel drive truck handled the snow just fine but the visibility was bad, and he drove slowly along the country roads back to the farm. I stared at the hypnotic snowflakes hitting the windshield, with Hank's ever-present AM radio old time Forties-era Big Band music playing. I wasn't worried about making it home; I felt safe with him driving. It was a new feeling, trusting a man not to take my well-being for granted. He had the heater on high, which I knew was for me. I thought about the arguments I always had with Brody about the car heater and I thanked God for this new dream.

Hank and I kept our budding relationship mostly professional during the day, although we flirted a little bit here and there. We both instinctively saved the romance for our date time, and when it was working farm business we kept it business-like, for the most part. He did put his hand on my behind when I was standing in line at the grocery store, just to mess with me, and although I moved away and gave him a shameful look, of course I loved it. And he knew it.

We turned onto the driveway up to the farm and I noticed the Christmas lights weren't on.

"Oh, I wish Pearl had turned them on so we could see what they looked like in the snow," I said.

As we slowly made our way closer, the whole house was dark.

"Did Pearl go out in this mess?" Hank asked.

"No, the car is here, and she wouldn't drive in this," I said. Not even the kitchen light was on.

Hank parked by the porch and we unloaded the grocery bags. The snow had piled up on the porch steps and up to the door. Pearl hadn't even been outside in at least a few hours, judging from the snow drifted up against the door frame.

I opened the door and called out to Pearl, but she didn't answer.

"Mom? Hello? Anybody home?!"

Hank set the groceries in the kitchen and I turned into the hallway and screamed.

"Hank! Oh my God!"

Pearl was lying in a heap on the floor at the bottom of the stairs.

I ran to her and knelt down, feeling for a pulse. She was alive, and her body was warm, but she was barely conscious. A basket of clothes had tumbled out near her, and it looked like she had fallen down the stairs somehow and ended up on the floor.

"Hank call 9-1-1!! Oh my God! She must have been lying here for hours!"

Hank ran out of the kitchen, saw Pearl and in a calm but no-nonsense voice he said "We're better off getting her in my truck, it will be faster. Does it look like her neck is broken?"

My heart almost stopped at the thought of his question.

He stayed calm. "Maggie, does it? If so we shouldn't move her, but if she had a stroke or a heart attack we need to get her to the hospital sooner. Does it look like her neck is broken?"

Pearl moaned. "Mom? Oh my God, Mom? Are you okay? Can you feel your legs Mom? Can you feel your arms? Squeeze my hand if you can feel your legs, Mom."

Pearl squeezed my hand slightly. "Hank she squeezed my hand. Go start the truck."

He ran outside. "Mom, can you hear me? What happened? We are going to get you to the hospital, okay? What hurts on you?"

Pearl mumbled. "I fell. Slipped. It hurts, oh God it hurts."

"What hurts, Mom? What hurts?"

"Everything," she said through gritted teeth. "Don't move me," she said.

"Mom we have to move you, we have to get you to the hospital," I said.

Hank came back in the house. "Okay," he said. "We are going to put her on this bench, use it like a stretcher, okay? And move her as little as possible, and get her into the back seat of my truck." He pulled the hall bench over, gently lifted Pearl onto it as she cried out in pain, and with his strong arms and back lifted her petite body and carried her out to the truck.

The wind and snow whipped around us. "Now Pearl, this is tricky," he said. I need you to be strong for me, Little

Girl. We gotta get you into the back seat here, and it might smart a little."

I climbed into the back seat from the other door. Pearl cried out again as I held her shoulders and gently slid her off the bench onto the seat. I covered her with a blanket and Hank jumped in the driver's seat and made his way down the driveway as gingerly as he could.

I called ahead to the hospital and when we pulled into the emergency entrance they were waiting with a stretcher. The orderlies carried Pearl off and I sent Hank with her while I sat with the intake nurse to answer her questions.

Robotically, I went through the information, name, address, and when it came to her birthday, I couldn't remember the exact year.

The nurse clicked a few keys on her computer. "Here she is. She was here year before last. Mild stroke, it looks like. She also has an unpaid bill of twelve hundred fifty-four dollars and thirty two cents."

Mild stroke?

How could I not know she had a stroke? *How could I not know the year my mother was born?*

Once the admitting paperwork was done I went back to find Hank.

He was leaning against the wall by the entrance, and when he saw me, he lurched forward toward me. "Where is she?" I asked him.

"She's in X-ray," he said, wrapping his arms around me. "She will be okay. Everything will be okay."

"I want to believe you," I said. "I really do."

"Let's get you a hot chocolate or something, and find us a seat. Pearl's in good hands, they will give her some pain meds and she'll be feeling fantastic in no time," he said.

"Hank," I said. "She was here two years ago. She had a stroke. I didn't even know. I wasn't here."

"And she survived," he said. "She will survive this too. God is not ready for Miss Pearl yet."

"But I wasn't even here. I didn't even know."

He smiled. "Maggie, you are here now. You know now. It's not too late. Really. It's going to be okay," he said.

We sat in the waiting room, drinking vending machine hot chocolate and watching "The Golden Girls" reruns on the old tube TV mounted in the corner.

There were a few other people there, enduring their own personal emergencies in the brightly lit waiting room. One woman's ten-year-old boy had an anaphylactic reaction to peanut butter, another woman's daughter broke her arm skiing.

After almost two hours, the emergency room doctor came to the hallway. She was a stern, stunningly beautiful Indian woman with a thick accent. She wore a white coat, and her luxurious long black hair was pulled back in a low bun.

"Pearl?" She called out to the room. "Anyone waiting for Pearl?"

Hank and I jumped up at the same time. "I am Dr. Sundarin. Please come with me," she said curtly, and motioned down the corridor through a set of doors that said Intensive Care Unit.

***

Pearl looked so tiny in the huge hospital bed, with its thick mattress and tall side rails. Her gnarled right hand had an IV in it. She was hooked up to monitors beeping and keeping track of her vital signs.

The doctor pulled the curtains shut, as if that gave us some kind of privacy.

"She broke her hip," the doctor said flatly. "She has a hairline fracture here," she said, pointing to the front of her own hip. "She got pretty banged up. Do you want to tell me what happened here?" I realized the doctor's attitude meant she suspected someone had abused her. Maybe even us. Me.

"Oh—I, we—I am her daughter, this is—my friend, Hank. I was out in town and when we came back she was at the bottom of the stairs. I think she was carrying a laundry basket up or down the stairs and she slipped. She said she slipped when we found her."

"She has an old healed fracture wound on her face, on her orbital bone. It was shattered at one point, broken in several places. How did that happen?" The doctor stared directly at me.

I looked at Hank, wide-eyed. "I have no idea, Doctor. I have only been home a few months. I lived away for fifteen years." I looked at Pearl's sleeping face. She was worn but still beautiful, and I could not imagine the bones around her eye being smashed.

"Look, Doctor—I know you need to ask these questions and I appreciate your concern. When she wakes up you can ask her anything you want. No one in my mother's life abuses her. She fell—it's that simple. She's had trouble going up and down the stairs for some time now. We will have to figure out a new plan when she gets home. But I can assure you—this was an accident."

I looked right in her dark brown eyes. She did not smile or acknowledge my speech.

"Your mother needs to be immobilized, so we need to perform a surgery, to put screws in place to hold the fracture while it heals. Then she will need bed rest. Does she have someone to care for her?"

"Yes, yes I live with her. I can take care of her," I said, knowing that didn't make the doctor feel any better. Maybe I should tell the doctor about how I didn't come home for my grandmother's funeral either.

"We have her scheduled for surgery in the morning at six o'clock a.m. You can go home, get some rest and come back," she said as she entered Pearl's chart information on her laptop. "You should know there is risk with this surgery, as with any surgery, with general anesthetic in advanced aged patients."

"Thank you. I understand. I'd like to stay here with her, if that's okay? She will be really confused and scared if she wakes up."

The doctor raised her brow. "Well, we don't allow visitation overnight in ICU. But I will speak to the night nurse and for this night you can stay."

She turned to walk out the door, but I stopped her.

"Doctor?"

"Yes?"

"Which eye bones were broken? Which side of my mother's face?" I asked.

"The right side," the doctor said.

"Could those breaks have been really old, like decades old?" I asked.

"Yes," she said, softening a little. "It's hard to tell exactly from the X-rays we took, and your mother's age and bone density. Why?"

"Well," I said, my eyes filling with tears, "my mother hasn't seen my biological father in almost forty years…I never knew him….but my grandfather always referred to him as 'Lefty.'"

"And you would not have known even this?" she asked.

I looked at Pearl. "Our family had so many secrets," I said.

She looked puzzled. "Well when she wakes up the social worker may need to speak with her. It's protocol," she said and turned into the hall.

***

Hank left, and offered to go to the farm in the morning to inform Cataldo and the other volunteers. He said he would come to the hospital afterwards to see how I was doing. He hugged me before he said goodbye, and it was a strong, life-giving hug that I sucked every ounce of energy from.

I pulled an itchy upholstered wooden chair up to Pearl's bedside, and found the one channel on the remote that was showing "Law & Order: SVU."

"Damn show really is on two-four-seven, isn't it?" I said aloud. It was comforting though. Something about its familiar characters and New York City sets were a welcome distraction.

Pearl's hands were at her sides, oxygen flowing into her nose through a tube, pain killers and who knows what else through an IV. Her breathing was steady but shallow. I held her hand and rested my head on the bed.

"Mom…" I whispered. "I'm sorry. I love you."

She lay unresponsive, unaware. "We will get through this, Mom. We will get through this together. I need you to pull through this surgery tomorrow, and after that you and I, we will get through the rest together. We've done so well these past few months…I never thought we could get along like this. I feel like I never knew you, really. Or you never really knew me. Look what a great team we make— and besides," I wiped my tears on my sleeve, "no one knows how to work that percolator. And honestly, I don't want to live in that house alone. I don't know how you did it all those years. All those ghosts. Were you just waiting for me to come back?

"You did call me when Gramma died. You did say you needed me. And I didn't come. I'm so sorry Mom. I 'm so sorry I wasn't there for you," I sobbed into the bed. "I wish I could do it all over so differently. I would do so many things so differently. I'm so sorry, there's so much I didn't know about you, about myself. I just didn't understand how much power I had to change my own life. I didn't know I had the strength to leave all that time. I didn't *believe it.*

"But look at us now Mom, we are doing so great. The barn is fixed up, the house needs a lot of work but we have Christmas lights—when is the last time you had Christmas lights?" I wiped the snot off my upper lip.

"The driveway is fixed! The sign is up, we have life back at Tree Haven. It's literally come back to life. Liberty, he's so magical. All the other animals, it's so amazing to have this place of healing. And Cataldo! Oh my God, Cataldo! He's so great, Mom you need to talk to him, he has such a story. You have friends now, the Old Bitties, you guys have your cooking and your crafts…things are better, right? Didn't I make things better by coming home Mom?"

I looked at her comatose face. She twitched, and her eyelids fluttered and open and closed. She mumbled something angrily.

"I couldn't understand you Mom…say it slowly…" I leaned close to her.

"My…percolator."

Pearl. She will be just fine.

***

Pearl finally woke at about five o'clock in the morning.

"Maggie! Maggie?"

"Mom, I'm here, Mom, I'm here, it's okay."

"Maggie what happened?" she was panicked.

"Mom." I sat up and turned on the bedside light. "Shhh. You are okay. Calm down. You fell down the stairs tonight. You broke your hip. Hank and I brought you to the ER, and you need surgery this morning. You will be just fine, just bed rest."

The panic in her eyes did not subside. "What? I fell down the stairs? Where? At the circus? I was dreaming about the circus!"

"Mom." I held her face in my hands. "Look at me. Look at me. Calm down. Settle yourself. Breathe slowly. Breathe." Pearl blinked and began to focus on my face.

"There we go. Okay. You fell down the stairs at home, at the farm. You were carrying a load of laundry? Do you remember that yesterday?"

"No," she said, a look of fear taking over her face.

"It's okay Mom, they have you on all kinds of pain killers. You will be okay. Just calm down. I'm here. I'm here. "

I heard a soft knock-knock and Hank's tall silhouette appeared in the door frame.

"Good morning, Maggie. I brought you some coffee and a muffin," he whispered, like he was talking to a five year old. "Pearl! You're up!" He had a bouquet of flowers under his arm.

"She's a little rattled," I said.

"Well I don't blame you, Pearl. It was quite a scare," he said. "You did a half-gainer off the stairs! How are you?"

"Shitty," said Pearl flatly.

"Well there's room for improvement there but there's worse," he said, handing me the coffee and putting her flowers on her nightstand.

"Thank you, Hank," she said. "They're lovely. They need water."

"We'll get them some water, Pearl. Don't worry," he said.

He studied my face. "Rough night?"

"Um, yes, I guess you could say that," I said. "In case you hadn't noticed all this," and I waved at the hospital room.

"I mean you look like you've been crying," he said. "Remember I've seen that face before." He smiled softly.

"Oh," I said, closing my eyes in abject humiliation. I couldn't imagine what I looked like. "Yea, I guess I got a little emotional about everything. And Pearl said no one touches her percolator."

"Of course," he said, smiling at her. Pearl looked confused. Hank had a way of making everything seem so easy, so doable. I needed to be around it, wanted to be around it, all the time. Even Pearl softened up in his charming presence.

"What about the morning chores at the farm?" Pearl said.

"It's all under control, My Dear," said Hank. "You just worry about nothing, okay? Maggie and I figured everything out last night. Cataldo and I will take care of everything." Pearl settled back in her pillow, visibly relieved.

"I know I said I'd stop by after I swung by the farm," he said, "but I thought Maggie might need a coffee and a muffin. And you might need some flowers. Pearl, you're a tough gal, I know that. And so are you, Maggie."

A parade of orderlies and doctors flooded the room.

"Pearl! It's showtime!" The prep nurse said cheerfully. They put a few more drugs into her IV.

The tall older gray-haired one shook my hand. "You're Maggie? I'm Dr. Osterman, I will be performing your mother's surgery. I spoke to Dr. Sundarin last night. We need a few more x-rays right now, and then we will take her in for prep, okay? You will be here?"

"Yes," I said. "I will wait here for her."

"Okay," he said. He lowered his voice. "We are concerned about her heart and blood pressure. It's high, and for elderly patients the anesthesia can be more risky. We are taking every precaution, of course, but I am being truthful in telling you that there is additional risk in this surgery. The fracture requires stability to heal, however, so if she doesn't go through with the surgery she could be looking at permanent disability. Has she ever had anesthesia before?"

"I—I don't know," I said, looking down.

"Okay, well we will be on top of it," he said, giving me his best fake reassurance smile. I felt my gut hollow out. Hank leaned over Pearl's bed. "So Maggie says you told her last night in your drug-fueled coma that you know damn well that I make better coffee than you do, and you are relinquishing your percolator to me?"

Pearl pursed her lips. Hank kept going. "Now Pearl, if you don't make it through this surgery, I'm going to take that percolator…and I might not clean it right…" Pearl rolled her eyes. She loved it.

The orderlies unlocked her bed and rolled her toward the door.

"Even Cataldo says my coffee's better, Pearl," Hank called after her.

A small, gnarled hand rose from the giant bed, with a bent middle finger sticking up as the bed wheeled out into the hall.

"That's my girl!" Hank yelled, laughing.

If I had to pick a moment where my cold, dead, heart began to really melt and beat again for this man, that was it.

***

Hank went back to the farm to take care of things, and I lay on the empty other bed in Pearl's room watching TV to distract myself from the fear in my heart. I flipped through the thirteen channels on the giant remote control connected to the hospital bed, and sure enough there was some incarnation of "Law & Order."

"Yep, two-four-seven," I said aloud. As I sipped my coffee and ate the muffin Hank brought I realized this was the first time I had actually stopped moving since I left

Montana. I couldn't do anything but wait. Other people were taking care of the farm, doctors were taking care of Pearl, there was nothing for me to do in this room.

"God, please don't take her away from me," I started to pray. "Not now. We are just starting to pull it together," I said, and I felt the fear and pain grip my heart and squeeze as hard as it could without killing me. My whole body shook.

"Fuck!" I said out loud. "I can't do this right now! I can't! Just bring her back!" I said to the ceiling through gritting teeth, wiping tears off my face and turned up the volume on the television.

I watched the detectives walking on the streets of New York. One of them was eating a hot dog. I'd never been to New York City. I day dreamed a little about Hank and I, maybe married one day, going to New York at Christmastime, eating a real New York hot dog from a real New York hot dog cart, seeing the big tree at Rockefeller Center.

Suddenly I identified this odd feeling—it was *possibility*. It felt like maybe one day, if Hank and I did eventually start a real relationship, and it went well, and we did get married, that we could take a trip to New York, and it could go something like the way I envisioned it.

It had been so long since I'd felt anything good was possible in my life. I had spent so many years with Brody telling me in subtle, or even direct, ways that I didn't deserve good things, I couldn't make them happen without his approval, my view of the world was wrong, I was too incompetent to make anything happen on my own that I'd internalized it all.

Brody was sly in his insults; if he was too direct, I could shake them off as him being drunk or mean. But he was too clever for that…his insults would enter into my psyche through a second floor open window, slither down the stairs and take residence, and grow like mold until they infested everything I did and felt and thought.

"Why don't you have any friends?" he'd ask.

"Because you have sucked the life out of me" I would think to myself, but not dare say.

Or, *"Because when I make plans with my friends, you take those opportunities to cheat on me. Or you get angry with me that I am doing something without you. Or you scream at me for two days after I've spent half a day with a friend."*

These are the answers that ran through my head, because they were the truth. But I couldn't say them out loud to him because they sounded ridiculous, even to me. They sounded whiny and lame, and they were. Even remembering them made me feel like I was so weak and lame for not leaving him. But I also remembered feeling so trapped, so closed in.

And since I couldn't say those things to him, I would just answer "I have friends, they're just busy."

But then I would think about his question, and answers would turn like worms in my brain and with all the seeds he'd already planted—no one likes you, my friends all think you are boring, my one friend Ted thinks you remind him of his ex-wife and he hated her, but *why can't you be more like Keith's wife, she's so much fun?* His question was the water over those seeds, and the garden of weeds flourished.

That is how he destroyed my self-esteem. In drip-drops, slowly over time, with layers upon layers of inflicted self-doubt—triangulation by comparing me to another person's qualities, grinding away daily, regularly at my intrinsic personality traits that I either couldn't change or once was proud of. Denying he said or did something he damn well said or did, so I questioned my own recollection, my own *sanity.* He took whatever self-pride I had and twisted it up so I felt ashamed and insecure instead.

Boy was he good at it too.

And then after I'd break down screaming and crying and threaten to leave or try to leave or I'd defend myself somehow, he would fight me for a few hours, exhaust me, and then he'd throw down the "I'm sorry, I love you, I need you, no one else understands me," bullshit. He'd buy me some supermarket flowers or a stupid card and write a sentence in it about how I changed his life. Lies.

What a fool I was. I changed his life?…He almost ruined mine. He gutted me. That's what they do, these people— they are vampires, they suck the lifeblood out of you, and when they can't get any more, you are spent, a carcass, nothing left, then they find a new supply. That's when the younger chippy appears, and suddenly the life you've built on eggshells collapses underneath you.

I wondered where Brody was, how he was doing, what poor victim he was feeding off of now, telling her how horrible I was to walk out him like that, with my fat brown coat and my terrible workout clothes and no friends.

"Fuck you, Brody," I said out loud.

"Thank you GOD for arresting him," I said to the TV, as Olivia and Elliot put cuffs on some perp and hauled him downtown for questioning. I made a mental note to email Joy and Bud some pictures of Liberty. He was flourishing.

***

"Ma'am?" The nurse touched my arm and I woke up. "We are bringing your mother in now. Everything went fine."

I had dosed off with the muffin wrapper still sitting on my chest.

"Oh—sorry" I scrambled to my feet as they wheeled Pearl into the room. I was elated. She made it. We made it.

Thank you God. Her eyes were squeezed closed, and she looked like she was in pain.

"Is she medicated?" I asked.

"Oh yes," the nurse said, pointing to the IV. "She's in La-la Land. She'll sleep for the rest of the day, if you want to go home and get some rest."

"It's okay," I said. "I'll stay here, if that's alright." The nurse nodded.

"The doctor will be by in a few hours on his rounds, you can talk to him then," she said.

Orderlies positioned Pearl's bed and monitors and cleared out of the room.

I stood next to her, my hands resting on the bedrails. She was sleeping, but she looked pained still.

We would have to somehow move a bed into the den or the living room for a while, so Pearl could avoid the stairs. The Old Bitties would come by for sure every day to make her lunch and help her.

I bowed my head. The gratitude that filled my heart was overwhelming; the realization that I had people in my life who were kind, helpful, who cared about me, about us.

But also that Pearl and I cared about *each other.*

Tears dribbled down my face as I whispered aloud "Thank you, God, thank you" for bringing her through the surgery, and for bringing all these people into my life. I had no other explanation for these good fortunes. From the moment Liberty found me, literally on the side of the road, to this moment, I had gone from a shell of a person who trusted no one, not even myself, to a person filled with future possibilities, who was daydreaming about marrying a roofer named Hank. I had a little tribe of people who cared about what happened to me and my mother. I had a horse, and people like Cataldo, who depended on me. And I depended on them.

I went from abused isolation to nourishing connection. I was involved. *Invested.*

And the best part was it wasn't scary, it was amazing. Healing. Energizing and fulfilling, like a warm blanket on the chilly, old aching bones of my soul.

***

Cataldo, Hank and The Kens heaved and huffed as they edged Pearl's cherrywood bed headboard down the stairs.

"Careful!" Hank said. "Don't scratch the wood work!"

"Yea we got it," Old Ken said. They assembled the bed in the office, which we reconfigured as a sleeping area for Pearl. She could use the first floor bathroom without the stairs, and get to her percolator every morning when she was cleared to walk again.

We brought in tables and the television, made room for her wheel chair, and one of the Old Bitties brought a little dinner bell for her to ring when she needed something. I went to the hospital to pick her up, and she was woozy from pain meds but feeling okay.

Hank and Young Ken carried Pearl in her wheel chair, Cleopatra-style up the porch stairs and into her new room.

"Ta-da!" said Hank. "Welcome to the Bridal Suite!" he trilled as he wheeled her into her new parlor.

Pearl didn't say a word.

She observed each object, her bed, the tables, the television slowly, as if she were taking it all in.

No one said anything.

I cleared my throat. "Pearl, the doctor said you couldn't do stairs—"

Pearl looked up at me, her black eyes wide with emotion. Hank touched her shoulder and she reached up to hold his hand.

Everyone mumbled "Aws" and "We love you, Pearl" as she whispered a simple "Thank you."

"Doctor says it's two weeks until you can use the cane, Pearl," Hank said, and he pointed sternly to the kitchen. "Percolator. Two weeks."

Old Bittie Barb handed Pearl a tissue and she dabbed her face. "Oh I may need someone to do the heavy lifting, but there will be Pearl's coffee tomorrow morning. 6:30 a.m. sharp," she said. Everyone clapped and whooped.

I was in such awe of my mother, the emotional cripple, the once angry, bitter selfish bitch, who had never shown this side of herself before. I had no idea it even existed. Her defenses were down. She was grateful. She was *funny*.

"Okay Folks," I said, "Let's get Pearl some rest now…thank you all so much for helping us do this. I—we—would not be able to do any of this without you. I am so grateful for each of you."

"But get out," deadpanned Old Ken, and the room erupted in laughter as the group said their goodbyes to Pearl and shuffled out.

Hank pulled me aside.

"You okay?" he asked, his piercing blue eyes searching my face for signs of distress.

"Yes," I answered honestly. "I am." I put my arms around his neck and I hugged him. He wrapped his strong arms around me and held me tight.

"I'll check in later," he said. "Call if you need anything."

"Thank you," I whispered in his ear. " In every way possible, thank you."

I watched his truck make its way down the driveway and I had the funniest feeling in my stomach. It wasn't butterflies exactly. I tried to identify it; I wasn't sad. I wasn't giddy. I felt...*safe.*

I heated up some tuna casserole that Old Bittie Betty had brought. We had more food than either one of us would ever eat. Our freezer was full of little plastic containers of soup, casseroles and rice dishes.

I brought a tray in for Pearl and we watched an old "Columbo" together. We reminisced about how Gramma Helen used to love "Columbo." She watched it every week in the very room where we were sitting. I had come to appreciate the family history of this house, and loved that the spirit of my grandparents was around us all the time.

During the farm's Golden Years, before Baby Johnny died, Tree Haven Farm was a place of joy—busy with family picnics, horses, riders, chili cook-offs, weddings, parties and fundraisers. A feeling of pride rose in me as I promised myself I would fight to return this place to its former glory.

"There is a small housekeeping issue, Mom," I said as I cleared away the empty plates. "The plumbing wasn't right in the downstairs bathroom so we had to have a guy come in and fix it so you had hot water."

She frowned. "How much was that?"

"Don't ask," I called from the kitchen. I didn't want to tell her it took all but the last of the duffel bag money.

***

Pearl was a champ for the next few weeks, and as Christmas Day approached she fought hard to regain her strength. She could hobble with a walker or a cane, and she preferred the cane although the doctor told her to use the walker.

"I'm old as dirt," she would say. "What am I, going to ruin the last five minutes of my life? I'm not shuffling around with that thing. This is more dignified." and she'd wobble off.

Hank and I went out again, this time to see his friend Clyde's band The Bottle Necks play at the Broken Spoke Bar & Grill. The place was one of those corner joints, with really good chicken wings, peanut shells all over the floor, friendly waitresses, and a long beer list.

His friends were kind, like him, and funny. We all sat around a table during the band's break and Clyde, the band's bass player, said "Well, well. A toast! We finally get to meet Maggie, the girl he won't stop talking about."

I raised my eyebrows. "It's all lies, every bit of it," I said, downing a shot of whisky and slamming the shot glass upside down on the table, to the whoops and hollers of his friends.

"Hold up, hold up," said Clyde. "Now would those be damned lies? Or *dirty* lies?" sneered Clyde, as he leaned forward in all seriousness, and handed me another shot.

Exaggerated "Ohhhhhs" swelled around the table. I waived them off.

"Both," I said, tough-guy like, downing the shot. I never did have a problem drinking Irish whisky.

They all hooted and applauded and Clyde high-fived me. Hank shook his head and smiled at how corny it all was.

We danced so much that night I ruined my shoes, but it was worth it. We ate chicken wings and drank too many beers on top of the whisky, and Clyde's wife Camille had to drive us back to Hank's house in town, which was much closer than the farm.

We were all laughing about the evening as Camille poured us out of her Hyundai and she drove off. Hank and I walked up the steps to his beautiful old Victorian.

He stopped me at the door and kissed me, one of his long, beautiful kisses that felt like floating and being on fire in all the right places.

"You should bottle that," I said, giggling.

"They do, it's called Irish whisky," he said, kissing me again.

He stopped, and squared his sparkling eyes with mine. "I will sleep on the couch. You will sleep in my bed, okay?"

"Okay," I said, smiling that he was so respectful. "I need to make sure Pearl is okay first."

"You need to call your Mom?" he said, his tone teasing me.

"Yes," I said mockingly. "Because I'm almost forty and I live with her."

He laughed and opened the door.

***

His home was beautiful but void of life; he had no photos, no books, no records, nothing that indicated his personality. I was surprised. A lot of antiques—very expensive antiques. But this did not look like the home I expected warm, friendly Hank to live in.

I called Pearl on my cell phone, and she was sleepy but up watching TV. She said she was fine, she took a pain pill and would probably nod off soon.

"Alpine?" Hank said, taking The Ugly Brown Coat and gently hanging it up.

"Sure," I said absentmindedly, staring at an odd, large modern painting above the fireplace. It had a wide bright yellow swish with angry red swishes across it, and black splotches. It looked out of place in the Victorian house. "This is…interesting. It doesn't really fit the rest of the house?"

"The Leuger? Actually," he called from the kitchen, "It's the only thing that is me in this house. Everything else was my ex-wife's idea of a life-sized dollhouse. If it were up to me, I'd live in a loft somewhere in the Big City," he said.

"Not much Big City around here," I said.

"Well, hence, I live in this old Victorian with all my ex-wife's dollhouse furniture that I got in the divorce. She didn't want the reminders, she told my lawyer." He lowered his voice but I still heard him in the kitchen: "Oh, but she sure took the cash…"

"Who's Leuger? I'm not really much of an art expert," I asked.

Hank laughed. "Marshmallows and whipped cream?" he called.

"Of course!" I replied.

"Leuger!" Hank shouted from the kitchen, sarcastically as though I should be very impressed, "you've never *heard* of Craig Leuger?"

Hank brought our Alpine mugs into the living room. I shook my head. "No…?"

"Well, that's probably because he was my college roommate," he smirked. I did not need that Alpine on top of the beers and whisky, but it tasted so good. Hank threw three short logs in the hearth and we clinked our mugs together.

"Cheers…So Craig and I, we lived together in this little dumpy apartment. I was going to school for architecture and he was going for art. He was nuts—he couldn't hold down a job, and he was always short on money. I liked his paintings though, they were cool, I thought. And one month he was short on the rent so he gave me an I.O.U. for that painting, which he called 'Happily Ever After,' for thirty-five thousand dollars, contingent upon him one day selling a painting for twice that amount."

I smiled and raised my eyebrows.

"I know, I know," Hank said. "I was basically paying his rent that month. But I liked the painting, so, I guess I bought that painting for two hundred bucks. And according to the signed official documents I have, written in ball point pen on a paper towel taped to the back of that painting, it's actually worth *thirty-five thousand dollars*. What a return, huh?"

He took a self-satisfied sip of his Alpine, and left a whipped cream moustache on his upper lip for effect.

"You're a regular Rockefeller," I said, and leaned in to kiss the whipped cream off his lip. He kissed me back, a little more than I'd expected, which was thrilling.

"And where is the great Leuger now? Painting portraits of the Queen? Heads of State? Selling his landscapes to the Louvre?" I asked.

Hank took a deep breath. "No," he said quietly. He set down his mug.

"It's actually…about four years after he sold me that painting, he… Hunters found him…he'd gone out in the fields with his dad's hunting rifle and…that was it. He lay there for two days, they think. His mother told me he had been manic and happy right before, she just couldn't figure it out. I think he was just…something wasn't wired right in his head.

"It's like he wasn't able to make choices like the rest of us do, with facts and reason and context. He couldn't see the world as it really was. He saw it… *like that.*" Hank pointed to the painting, with its angry swishes made out of happy, bold colors, pierced by the black inkblots.

"Leuger used to call them Fear Goggles. That's how he saw the world, through Fear Goggles," Hank said.

"Like Beer Goggles," I said, nodding. I studied the painting. To me, it looked like something sunny and happy, pierced by rage and bullets.

"We get so wrapped up in the things we are afraid of…things we are afraid of feeling, doing, experiencing," I said. "I'm so sorry about your friend. I've been down that low, but I never thought of actually killing myself as a solution. It would cross my mind, like 'I wish I was dead,' but it was never something I would actually think about long enough to get all the way out in the woods with a rifle in my hand. He must have been in terrible pain, whether it was justified pain or not, it was justified to him in his mind.

"And yes, Hank, you're right…of course he wasn't seeing things clearly. It's strange, now that I am so far away from Montana, how I felt when I was there, I see things so clearly now. And it's a much different life I remember than the one I thought I was in when I was in it, if that makes sense. I had so much more power than I thought I did. If I'd only woken up to it.

"I'm not saying Brody's abuse was my fault—it wasn't. But the Fear Goggles I had on were thick, and the isolation and the abuse I endured made them thicker every day I stayed." I looked down at my cup. "I guess didn't know all I had to do was take them off."

I raised my mug to the painting. Hank raised his. I said, in a formal voice fit for the Queen's portrait painter, "A toast—to The Great Craig Leuger. To taking off Fear Goggles forever, and finding Happily Ever After," I said. "Here, here!" Hank said.

"I do miss the guy. He was crazy, but he was the sweetest guy you'd ever know. I had lost touch with him the year before he died, and I often wonder if I'd made the effort, If I'd kept in touch or tried to, would he have turned to me? Could I have helped him?" His eyes were red. He blinked.

"But…hindsight is always crystal clear," Hank said as he shook his head. "You can't evaluate your decisions then based on information you have now. Like, you did the best you could in Montana, based on the information and the resources you had. Maybe you could have done something differently, sure, maybe you could have left him earlier or fought back harder or I don't know what.

"But you also could have done something *worse*. You could have drowned yourself in alcohol. You could have developed a drug problem. You could still be there now! You could have started hurting people around you to lash out. You could have done so much worse than just… leave."

His words sunk into my brain like a red wine stain on a white carpet. I didn't say anything for a moment. I had been, for years, so focused on what I should have done, should have said, what I did wrong. And lately how my sudden leaving was so unfair to Brody. All the things that Brody's abuse had trained me to think: *it was my fault.*

I never once considered all the terrible things I *chose not to do*, and the strength it took to make those choices at that time because I was trying to make the relationship work. I was trying to figure Brody out, trying to love him. Trying to get him to love me again the way he did in the beginning. I chose to leave suddenly, selfishly, exactly when I did *because I could*—Brody was literally handcuffed and couldn't come after me long enough to give me a head start—and I finally needed to stop beating myself up about it.

"Hank?" I said sweetly.

"Yea?" he said, his eyelids getting heavy.

"You make really, really good Alpines."

****

CHAPTER ELEVEN
You Are Enough

On Christmas morning I woke up early and tip-toed downstairs, much like I did when I was a little girl. I missed Gramma Helen and Grampa Bill so much in that moment.

Pearl was still asleep, with the colored lights aglow on the huge tree next to her bed. We had thought about putting the tree in the living room by the window, but she said she could enjoy it more if it were within her sight. The TV was still on, tuned in to "It's A Wonderful Life" which started repeat-showings on a cable channel at midnight. I watched the scene when the people all come in the door with money to help George overcome the loss of eight thousand dollars and my eyes filled with tears.

"Never fails," I whispered out loud, and wiped my cheek with my sleeve.

I looked at the shiny wrapped gifts on the floor, one of which was Pearl's hat from Lainey's. I was very curious about what Pearl got me. When I was a girl she gave me impersonal gifts, perfume I didn't like, or sweaters that I hated. Christmas seemed perfunctory, a chore to her then. This year was different though. She and the Bitties baked up a storm for three days before Christmas, and like Thanksgiving, the strays were coming in the afternoon for turkey dinner.

My heart swelled with peace and gratitude as I watched Mom quietly sleeping. If someone had told me last year, when I held the lone Harry Connick, Jr. Christmas CD Brody bought me, and watched while he opened the dozen gifts I gave him, that in a year I'd be home on the farm, not only free of Brody and his judgmental misery, but I would be celebrating Christmas happily *with my mother*, I'd have fallen down laughing.

I made some tea and bundled up for my morning walk with Liberty. I brought him an apple for a present, and I dressed him in his fancy new red plaid blanket over his regular blanket. The rich crimson wool was striking against Liberty's iridescent coat and the white landscape around us.

We trudged through the deep snow along the trail in the woods, and the bright morning sun glinted off the icicles in the tree branches. It was so still.

"Have I told you how much you mean to me, Boy?" I said, pulling the apple out of my pocket. I held it out in my flat hand and his soft lips and giant teeth scooped it up. "Merry Christmas, Liberty," I said.

"It still blows my mind… I mean from the second I found you, or you found me, however that worked, and Bud and

Joy… by the way, I sent them a basket of stuff, cheeses and pepperonis, little mustards, things like that." I petted his velvety neck and walked close to him to keep warm.

"I wish I knew more about you, and your life in the circus. Were you one of those dancing horses? Did the ladies stand up on your back as you trotted around the ring? Is that why you don't want anyone riding you anymore?" His soulful eyes stared back at me but didn't give anything away.

How strange that I had no idea what Liberty's life was like before I met him. I knew some details, but not much. Did it matter? Should I try to find out, to understand him better? He seemed fine, as long as nobody tried to ride him.

Humans spend so much energy analyzing, rehashing, repairing, healing, rewriting their pasts. *What if we just made a choice at some point, accepted where we have been, and let the pains of the past go? Is that even possible, with our trauma and injuries and emotional scars? And how do we find that pivotal point in time? If we let the pain of the past go, do we have to let the good stuff go too?*

I thought about my date with Hank and how the ghost of Brody almost ruined it. I was conditioned to doubt myself, to mistrust my own instincts, to fear the worst. I was able to finally trust Hank that night because he looked in my eyes and said "You are enough."

Or was it not so much about being "able?" Did I really *choose* to trust Hank that night? Or did I just *want* to believe him? Like I *wanted* to believe Brody all those years ago, when I was so sure of myself, so sure of him, and yet so very, very wrong.

Pearl…Pearl and I just seemed to have mutually decided in our own heads that the best thing for each of us was to hit the reset button; get along and not trigger each other. We needed each other too much. And it worked like a charm. When two people really wanted harmony, it was like witchcraft.

"I guess that's it, Boy…real harmony takes two—one to draw the boundary and the other to choose not to cross it," I said out loud to Liberty. "But the whole trick to inner happiness is to stay on this side of the line in your own head. Like you, you drew your boundary, your line in the sand, no one rides you. And you were willing to go to the glue factory before you let someone on your back again. But in your mind, you stay on the *future* side of the line. You don't cross back into the past. You aren't sad and scared. You live on this side of the fence, happy and free, and you know, *you are enough*."

He raised his massive head and shook his mane with a snort. I laughed at his timing, as if he was answering "Now you're getting it!"

Then I laughed at myself. mean Jesus, what was crazier, that I was talking to a horse, or that he was *kind of talking back?*

***

When I got back to the house Pearl had somehow gotten the turkey in the oven on her one good hip. She was sitting in the front room staring out the window down the driveway, sipping her coffee. The colored twinkle lights around the window framed her small silhouette.

I poured myself a cup and sat with her.

"You know, Maggie," she said seriously, "it's been many, many years since this farm has seen any real life, let alone be fixed up like this. This is the first Christmas morning in many, many years there's an energy here, I can't explain it," she said. "I am so proud of what we've done here. And it would never have happened without you coming home."

She turned her eyes to mine. "I want to thank you."

I was a little taken aback.

"Thank *you*, Mom." I warmed my fingers around my mug. "It was you who took Liberty and me in. It was crazy for you to be open to all of this. None of it would have happened without you either. We did this together," I said. I told her my thoughts about Liberty's line in the sand, and how once you draw the line you have to promise yourself to face forward and stay on this side of the fence. And people's boundaries and choices, and respecting them.

"Well," she said, "I think there's a twist there. Some of us *have to* draw a line, build a fence between the present and the past, so *we can* face forward."

I smiled.

She nodded. "It's definitely a choice. I chose to let you come back here, maybe for the wrong reasons at first, but I can't quite explain the feeling—it's a happy feeling, what's going on here…but it's not exactly happy, is it? We have all these animals now, and God Bless this motley crew of people who help us, each an oddball in some way. I just can't find the word to describe what is happening here…" she trailed off.

I thought of how long I'd felt so trapped with Brody, and now with my past on the other side of that fence, me in the present, I saw how I wasn't as trapped as I'd thought. But that's how far down I'd been beaten by his mind games.

"Maybe sometimes we don't know how much power we really have to change our own lives," I said. "Every minute we make choices about a million things, sometimes it's the wrong choice for the right reason or the other way around. And these decisions either empower us or they don't, keep us on track or throw us off. I think I chose to come back here for the wrong reasons too, Mom. But I am so glad about how it's all turned out."

I looked out beyond the trees, at the Tree Haven Farm sign at the end of the driveway, standing tall and welcoming all who entered—the rescue animals, the volunteers, Liberty, me, Hank.

"Well Margaret," Pearl said, "the thing is, over time, those protective lines in the sand can get washed away. Fences fall."

She furrowed her brow. "But—and I hadn't really thought of this until just now—sometimes wiping out those old edges can be a good thing."

I looked up at her, and felt a weight lift off my shoulders.

"I know what that indescribable feeling is around here, Mom," I said.

"It's healing."

***

The strays arrived one by one, filling the kitchen counters with Rubbermaid containers full of side dishes and desserts. Everyone wore some kind of ugly Christmas sweater, although I first thought some of the Old Bitties may not have understood the irony. Barb's sweater had a giant cat face embroidered in it, with exaggerated yellow cat eyes boring into your soul from under a fur-trimmed Santa hat. It was quite a work of Ugly Sweater art.

"Do you like it?" Barb asked me.

"Um, sure, it's…festive!" I offered.

"Ugly as Hell, right? I've won a small fortune with this thing every year all over town in Ugly Sweater contests. I found it at Salvation Army. I sewed the Santa hat fur on myself," she said proudly.

I laughed at my own naivety for misjudging hers.

Hank arrived wearing a plaid vest that he said once belonged to his grandfather. He set a bottle of Rumple Minze and bag of marshmallows on the counter and winked at me.

"We're gonna make Alpines for everyone later," he said.

The Bitties and Pearl bustled around setting the table and finishing the turkey, while Hank and I set the holiday mood with music and lights and lit a fire in the fireplace.

As everyone took their seats and scooped mashed potatoes, passed turkey slices on serving dishes, poured wine and gravy and shook salt and pepper, I looked over at Pearl. She just sat at the head of the table, surveying everything with a broad smile on her face.

I leaned over to her. "Pearl, is it the painkillers or are you just really, really happy right now?"

She turned to me. "Life is really good, Maggie. I'm just freezing this moment in my mind."

I took her hand. "Mom, we're facing forward. Finally."

***

After dinner the group wedged themselves all around the Christmas tree in the den, some on Pearl's bed, others on chairs askew, a few on the floor. Pearl sat up straight in a dining chair, with her hands on top of a small old cardboard box in her lap. As everyone settled with their Alpines, Pearl made an announcement.

"Everyone. This year has been…well, the past few months have been…wonderful. And I owe so much to Margaret, for coming home finally, and to all of you, who have quite literally given your time to the animals, to this farm, to us. And I do have something for each one of you." Cries and moans of protest erupted, but Pearl waived them down. "Now, now, please, it's pitifully, woefully inadequate thanks but it's just a small gesture of what you all have really meant to me here. And now—I'm going to ask Hank to do the honors here. We will do the Secret Santa first, then my gifts to you, okay?"

She struggled opening the cardboard lid with her pained fingers, lifted a layer of tissue paper and pulled out a Santa hat. I recognized it immediately.

"Hank," she said. "This was Margaret's grandfather's Santa hat. My father's. His name was Bill. He used to wear this hat, and he would do the honor of handing out all the gifts, you know, picking them up from under the tree one by one, and handing them out. Would you be so kind?" She held up the hat by its worn white pom. It still said "Bill" in dingy glitter glue on the white trim.

"Of course, Pearl," Hank said solemnly. "I would be delighted." He put the hat on with flair, like it was Fred Astaire's top hat, and knelt by the tree.

"Okay! Pearl, how does this whole Secret Santa thing work? I just grab a gift, read the tag and hand it over?" Pearl nodded, and Hank started to pass out the gifts, announcing each name like the Town Crier. Guessing who the Secret Santa was turned out to be more fun than the actual gifts, which were mostly candles, scarves, gloves, and kitchen gadgets.

Young Ken was Old Bitty Barb's Secret Santa, and he got her a Barbie Doll. That changed the whole mood of the night. It could have been the Alpines or innocent Young Ken saying "What, it's a *Barb*-ie Doll, get it?" that set her off, but she just lost it laughing and never recovered. Barb had drawn Cataldo, and she bought him a beautiful pair of thick-lined leather winter gloves. Cataldo's eyes teared up and he didn't say a word. He just held up the gloves with one hand, nodded, and placed his hand on his heart.

"Well Margaret, here's your Secret Santa," he said, handing me a small, lumpy gift wrapped in a piece of burlap, artfully tied with string and finished off with a little wooden "M" tied in the bow.

"Ohhhh," I said, carefully untying the bow. As I unfolded the burlap, I put my hand to my mouth and began to cry. Inside was a tiny, beautiful wood carving of a horse, painted gold to look like Liberty. The little horse was rearing so he balanced on his tail, with his front legs high in the air, triumphant and majestic.

"It's so beautiful," I said quietly, handing it to Pearl, who passed it to Hank and then around the room.

I pretended I didn't know who the Secret Santa was, but when everyone shook their heads and shrugged for the right amount of time I looked right at Cataldo.

He smiled and his kind brown eyes lit up. "Yes! Me!! I carve Liberty for you!" he said and the whole room lavished praise on him. "My father taught me to do this," he said.

Barb spent a little longer looking at the carving. "Cataldo, how long did this take you?"

"That one took me three weeks," he said. "But I wanted it to be perfect. I do simple ones in a few hours."

"Really?" she said. "You know you could sell these for a lot of money?"

He shrugged.

"No, seriously, Cataldo, the gift shop by the quarry, you could sell these, you could make a lot of money. I can talk to them if you like, I can help you. In the summer I sell my crochet beach cover-ups there. The mark-up is crazy," she said, drawing a big swig on her Alpine.

I looked at Cataldo. "That's not a bad idea…you can use space here if you like, if you need tools or wood or whatever. Just tell me what you need," I said.

Cataldo held his gloves tightly. "Can I say something, Miss Pearl?"

Pearl looked surprised, although she probably loved that he asked. "Of course, Cataldo."

"I feel like you, Miss Pearl. I feel this place has…been a home, or like family for me. I used to have no hope, no home," he said, pointing to his heart. "But I have a place to go, where the animals need me. I always like to be working, doing, but when working and doing is also making you happy. That is the greatest thing. So you say thank you to us, I say thank you to you."

Hank raised his Alpine. "Here here! Thanks to all of us, God help us, we need each other!"

The group laughed and clinked mugs but it was true. We did. And it felt so good to say it. And to not hate it.

Pearl asked Hank to reach under the tree and pull out the pile of small presents, one tagged for each person. I won't lie, I thoroughly enjoyed the view while he was bent over, his head and shoulders leaning way under the tree. He was, and is, a perfectly built man. At least in my eyes. He wasn't as muscled as Brody but he had a strength to him, a solid-ness that made me feel safe in a different way than I had felt with Brody at first. And Hank smelled so good, I loved his musky, manly cologne or aftershave or whatever it was that made me dizzy if I got too close to the warm skin on his neck. I wondered where, and when, and how, or even if, our bodies would be completely naked with each other, moving together, making each other crazy. My ungroomed, unpedicured, unmanicured, unshaven, long-untended-to femininity jolted me out of daydream. *I really need to get to that*, I thought. I bit my chapped lower lip and curled my unpolished fingernails under my hands.

Hank navigated his tall frame out from under the tree and began handing out small boxes to each person. They were meticulously wrapped in brown paper that had little gold horses all over it.

"Everyone just open them all, please," said Pearl. Hank handed me one too.

I opened mine to find a white coffee mug, with a "Tree Haven Farm" logo on one side, and "Margaret" on the other. Pearl beamed as she watched everyone examine their mugs, personalized with their names.

"I designed the logo myself!" she said proudly. "I did it on the internet!" I smiled at her resourcefulness. She had really taken to running the business, and she was becoming a real whiz on the computer. She would sit up late into the night, her glasses perched on the end of her nose, tapping on her keyboard and forcing herself into the Twenty-First Century.

"Pearl," I said. "I have a gift for you." And I handed her the hat box.

"Oh!" she said, feigning great surprise. She slowly pulled the beautiful ribbon off the ornate box and lifted the lid.

The look on her face was so strange; at first I thought she was angry. Then I realized she was trying not to cry. She reached in and held up the hat. Ooohs and aaahhhs peppered the air and she forced a smile on her face, but it was as if any emotion escaped, the dam would burst.

"It's lovely," she said quickly. "Thoughtful. Thank you, Margaret." She left the lid off the box and quickly turned to Hank. "What's next?" I smiled to myself. She loved it.

"Well there's my gift to you, Pearl," Hank said.

He handed her a small, delicately wrapped box.

She smiled a devilish grin and picked gently at the wrapping. As she opened it, her face melted into large, watery eyes and a trembling frown. She lifted a beautiful gold necklace, with "Pearl" spelled out in thin gold cursive letters, and a single white pearl on each end.

"Oh," she whispered. "Beautiful. Thank you, Hank." She held it toward him and he stood up to put it around her neck. Everyone gasped and oooohed and aaahhhed and awwwed at Hank's thoughtfulness. Pearl kept touching her neck, as if she was afraid the necklace would disappear. She was very quiet for the rest of the night, but in the most beautiful way. A way I never saw before.

I wondered, if my mother had known this love and support from way back, would my childhood have been different? Would I have known a different love and support from her? Would I be different? Are there people who don't have do draw lines, because their pasts aren't trying to kill them?

Hank picked up a huge box that had been sitting next to the tree. It looked like it might be a toaster oven or something.

"This is for you, Margaret," he said. "Now if you don't like it, we can exchange it, no problem."

I looked at him, puzzled, as he set the giant box in my lap. It was too light to be a toaster oven. It was wrapped in department-store style, with a giant red bow. I tore into it, and lifted the top.

Under layers of white tissue paper, I felt some fur and material, and stood up to pull out the biggest, fattest,

puffiest, warmest blue down faux fur-hooded parka I'd
ever seen.

Everyone applauded, and Hank reached over to grab the
shoulders and put it on me. It was huge but it fit me like a
glove and he pulled the hood over my head and looked
into my eyes, zoning out the laughter and everyone else in
the room, and said "Do you like it?"

"I love it," I said, and we kissed, in front of everyone, me
wearing a coat that only a man who truly cared about and
understood me would even think of buying for me.

"I never want you to be cold again," he whispered to me.
And the power of his words was like a giant gong ringing
in my psyche. I held his gaze for a moment and smiled at
him.

The coat was so big I had trouble maneuvering to grab his
gift, which I had kept hidden behind the door all night.

"Now, I had to do some sneaky stuff to get this," I said to
Hank. "But I'm hoping you will forgive me," I said.

He looked at me, intrigued. I pulled out a large wrapped
picture frame from behind the door.

"There might have been a little thievery involved," I said.

He tore the wrapping and his whole body slumped. He
smiled and shook his head as he uncovered the rest of the

frame. It was the paper towel from Craig Leuger, promising him the $35,000, and a placard that said "Happily Ever After," Artist: Craig Leuger, for him to hang with the painting over his fireplace.

"How did you—"

"I looked behind the painting," I said. "I saw you had an envelope taped to the back. And…well, I stole it."

Everyone looked very puzzled, especially Pearl. "Does someone want to explain this?" she asked.

Hank laughed. "Well, I have this painting in my house," he said. "It was done by —it's a long story, but—this is just—this is really, really special. Thank you Margaret," he said, and he stood up and kissed me.

"Well," Pearl said. "Last but not least. Margaret. Here is my gift to you. Hank, will you please hand Margaret that box there, in the gold wrapping?"

Hank placed a beautifully adorned gift in my lap, with two pine cones attached to a silver bow on the box top. I lifted the lid and there was a huge leather-bound photo album inside.

"Open it!" said Pearl.

I pulled the album out and gently opened the wide cover. On the first page, I saw a single faded old color photo, carefully centered on the beige paper. It was Pearl, with her hair in a bouffant of the times, holding me, a tiny baby in her lap. I recognized the chair she was sitting in as Grampa's old brown winged chair that used to be in the front room of the house.

I turned the pages, and they were filled with old photos, some in color, faded with torn edges, others black and white, stiff with curled corners. I was in each one. As I turned the pages, my image changed from a small baby to a toddler, and my mother disappeared from the photos. My grandparents appeared in them or I was in them alone. I ran through sprinklers, grinned and stuck out my tongue with a chewed up fresh tomato on it, my grandfather's prized tomato plants in the background. I sat proudly atop Sherman Tank, one of my Grandfather's horses and my favorite even after he threw me smack on a hornet's nest. The photos from the nineteen seventies were sepia toned, mostly from the summers as I started equestrian lessons, jumping three and four foot fences and fearlessly riding horses that should have been far too big for my tiny body and short little legs.

"Pearl, this is amazing," I said to her. "How did you—"

"I wanted to piece together your childhood," she said. The guests shifted uneasily in their chairs, like they were witnessing a very personal moment. And they were. But I had had quite enough of secrets and hiding anything about myself.

"This is the most wonderful thing ever, Mom. Thank you," I said. I tried to stop the single tear from rolling down my cheek, but there it was.

Barb and Ken and the volunteers started chattering away around me but I tuned them out, I was mesmerized by the pictures in the book. I didn't recognize the happy girl in them at first. When I got to a picture of Grampa, holding me at probably five years old in his arms, both of us laughing, me wearing my helmet from some riding adventure, I studied the smile on my face. It was so…authentic. That girl was filled with… *joy.*

The pictures became fewer as I reached puberty, and my mother turned up in one or two again, when I graduated from junior high school, and she was there in my high school graduation photo. She looked uncomfortable, distant. I looked miserable.

I turned back the pages, and realized that somewhere around junior high school, when my mother returned from her globe-trotting disaster of a life, the joy faded from my eyes, and the smile disappeared from my face. I looked up at Pearl. Her expression was desperate, as if her whole life hung on whether this gift made me happy or not.

I closed the book and I helped Pearl to her feet, and I hugged her for a long, long time. "Merry Christmas, Mom," I said to her. "I love this. Thank you."

"Merry Christmas to you, Margaret," she said. I knew she meant so much more than that.

***

The next morning I bundled up for my walk with Liberty as usual, this time with my new Fat Ugly Blue coat. Tea in hand, I went out to the barn and he was bobbing and snorting in his stall, excited to get out into the winter sun. It was bright golden white in the early daylight, just like Monet's paintings of haystacks.

We ventured on the trail a little bit into the woods, but the snow was too deep, so we turned around and walked up the plowed driveway and back. It had been a very rough winter. I looked at the snow piled high on the barn roof, and it made me nervous. I knew it would hold at least somewhat until the spring, but a few more storms could really do some damage.

I put Liberty out in the small paddock with a bale of hay, climbed up on a fence rail and watched him prance around in his red blanket. His injury had all but disappeared. He knew no one would try to ride him. He was free to live on his side of the line. As I sat up on the fence and finished my tea I was overwhelmed with gratitude. I put my hand over my heart and looked up at the clear blue winter sky.

"Thank You," I said, as tears streamed down my face. "Thank You for opening a door for me to choose to walk through. How can I show my gratitude? Go to church every Sunday? Study the Bible? Be a perfect person?"

I sat on that fence for a good half hour, just letting the tears fall. They were good tears. Then, from the middle of the paddock, Liberty charged straight up to me and came to a sudden halt, kicking up snow, and stared at me.

"Whoa, what was that!" I said to him, petting his neck. "I'm okay, I'm just trying to figure out how to say 'thank you' to people who you owe your whole life to. How would you say it if you could?"

He snorted and ran off into the paddock, kicking up snow everywhere. It was a beautiful sight, this glorious horse, swirling up crystalline clouds of shimmery snow in the bright winter morning sunlight.

He was showing off for me, I thought. He was thanking me for taking care of him by putting on a show. Giving me what he could offer. That's all I could expect from him, and I realized sitting there watching him, that all I really did expect from him was just whatever he could give me. Nothing more, nothing less.

I remembered the cashier from the gas station, who had recognized my need to escape, and with a free tank of gas and a coffee unwittingly helped me find Liberty, get to Bud and Joy, and ultimately get home, and at the time, all I could offer her was the promise of helping someone else down the line.

"Pay it forward," I said out loud, and hopped off the fence.

"Liberty!" I shouted. "Come on, Boy! I've got some work to do!"

***

I sat at Pearl's computer and printed up fliers with little tabs at the bottom so people could tear off the email address.

"Support Group for Victims of Emotionally Abusive Relationships" I typed in large font.

"This is not a professional therapy group, but just an old fashioned 'sewing circle' for people who are in, or have been in, emotionally abusive relationships and want to talk to other people about it. This is an anonymous, informal setting, free coffee and refreshments will be available, and hopefully we can all help each other heal."

"First meeting: January 5, 7:00 p.m. at Tree Haven Farm. Please email RSVP so we have a head count or if you have any questions."

The public library, Target, the supermarket, the tack store and the local coffee shop I figured would be good starting points.

I tacked the fliers up, did some shopping in town and went back to the farm a few hours later.

Pearl was sitting at her computer eating a tuna sandwich.

"Maggie," she called to me as I shook off the cold and hung up my coat.

"Why do we have two dozen emails about a Support Group?"

The grocery bag slid out of my arms and onto the counter with a thud.

***

I sat up late hunched over Pearl's computer reading the emails, with Pearl quietly snoring in her bed next to the Christmas tree. I couldn't believe how many women, and a few men, had similar stories to mine. Most of the emails were questioning whether their situations met the criteria for "emotional abuse," and if not, could they come anyway because they were so desperate for help.

"He started off always telling me how sexy my red lipstick was," one woman wrote, *"and then after a few months he started telling me how annoying it was that it got all over his face when he kissed me, and it looked trashy. Does this kind of thing qualify? I know it sounds so minor but it's comments like this all day, day-in and day-out, about things he once loved, and suddenly three months later now he doesn't, and I try to change everything about myself to make him happy but no matter what I do he's never happy with me anymore. It's like I'm being slowly chipped away, piece by piece. I would like to come to your group."*

A man wrote *"My girlfriend will stop talking to me for days at a time, not telling me why she is angry with me. She withholds her affection like punishment until I beg and plead for her to talk to me. Is this emotional abuse? It feels like it. I am on eggshells every day."*

The eggshells turned up in a lot of the emails. The same eggshells I once lived on, with Brody's irrational, ever-changing rules.

A college-age girl wrote, *"My boyfriend was so into me when we first met, it was almost annoying. Now he says I'm plain, he compares me to other girls, the size of their boobs, what they supposedly do in bed that I won't, how they will do anything their boyfriends want and I am a bad girlfriend for not being super slutty like them."*

I was stunned. Their stories were my stories.

"I am so sorry that you are experiencing this," I wrote back to each of them. "It's not up to me to judge whether this is emotional abuse. It's up to you. If you feel you need help, or answers to questions about how to handle certain decisions in your life, like whether to leave or stay, please call a professional therapist. And you are welcome to come to our first meeting. Maybe this can be your first step in understanding the whole process."

I told Pearl about my idea and she loved it. Mostly the idea of making coffee and cookies for everyone. Although she wasn't sure how we would fit that many people in our house.

***

On New Year's Eve I trotted out the infamous black dress with the red trim. Hank said we were going to ring in the New Year in our finest, so I spent extra time dabbing on eye shadow and perfect lip liner, dousing my hair with spray in big rollers.

I went downstairs in Grampa's old robe to make some tea, and sit with Pearl for a while.

"Where is he taking you?" she asked.

"To the Spaulding Quarry Country Club," I said, raising a perfectly penciled eyebrow and feeding an Oreo into my perfectly red-lined lips. "Will you be okay here by yourself, Mom?"

"Oh I'll be fine," she said. "I've got the tree lights, the cats and those Alpines leftover from Christmas. I'll watch the ball drop and fall asleep. It will be peaceful. There's so much I'm looking forward to this New Year. I don't need a fancy party at midnight. But you should kick up your heels a little."

"And this time I'm not going to cry in this dress," I declared. Pearl let out a small "Hah."

"You really like this guy, don't you?" she said.

I smiled. "Yea Mom…I do. It's new—I'm so aware of that. And I'm trying so hard to stay even-keeled and just let things unfold, and to not let any ghosts of the past block my view of the truth. But yea… I really like this guy."

"I like him for you, Maggie. He's a good egg." She bobbed her tea bag in her cup. "Don't let some asshole from your past steal the Blessings from your future. I did that a long time ago, and it cost me everything. Including you, for so long. All those wasted years. But mostly it cost me myself. I let him steal *me*. The more you get out there, rebuild your life from the inside out or the outside in, whichever comes first, the less power he will ever have over you, and the more of you that you will get back."

Once again she surprised me with her insight. "Thanks, Mom." I put my hand on her hand. "Just being able to reconnect with you is something I never expected, and something I am so grateful for. It makes everything worth it to me."

Pearl took a sip of her tea and shifted herself out of getting mushy.

"Well! You better finish getting ready, he's going to get here and see some old lady in Dad's old robe instead of the hot date he's supposed to pick up."

I laughed. "Okay Mom," I said.

Hank arrived exactly on time, with a knock on the door at precisely eight o'clock.

"The *dress*," he said with a smile as I teetered slowly down the stairs in my heels. He looked like he stepped out of an old Frank Capra movie, dressed in a black tuxedo, with a black bowtie and holding a bouquet of luscious, red long stem roses. I lost my breath for a moment as I took in the sight of this tall, strong man with his wide smile, dark hair and those happy blue eyes. He had such a cheerful way about him, so different from Brody's judgmental, serious, unhappy way of looking at everything. Brody took everything about himself *very* seriously, from his workouts to his shaving cream. Hank didn't take himself seriously at all. Hank did not see others as there to serve him, or beneath him like Brody did. Hank saw himself as someone who wanted to make the mood in a room better than it was before he walked in.

These were traits I knew I shared deep down, but why had I talked myself out of them? I'd become pretty guarded and bitter during the past five years. I'd forgotten how nice I used to be. People used to call me, seek me out, enjoy my company. Now I felt like I was lucky if someone could stand to be in the same room. But what had I done that was so bad? Really, what was so awful about me? Other than what Brody decided? What he had drilled into my head and my psyche over all those years? Subtly, mixed in with enough positive messages to keep the cycle repeating. And even though it was Brody who had really changed a few months in, when his mask came off, I did see his awful way of looking at the world from the beginning. I did initially see his sense of entitlement, his vanity, his imperial way of thinking that he was the smartest person in the room, and how he judged others so harshly in the beginning, before he turned his cruel eye toward me.

Now, standing in front of a man who brought light into the room when he entered, instead of sucking the air out of it, I was learning that it's not so hard to ferret out the good guys from the bad ones. Even if they are good liars, their actions will not line up with their words, even at the beginning. There will be *something* off; if he says he's easygoing but he gets inappropriately upset that his order is wrong at a restaurant or that his table is not to his liking. He claims he is generous, but he is a miserly tipper. He says he likes you and he contacts you a lot but he doesn't actually make an effort to see you or ask you out. He claims he has been wronged in all his past relationships but he has very few close friends, indicating that people have not stuck by him.

This man, Hank—this kindhearted, truth-telling man, he was not like Brody at all. He was authentic, and real, and *he* liked *me.*

"Shall we go, Margaret?" he asked, holding his elbow out to escort me.

"We shall," I said, feeling like I had won every lottery, ever.

***

The trees outside the Spaulding Quarry Country Club
were peppered with twinkle lights as we walked up to the
grand door. A frozen gusty chill sent a shiver through me
and Hank instinctively wrapped his arm around the New
Ugly Blue Coat I draped over my shoulders.

"We're almost inside," he said. "I'm sorry, I should have
dropped you off at the door, but I didn't want to leave
you," he smiled.

I laughed off his cheesy sentiment but inside I was mush.
We walked through the heavy wooden doors and it was
like a scene from a Disney movie—a beautiful ballroom,
decked out with bunting hung from the dark oak beams,
sparkling chandeliers, glittering lit Christmas trees that
lined the room and red and gold ribbons everywhere. An
orchestra was playing Big Band music, and I recognized
Hank's bass player friend playing his upright.

The men were dressed in black bowties and satiny
cummerbunds and their dates were sequined and glossed
to the nines. I wondered if the woman who abandoned my
dress at the Plaid Shoppe was here. Whoever she was, her
measurements were identical to mine.

Hank and I made our way to the bar, and many of the
hoity-toity people seemed to know him, with the husbands
handing out firm handshakes and the ladies raising
Botoxed brows to say "Hank! Our roof is keeping us
warm!" or something along those lines. He introduced me

proudly to each one, making sure he mentioned the "old Tree Haven Farm" and how I was "bringing it back to life." Most of them had no idea what he was talking about, but one woman in particular I noticed looked really uncomfortable.

"Tree Haven…" she said. "Yes I think I know the name, out on the outskirts of town, right?" and she seemed to be looking deep into my eyes, with an urgent look of fear. I recognized her name as one of the emails I received for my support group. I glanced at her husband, who seemed polite, if a little distant.

"That's our farm," I said to her. "It's very nice to meet you." I held her gaze for a moment, and gave her a quick wink. She relaxed her face.

"You too," she said. "Enjoy your evening and good luck with the farm. Maybe I will take a ride out sometime. To see the horses."

"Sure, you're welcome to," I said. "We love the company." As Hank and I turned away I whispered to him, "So what do you think of him? She seemed nice, but what's his story?"

"Eh, he's hard to read," Hank said as we waited for our champagne. "I did a tear-off for them two years ago. I dealt mostly with him, she was pretty quiet. He seems okay, but she seemed—*sad*. A lot of rich people are sad though. It's like because money can solve a lot of life's problems, they think money can solve *all* their problems. But you can't roll up hundred dollar bills and stick them where your heart should be. That might work temporarily but it always, always goes bad in the end. I've seen it happen over and over again with these people."

I thought about all the problems that fifty thousand dollars solved for Pearl and me. I used to daydream about winning the Lotto in Montana and running away from Brody. I blamed money all the time as the reason I couldn't, or wouldn't, leave him and my situation there. Yet when I walked out on him I did it without even knowing I was literally sitting on all the resources I needed to escape. And whatever I wasn't sitting on, I later found. Or it found me.

Now the farm was almost out of cash, and what would I do to solve the next round of problems that came up? I prayed my luck hadn't run out.

Hank handed me a glass of champagne with a fat red strawberry in it.

"Well we have some time until midnight, but, Happy New Year, Margaret. Thank you for spending tonight with me," he said.

"I am honored you chose me as your date tonight," I said. I wanted to deflect my deepening feelings and joke with him that somewhere in this room was probably a woman looking at me thinking "that's my dress!" but I didn't. I let myself be deserving of all the sparkle and grandeur in the moment.

"Happy New Year," I said softly to him, and took a big, big swig.

***

The band was playing "Take the A Train" and Hank and I were doing a really clumsy but charming West Coast Swing dance. We were both laughing so hard at our attempts to be good dancers that I was almost happier we were so awful at it. Hank was starting to sweat and my hair was beginning to wilt. We were less concerned than the other couples about maintaining our coifs, like two little kids at the grown-ups party.

The band switched to "Someone to Watch Over Me" and Hank pulled me close to him. "This is a great New Year's Eve," he whispered in my ear. I got chills from his warm breath on my skin. "Are you having fun Margaret?" he whispered.

"Yes," I whispered back in his ear. "The best kind of fun."

He pulled me a little closer. "What do you think Pearl is doing right now?"

I felt my heart sink a little. "I don't know…watching TV probably. And drinking whisky." I stared at the flickering candles around the room. "I have to say I feel a little bit guilty, leaving her there alone."

Hank touched my chin and pulled my face up to look in his beautiful blue eyes. Good God, those eyes. "Is that true?" he said. "Do you really feel guilty? Do you think she's okay? Or do you think she's lonely out there on the farm alone?"

I looked into those deep, vivid blue jewels, the color of some Gauguin Tahitian sky, and told him the truth.
"I think she is okay, *and* she is lonely. I think it's both. I think a lot of good things are happening this year, and she knows it, but I think she's probably feeling the void of people tonight. Like anyone alone would on New Year's Eve."

He pulled my head to his chest and held me tightly in his strong arms for a moment. "Margaret," he said suddenly, "come with me." Then he took my hand and led me off the dance floor.

We ascended the steps to the coat check room, and he pulled our ticket and a five-dollar bill from his pocket. "May I ask you to get our coats, and I will go get our chariot, and we will go back to the farm. We need to be with Pearl tonight. She needs us to be with her tonight."

I opened my mouth to say something but he wouldn't let me. "You know it. And you and I, we have all kinds of time to do things like this. But you and Pearl—you need to be together tonight, and on this night, this particular New

Year, it needs to be different for her too. For both of you. Together. Trust me."

He handed me the ticket and the money and raised his eyebrows. "Okay?"

I nodded slowly, astonished at how right he was. I turned to the coat check girl. "It's a black men's wool coat and a really ug—*warm…puffy* blue one."

***

We drove up to the porch and the house looked dark except for the Christmas lights on the porch. Hank and I shook off the cold and I called out to my mother but got no answer. I heard the television in her makeshift den bedroom but she was nowhere to be found. The Christmas tree lights were on. My photo album was open on the table next to her computer, on the last page. It was a photograph of my grandmother and me, standing in front of my old Subaru the day I left for California.

"Mom?!" I called. Hank called upstairs. "Pearl?" She was nowhere. Hank went outside to check the cars. I was about to dial the police when Hank called to me.

"Margaret! I found her! It's okay! Come on out to the barn!"

I grabbed my coat and walked to the barn, and there, sitting on a blanket on a bale of hay next to Liberty's stall, bathed in the multi-colored glow of a small battery-powered fake Snowman decoration she had borrowed from the porch, was Pearl. She was wearing The Hat. Her Christmas gift from me. And she was three sheets to the wind.

"Mom? Are you okay?" I knelt by her. She had a bottle of whisky in one hand, and a coffee mug in the other.

"I'm perfect," she said, struggling to sit up. She was wrapped in a quilt from the house, shivering, and wearing her muck boots. "I came out here to say Happy New Year to Liberty. You were right, he's a good lissss-ner."

She smiled and raised her mug to Liberty, whose head loomed protectively over his stall door above her head. I smiled at her and straightened The Hat on her head. "Mom, you want to come in the house? It's cold out here."

"NO!" she said emphatically. "This is where I wanna be. Ring in the New Year. In the barn. Grampa's barn." I looked at Hank. He shrugged.

"Margaret," Hank said, "Why don't I go in and make everybody some Alpines? I'll bring them out, and we can all ring in the New Year right here, together? It's eleven-thirty right now, and Pearl, right after midnight we will get you to bed, how's that?"

Pearl nodded. I gave Hank the okay sign and he went back up to the house. I realized I didn't have to ask him to bring extra blankets, because I knew he would. And my heart almost exploded with gratitude that this man was in my life at all, for however long he would be.

"Mom, why did you come out here to the barn? How long have you been sitting out here?"

"Oh…I was watching the TV, and I kept thinking about Liberty," she said, loose-jawed. "And these guys," as she waved wildly to the miniature ponies and cows in the front of the barn. "But mostly him." She pointed up to Liberty. "I thought this poor guy, he's out here and his stall is kind of separate in the back from them and he's alone and I thought well I'll just come out and have a talk with him, you know. And it turns out he's a damn good converser— conversationer—he's—"

I smiled. "Conversationalist."

"Yes," she said, relieved. "That. And then here we are. And here you are!" Her brows furrowed. "Why are you here? What happened to the Country Club?"

"We came back for you, Mom," I said. "Hank thought we should come back so you wouldn't be alone. We both wanted to celebrate with you. All of us. Together."

Pearl's head bobbed in agreement. "Okay," she said, and patted the hay bale next to her. "I don't understand two young people wanting to sit in a cold barn with an old lady but okay. Sit."

Hank came back, juggling a tray of mugs, a thermos of Alpines, an apple for Liberty, an electric blanket and the emergency radio. I fell completely in love with him at that moment. Many moments before and since, but that was one of them for sure.

"Okay, Ladies, here we go," he said and set everything up. He handed me a mug of pepperminty chocolate, slowly took Pearl's whisky mug from her and handed her a hot chocolate mug. "Extra chocolate for you Pearl, and we'll plug this thing in and be cozy warm until the clock strikes twelve."

There we sat, the three of us, on bales of hay, next to Liberty's stall in the old barn, cozy under a heated blanket and sipping Alpines, except for Pearl who unbeknownst to her was just sipping hot chocolate. The Snowman grinned next to us, silently blinking red and white and green. We listened to the AM radio station play Christmas oldies. Pearl surprised both of us with her ability to remember all the lyrics to "Jingle Bell Rock."

At midnight we clinked our mugs together and sang "Auld Lang Syne" loudly and very out of tune along with the radio. Pearl knew all the words to that too. Then we all kissed Liberty's muzzle for good luck, like he was the Prayer Wall. I took an extra moment, my lips pressed to the soft hair on his nose, and petted his velvety cheek. I still had no real answer why I brought him with me, why I fell in love with him like I did at Bud and Joy's. Or why they understood how much I needed him. I could only guess that Joy knew Liberty would counsel me the way he'd counseled her, on their walks after her loss.

A few minutes after midnight, Pearl fell sound asleep on my shoulder, hat and all, and Hank carried her all the way up to the house and gently lay her in her bed. I switched off the snowman, gathered everything up from the barn and walked back up to the house.

"Well, she's going to sleep until Valentine's Day," Hank said, laughing. "I can't say I blame her for tying one on, though. Pearl's seen a lot of changes. Is she okay?"

"I think so," I said, washing the mugs in the kitchen sink. "I'll talk to her about it tomorrow. You're right, it's been a lot for her to process, more than you know. I'm not sure if that was a happy drunk or not tonight."

Hank wrapped his arms around me slowly. He kissed the back of my neck gently, and I could feel my knees wobble.

I turned around and kissed him for a long time. He held me protectively.

Wrapped in the safe affection of this handsome, kind, warm, funny, once-wounded man, who fought so nobly to come back from his divorce a healthy, whole, loving man again instead of staying bitter, and punishing the next girl for the last one, I silently said a soul-deep prayer of gratitude to God.

I decided then and there that whatever happened with Hank and me, I was going to cherish the experience, keep my heart open, and as long as his words matched up with his actions, I would allow him further and further into my heart. *Hank was not Brody.*

****

CHAPTER TWELVE
No Whining

The day of our first Support Group meeting, Pearl fidgeted and made pots upon pots of coffee, pulling out the big holiday coffee urn and the cookie trays, and baking herself into a frenzy with dozens of little round sugar cookies.

I made some notes to start the meeting off, and some rules for the meeting that I thought would help keep the evening from turning into a morose group therapy session.

"My goal is to inspire each other," I wrote, "and learn from each other, and help each other find the strength within to do what is best for each of us, for ourselves and for our families."

I read it off the legal pad to Pearl as she frosted rows of sugar cookies. She was hunched over them like a jeweler, her glasses and apron smeared with flour.

"I like that," she said. "But you know you are going to hear a lot of 'woe is me.' You have to decide how to set a limit on the 'woe is me' stuff. Not everyone *wants* to solve their problems. Some people would rather just complain about it because…somehow, it keeps them important to other people. For some people, they like the attention, the casseroles, the pity. You need to shut that stuff down, make this little club a place where they can't go for whining. No whining allowed," she said as she rounded a perfect layer of icing on a perfect cookie.

"No whining allowed," I said, and wrote that on the legal pad in capital letters.

***

Hank arrived first, with a bag of tortilla chips and a jar of salsa. I had told him of my idea, and he asked if he could be one of the first attendees. I told him I was counting on his expertise and I hoped he'd share some of his therapy knowledge.

"I felt like I needed to bring a dish," he said sheepishly and handed me the food. I shrugged, kissed him and pulled out a serving bowl.

One by one, cars slowly pulled up the long driveway, followed by a knock on the door. Each person wore a similar expression: polite smile, somewhat pained, relieved, and uncertain, but also hopeful, like it was the first day of a class they looked forward to taking.

And everyone brought a dish. Pearl was in her element, buzzing around the buffet table setting up everything.

"Margaret," she said, pulling me aside in the kitchen after the nineteenth person came through the door, "we don't have enough room for all these people."

I surveyed the layout of the living room, and with Pearl's bed in the den, and the porch out of commission in the cold, she was right. People would be sitting on each other's laps in the living room or standing around the dining room table, crowded next to each other.

When the final R.S.V.P. arrived, we had twenty-six people. Everyone was crowded in the dining room with plates of food and sodas, nodding politely at one another. Some recognized each other and traded uncomfortable empathetic glances. They were all walks of life—teacher, housewife, wealthy, poor, doctor, student, housecleaner, waitress, police officer. Different personalities, some were outgoing and bold, some were quiet and sad. Others seemed angry. They all had an aura of being…worn. Tired. Hollow.

"Hank," I called to him from the kitchen. "Could you come in here for a second?"

He slithered his way through the plates and elbows. "I know," he said. "It's just too many people. We could go to my place?"

"It's so far," I said. "That might work for next time." I thought for a moment and looked over at The Ugly Coat hanging by the front door. "Wait—I have an idea!"

I sidled into the dining room. "Excuse me everyone, may I have your attention? I'm Maggie, I'm the…host, I guess I call myself. Welcome. As you can see we have a bit of a space problem here. If you can all put your coats back on, grab your food plates and drinks and follow me, I have an idea and we can get started with this first… um… gathering. I guess. Yes, it's a gathering. Okay!"

I led the diverse parade, all juggling plates and some kind of chair, me with blankets and my notepad, down to the barn. Hank carried the coffee urn, and another man followed with the tray of condiments. Hank ran back for Pearl's cookies.

I motioned for everyone to make themselves comfortable in the back of the barn by Liberty's stall. "I hope no one is allergic to horses," I said apologetically.

"We can figure something else out for next time but for now, this will be okay. I have three electric blankets here, we can plug these in and if you just kind of put them over your knees and don't mind sharing with the people next to you we should be warm enough in here for an hour or so." I looked around for expressions of disapproval, but I didn't see any.

Hank helped Pearl set up a little coffee station, and the sight of him, his tall strong frame following the orders coming from her frail tiny body to put the creamers here and the stirrers there was unbelievably charming. I smiled at his careful layout of doilies.

When everyone was settled, I introduced Liberty, who occasionally stuck his head over his stall door to join us. I read my little introductory speech, and a few rules: No

Judgment. We were all on our own journeys, and we were not to judge each other's choices. No repeating what we heard. Everything spoken was sacred and anonymous, just like AA. No diagnosing. If someone was seeking diagnostic solutions, they needed to be seeing a medical professional. We were not psychiatrists or psychologists.

And I paused before my final rule: No whining. We all knew the difference, deep down, between venting, or disclosure, or trying to identify a problem, and simple whining. No whining allowed.

Everyone nodded, most laughed at the no whining rule, and I suggested we all go around the room and just give first names, and what we hoped to get out of these gatherings—closure? Healing? Coping tactics?

The next hour was a whirlwind of pain, bewilderment, unrequited affections, wounded souls, people expressing symptoms almost akin to Post-Traumatic Stress Disorder:

"I feel so much anxiety when I see it's him calling on my phone, my heart literally starts pounding in my chest. I never know which one of him is on the other end—the sweet one, or the one who is going to tear my head off. I want to leave, but I don't know why I don't leave. In this group maybe I can figure that out?"

"He just stopped touching me, and said it was my fault, that I am cold, he calls me an old frigid woman, and he can't get aroused by me because he says I am so inhibited

sexually. He never had this complaint before. It just came up about six months into our marriage. He suggested we hire a prostitute to come to bed with us, to make me freer sexually. I refused, and he told me that proves he is right, that I am sexually cold. I don't know how this group can help me, but I have felt completely alone and worthless, and I believed him a little more each day, how worthless I am, until I saw your flier, so I had to come here. That's all I know."

"She told me that if I don't buy her a new car, she is going to leave me, because I must be spending all my money on other women. I have never, ever cheated on her, and I break my back trying to keep her happy with whatever she wants. I am in thirty-five thousand dollars of credit card debt, all for her clothes, jewelry and vacations. I cannot afford a new car for her, and I don't know what to do because I love her. If I tell her fine, then leave me, she cries and says she loves me and why don't I love her enough to make her happy? I can't win. I just can't win, and I feel betrayed by my own heart. Through this group, I want to find the courage to see things more clearly, and one day, just let her leave."

The hour turned into two hours, with a bathroom and snack break.

During the break I could see the ice had been broken and people were really talking. Two women who recognized each other from the Country Club with polite nods were hugging each other in tears, exchanging phone numbers and telling each other they "had no idea." Two men were politely nodding and talking on the porch, finding some common ground in their predicaments. I heard one man tell the other "you should come to my church, Man. I get a lot out of it. It helps." Another young woman was talking to an older woman, learning from each other.

"My husband says I'm not pretty enough," the young one said.

"Mine tells me that too," the older one said with a wry smile. "They're both lying."

As I carried another tray of cookies back down to the barn I stifled the tears in my eyes. I realized I was not emotional for myself. I was grateful to have been able to help these people. Be a catalyst. My heart filled with love for them, for me, for the God that had led me to this moment. I had truly paid it forward. And I understood, for the first time, why that woman in the gas station did what she did. Why Bud and Joy did what they did. It was so simple. It was like gratitude multiplied by victory divided by hope.

Just before we all settled back from the break, Ted the retired police officer was standing by Liberty's stall, petting his long nose.

"Breathtaking horse," he said. "I did some horse detail years ago. Love 'em. How'd he get the scar?"

"I'm not totally sure," I said. "He was in a rail car accident, and he was lost in the woods for six weeks. He probably got it in the rail car accident. He can't be ridden anymore. But he's the best listener in the world. I walk with him every morning, and I tell him my troubles," I said, smiling. "If you kiss his scar, it's good luck," I said. "He'll let you."

Ted raised his eyebrows. "Well Hell, who couldn't use good luck?" He leaned his head in and gave Liberty a kiss on the edge of the scar below his eyes.

"Geez are you that desperate Ted," one of the Country Club women joked.

"Hah, Marion, no. It's good luck. Go on." Marion shrugged her shoulders and approached Liberty's stall.

"Hello, Handsome," she said formally. "I'm Marion." She leaned in kissed his soft nose just next to his scar. Liberty stood still for her, as a gentleman would. I looked at Marion—a true beauty, gentle, intelligent, funny, Chair of a dozen charities in town, mother of two bright sons in Ivy League schools, the kind of woman who would always help a stranger. Yet she couldn't leave her husband who screamed at and berated her several times a week over household chores, landscaping, his shirts not starched enough, the leather on her car seats not clean enough, a few pounds gained after the holidays. Who were these emotional vampires that preyed on the good souls like her? Like me? Like Ted? Like Hank?

Anyway, everyone had to kiss Liberty for luck on the break. Liberty loved it. He shook his head at one point, then stepped forward and stood still for the next round. Pearl stayed in the house for the second hour. She was feeling the chill, and was suddenly tired, she said. She didn't share anything, but had listened intently.

"All these people—it's like their hearts have been mugged," she said. "I've been there. I don't need to tell my story, but Margaret, this is a good thing you're doing. I'm so proud of you." She said she was just exhausted.

When we began again after the break, a woman who was a yoga teacher suggested that at the end of each person's sharing, we all say something encouraging, to counteract all the negative energy we were releasing.

"That's a great idea. Any suggestions about what we should say? What would be appropriate?" I asked.

Eyes darted around the room, looked deep into coffee cups, but no one had any answers.

Hank spoke up. "I have a suggestion," he said, clearing his throat. "I know what started to change everything internally for me, when my therapist said I should look into the mirror every day and tell myself this, to recover from all the damage done to my psyche by the terrible things I had heard and believed for so many years. It's a simple thing, and I felt stupid saying it to myself in the mirror, but it really resonated with me, and it might be appropriate in this setting."

"Sure Hank," I said. "Go for it."

He cleared his throat again. This time he couldn't disguise the lump in it.

"You are enough," he said. Tears welled in my eyes.

Everyone mumbled *yes* and *yea* and *perfect* and it was decided. So every difficult story laid to bare through teary eyes and cracked voices, that confessed the ever-present guilt, and described the weapons—emotional manipulations, lies, twisted conversations to confuse and obfuscate, downright gaslighting to throw the victim completely off balance, all the carnage, blood, guts and pain and suffering—was followed each time by two dozen voices soothing the wounded soul with: *"You are enough."*

***

I woke early the following Saturday morning. I had a terrible nightmare that some strange wolf-like creature was chasing me. Pearl was already up, and I smelled the coffee as I came down the stairs in my pajamas and Grampa's old blue robe. It kept me warm and comforted me, like a hug.

"Good morning, Mom," I said, and poured a hot cup of coffee. She never looked away from her newspaper.

"What are you doing up?" she asked.

"I had a nightmare, " I said. "I couldn't sleep well last night. I feel...I don't know, my stomach or something. I'm...off."

She put down the paper. "You know I went out to check on Liberty this morning when I walked to the mailbox to get the paper. It's so damned cold out, I thought I'd just check on him before you take your walk and before Cataldo gets here. He was pacing in his stall. I've never seen him do that. Like a tiger or something. Back and forth. I calmed him down a little bit but he was really nervous."

"That's really strange. Okay, I'll go out and check on him. Maybe he's just itchy to run out in the paddock or something. I hope nothing's wrong. I'll call the vet anyway today just in case." I threw on an extra sweatshirt and boots and The Ugly Blue Coat and went out to the barn. As I walked toward him I could hear Liberty making noise.

He was swaying back and forth in his stall, snorting and stomping his foot, and the other animals were agitated too. The miniature ponies were hopping on their feet.

"Whoa, hey guys!" I said. "What's going on in here?" I walked up to Liberty and tried to soothe him but he wouldn't respond. He kept raising his head and neighing, and he seemed to become even more nervous as I tried to put a halter on his head. He jerked his head away and kicked the back of his stall.

"Whoa! Liberty…it's okay Boy, we won't do this then. It's okay. Just let me see what's going on with you here."

I turned around to hang the halter back up on its hook and I felt all the breath woosh out of my body.

My knees felt like sand. I froze, my voice paralyzed so I couldn't even speak.

I stood face to face with Brody.

****

CHAPTER THIRTEEN
Everything Went Black

"Hello Margaret," he said calmly.

He looked disheveled, maybe drunk or hung-over or both. He wore a thick beard, longish hair and his clothes were dirty. He had lost weight. His boots and beard and jacket were caked with icy snow, as if he'd been walking for miles in the wintery weather.

I couldn't speak, I could not get the words out to even ask what he was doing there, but I knew exactly what he was doing there.

"You have some explaining to do, don'tcha, Mags?" he asked me, his low voice scratchy and tense with rage.

"Like, oh, why the FUCK YOU LEFT ME IN JAIL AND STOLE MY TRUCK AND WHERE THE FUCK IS MY MONEY?" he leaned in screamed at me, inches from my face. I was terrified. Liberty went crazy, kicking and bucking in his stall.

Brody turned to look at Liberty for one second, and my body instinctively jerked and ran toward the house. I wasn't even in control, it was fight or flight and I knew I would lose that fight.

"Pearl!" I screamed breathlessly. "Call the police!" I shouted as I ran toward the front porch.

But Brody overpowered me and knocked me to the ground. He sat on top of me with one hand gripping my throat and slapped my face hard. The pain was a dull, excruciating bang that went through my skull from one side to the other. He slapped me again, this time splitting my lower lip. I could taste the metallic blood dripping in the back of my throat.

The weight of his body, the body that I used to love feeling on top of me in the beginning, that used to make me feel enveloped in his strength and his love, now made me feel terrorized. His knees pressed on my chest so hard I could barely breathe.

He pounded the snow next to my head three times, and I felt each thunderous hit stop my heart. He was so big and strong, and that power that once professed to protect me in those early, magical days was now threatening my very life.

"You bitch! Do you know what you did? You got me fired from that job! I had to spend the night in the drunk tank! I missed the flight! Luckily one of the guys washed out on his drug test and they grabbed me the next day, otherwise I was gonna come after you and fucking KILL YOU! You stole my TRUCK? Made me a laughing stock in front of everybody? Oh but I waited. I did my job, then I came home, and I cleaned up the FUCKING MESS YOU LEFT for me with the landlord, and I went looking. Now I'm gonna finish what you FUCKING STARTED YOU FUCKING PATHETIC LITTLE CUNT!"

He gritted his teeth and seethed. "You know what's hilarious?" he hissed through his clenched jaw, leaning down on top of my face. "Nobody gave a fuck you left. NOBODY! Your job came looking for you but that was it. Nobody else. No ONE CARED you WORTHLESS. PIECE. OF SHIT. You know who cared? I CARED! And you fucking RAN OUT ON ME?" He squeezed my face, pressed me into the ground and shook my head so hard my teeth cut the inside of my mouth.

"Brody please—" my muffled voice only made him press harder. It was getting harder to breathe with his fingers tightening around my neck.

His eyes were crazy, dilated and blank like he wasn't behind them. He was high on something, and probably hadn't eaten or slept in days. He smelled like he hadn't bathed in a week. I felt him closing harder around my throat, and my head was getting lighter as I came closer to passing out.

"Nobody does that to me! You hear me?" He started to shake my throat with both hands and hit my head against the ground. "Did you think you were just going to get away with it? Where's my fucking money? WHERE IS

MY FUCKING MONEY?" His hysterical voice got farther and farther away, everything started going dark, I felt a stabbing pain in my side, and suddenly I felt him release his grip, and everything went black.

***

"Miss. Miss. The police and the ambulance is on the way. Miss." Cataldo was kneeling next to me, and Pearl was next to him, crying, talking to Hank on my cell phone.

"I don't know," she was frantically trying to explain to Hank what she was seeing. "A man attacked her, he was choking her—Cataldo's car came down the driveway just in time. I was inside, I had no idea. I didn't hear her, I didn't see, oh my God, I'm so sorry, Margaret." Pearl was wiping tears from her face.

"Mom," I said. My voice was hoarse and it hurt to talk. It hurt to breathe, like a searing pain on the side of my torso. I had a terrible headache. "It was Brody. He's *here,*" I whispered.

Pearl looked at me with real fear in her eyes. "Hank," she said slowly, never taking her eyes off me, "it was Brody… yes. *Now.*"

She hung up the phone. "Hank is on his way to meet us at the hospital," she said.

The police and the ambulance arrived, and I gave what short statement I could to the police, but I left out the part about how he was asking where his money was. I was scared to death where that money really came from, and that our whole house of cards would tumble down when the whole story came out. I told the officers he seemed high on something, and that it was, in fact, my truck.

Suddenly I remembered the Glock in my bedroom. I pulled Pearl aside before the ambulance took me to the hospital. "Mom. The gun in my room. Go get it. Bring it with you." She nodded. Cataldo and Pearl followed the ambulance in Cataldo's car, and I was sick with worry about the animals on the farm until the police offered to hang around and see if Brody came back.

"Oh God, thank you," I said to them in my hoarse voice. "I am so scared he will do something terrible to Liberty, or break into the house." The tears poured down my temples onto the pillow underneath my head.

"We'll stay here until you get back, Ma'am," said the officer. "Oh, and, uh, retired officer Ted Krandall says 'hello.'"

I exhaled a huge sigh of relief. Ted. From the Support Group. I didn't even care how he knew about this so fast.

The emergency room doctor checked me out, sent me to get X-rays and told me I'd probably have some bruising around my neck, a concussion, and I had a cracked rib from Brody sitting on me, which explained the pain in my side, but otherwise I was physically okay.

Hank got to the hospital as I was lying in the little curtained-off room, waiting for a painkiller prescription. The way he rushed into the room, and his anxious voice was asking for my name, and where was I, made my heart swell with gratitude that he was looking for *me*.

As soon as he saw me, his face relaxed. "There you are." He reached to hug me but I stopped him.

"Watch out, I cracked a rib," I said, smiling feebly.

I saw a flash of rage flicker across Hank's face. He pulled himself together.

"What else," he said, trying not to lose his cool.

"Just bruising," I said, pointing to my throat. "He choked me—er… tried to choke me," I said, and suddenly the floodgates opened and I started to cry.

All the fear, the terror, the swirl of emotions that came with seeing Brody again, and being overpowered by him, being physically hurt by him, terrorized by him, threatened by him—my heart felt like it was split in half with conflicting emotions. I hated that somewhere in that mix was guilt. Guilt for leaving Brody the way I did. Guilt for seeing him so disheveled and out of control. Wanting to *save him?*

I'd never seen him like that. Drunk, sure. But never out of control like that. The Brody I knew was too vain to not trim his beard, cut his hair, wear clean clothes, and love

284

what he saw in the mirror. The wild, dilated pupils? The stench? I shuddered.

"Hank, I think he was...on...something? He wasn't right, he was crazy. He was definitely drunk or something but...this wasn't the Brody that I knew. He was...suffering from something, on something I'd never ever seen him like this before. Maybe I shouldn't press charges? He needs help?"

Hank slumped back in his chair. "Margaret. Are you kidding me?"

"What?" I said.

"Margaret. You feel sorry for him."

"Hank! He attacked me! He hit me! I don't! I just—I mean he's obviously been through a lot—" I stopped.

Oh my God. Hank was right. I did. *I felt sorry for Brody.* He was high on drugs, it wasn't his fault he choked me and broke a rib and almost killed me. *Poor Baby.* I did leave him a big mess to clean up. I did steal his truck and all his money. It was my fault. Of course I felt sorry for him. Everything Brody just did and said reminded me that it was all my fault. Everything always was! Even his getting fired was my fault. Not his fault, for getting hammered the night before he was supposed to leave for his big job. But *mine* for not springing him from the drunk tank where his own choices landed him. I *made him* want to choke me.

I lowered my gaze and sighed loudly. "Hank," I said, "you're right."

"He threw that same old shit at me. The exact same shit, do I have any idea how hard it is for him because of something I did…leaving out the part about his choices…and I fell right in lock step. I thought I'd come so far…but I'm the same girl. That same, weak girl. I haven't made any progress at all."

"Bullshit. Jesus, Margaret, don't go down that road either! Don't you get it, you are standing at a crossroads here? You can choose the same old path that leads right around in a circle, back to being his victim, his punching bag, his toilet for every shitty emotion he pukes up, OR, *you can choose the other road*. The one that leads to you raging at him. Press a hundred charges, and defend that farm with everything you've got against anything he might try before the police catch him. Get angry. He is the perpetrator, not the victim. So don't let him sneak in these back doors like he always has to manipulate you. He knows exactly how to get to you. But you know what?"

I was so ashamed. Again. It was like a drug that I swore off of and gobbled up as soon as someone put it in front of me. I was addicted to shame.

"What."

Hank crossed his arms. "Margaret. The state of his life is the *direct result* of the choices he's made. And so is yours, especially from this minute forward."

****

CHAPTER FOURTEEN
Liberty Lost

Hank helped me into the house, and got me settled at the kitchen table. He said he had an emergency at work and he'd be back later that night. He said he would hurry, because a terrible blizzard was just beginning to hit the western end of town. He checked on the animals before he left. We still had a Deputy at our house. He left his vehicle outside and stayed inside with us. Lucky for Pearl he favored Scrabble. Unlucky for him he was not very good at it.

Pearl had cooked a pot roast, I suspected more for the Deputy than for me but I still smiled at her making a fuss. I was starving although I only ate a few bites. She cooked me some tomato soup and that went down better. My throat was still sore, and my neck and head ached. The rib was painful if I turned the wrong way or took a deep breath. My chest was wrapped with a bandage to keep it stable but it didn't help much.

"It will just take time," the doctor said. "You'll just have to take it easy for a few weeks." I sighed. I would have to rely heavily on Cataldo. And Pearl.

The Deputy, Pearl and I sat around the kitchen table playing a serious round of Scrabble well into the night. I watched the clock, waiting for Hank to get back. The yellow phone on the kitchen wall finally rang at about ten thirty.

"Hello?" I answered.

"Hey, it's Hank," he said. His voice warmed my whole body. "I'm trying to make it out there, eventually I will. The roads are bad. Terrible visibility and a lot of accidents. I stopped to help a couple out here."

"Okay," I said. "We're fine, just beating the pants off Deputy O'Connell at Scrabble. He's probably going to shoot Pearl." I smiled at him and he rolled his eyes.

"Ha, well I wouldn't mess with Pearl," Hank said. "Okay, I'm making my way. Do you need anything?"

I closed my eyes. Gratitude was the ultimate painkiller. "No, thank you…just you," I said. "Please be careful," and hung up the phone.

"Hank says the roads are really bad," I said as I sat back down. "Deputy do you think you'll get called out?"

He shrugged. "It's possible," he said. "But then if the roads are that bad, nothing is going to get to you guys out here."

"I guess so," I said.

Scrabble ended with Pearl creaming us both, announcing she was ready to go to bed, and sending the Deputy into the front living room and me upstairs to my bed. As I tried to find a position that didn't make my rib scream out in sudden pain I thought about Liberty out in the barn, with the wind howling around him. The snow was really coming down and gusting sideways. I prayed the roof would hold.

I knew the animals would be warm enough with the barn heaters and their blankets, but I wondered if he felt scared out there, all alone in the back stall by himself.

I heard the Deputy's radio squawk downstairs a few times. He answered, but I couldn't make out what he was saying. He went back and forth with the radio, chattering codes and finally he said something that sounded final.

He politely called to Pearl downstairs in her bed.

"Ma'am?" he said, "I have to go to the highway, there's been some kind of tractor trailer pileup. I or someone from the next shift will be back to check on you as soon as we can spare someone. If you have any problems, please call 9-1-1, okay?"

I heard Pearl mumble okay, be careful. Hank wouldn't be on the highway so I didn't worry that he was in the wreck. The Deputy said goodbye, locked the door behind him and his car made its way through a foot of fallen snow down the driveway.

I lay there for a while, trying to sleep, but finally, painfully, sat up and went to the window. The swirling snow outside looked like a white curtain, just hammering the dark shadows of the barn and the yard and the silhouettes of the bare trees in the moonlight. If it weren't for the moon I wouldn't be able to see anything at all.

We had turned the Christmas lights off because of the wind. The Deputy's car was long gone and there was no sign of Hank yet. It was eleven thirty. I stared at the barn roof. I could see the snow piling up on top of it, and it made me very nervous.

The paddock was a wide stretch of greyish-white in the moonlight, obscured by the wall of snow blowing hard across the field. I stared at it for a while, mesmerized by the rhythmic way a snow storm falls from the sky.

I could barely make out the outline of the fast disappearing paddock fence, and my heart stopped a full beat in my chest. Something dark moved along the fence, by the side of the barn. Was it a shadow? It looked like it came from behind the barn, in the direction of the woods. I blinked. I looked harder. It was gone in the blur of snow, wind and darkness.

I pulled a sweatshirt on, wincing as I moved my arm near the fracture, grabbed my cell phone and made my way downstairs.

"Pearl?" I said. "Pearl! Wake up! I think Brody is out there! I saw something by the barn!"

I dialed 9-1-1 and the operator answered.

"9-1-1, what is your emergency?"

I explained our location and gave the operator the history of the problem and told her Brody, the suspect, might have returned. She said she would put a call out but that all Deputies were dealing with the pile up on the highway, and as soon as someone was available they would be there.

Pearl was sitting up in bed like a meerkat, her eyes wide with terror.

"What do we do?" she said.

"Nothing, we just sit. Where is the Glock?" I said.

"Oh my God, Margaret."

"What, Mom?"

"I left it in the car."

My heart fell deep into my gut. "Where in the car?"

"In the glove box," she said, protesting "I was so upset by everything, and I couldn't bring the thing into the hospital, I didn't know what to do with it. I stuck it in there."

"Well at least it's not laying on the seat," I said. I dialed Hank on my cell phone but it went straight to voice mail.

"Mom," I said. "I have to go out and get that gun. I'm going to run out there and grab it. You watch from the door and if you see anything, call 9-1-1."

Pearl looked at me uneasily, and followed me to the door. I put on my Fat Ugly Blue Coat and looked out the front porch. I couldn't see anything but the whipping snow and dark shadows. I flicked on the porch light, but it only illuminated the snow whirling in front of the porch. I could see the car parked, snow piled a foot high around it, in front of the porch. I figured if I ran out, grabbed the gun and ran back inside, we would be safer armed if Brody was out there.

"Okay Mom, I'm going."

Pearl held my cell phone in her hand and I opened the door to the howling storm. I ran outside, trudged through the snow and brushed off the car door to get to the lock, opened the car door against the wind gusts and reached for the glove box. I grabbed the Glock, closed the car door and turned back to the house.

Pearl's silhouette stood in the doorway, with the door half open.

I was halfway back to the porch steps when it happened.

***

A huge explosion in the barn lit up the sky with an orange glow, and I fell over from the impact, a blinding pain ripping through my body. I lost the gun in the snow and as I struggled to my feet I watched in horror as the barn engulfed in flames. I ran toward the barn doors, and all I could think was the animals were inside, and how could I get them out?

I pulled the barn doors open, ignoring the agonizing pain in my side, and the flames pushed me back. I couldn't see where they were coming from—the back of the barn, the front or the roof. They were just everywhere—high, and wide. The miniature horses were going crazy and I managed to unlatch their stall doors, and they ran out into the storm. Pearl was trying to make her way through the heavy snow to the barn.

"Mom!" I yelled to her through the gales of snow and wind, "Try to get the ponies into the small paddock!"

But Pearl wasn't able to grab their halters. I couldn't get back to Liberty's stall, the flames were too high so I went around through waist-high snow drifts to the back of the barn. One door was blown off by the explosion, and flames were coming out everywhere, through the upper hay loft, and creeping through slats in the wood. The roof was holding for the moment. Snow was melting off the roof but it was only creating a watery mess. It wasn't enough to put out any of the flames.

"Liberty!" I called to him. "Liberty!" I couldn't hear him. I listened for his neigh or him kicking, but I heard nothing through the wind, the flames and the crushing sound of burning wood falling around me.

I saw the headlights of Hank's truck come up the driveway, plowing through the snow with his four-wheel drive.

"Hank! Thank God!" I screamed. I made my way back around to the front of the barn, trying to breathe through the sharp stabbing in my chest.

Pearl managed to guide a cow to the paddock, yanking and pulling on her halter. I have no idea where she found the strength. The wind alone was almost blowing Pearl over.

Hank saw me and came running toward me, his face twisted with horror and confusion.

"Hank!" I screamed. "Help me get the animals into the paddock!" He nodded and ran after one of the miniature ponies.

I looked up at the barn, a mountainous inferno of popping sparks, swirling ashes, snow, wood, and hay.

I heard a distant fire truck on the main road, and I could see the glimmer of the flickering lights but my heart sank. I knew they would never be able to get down the driveway in time to save the barn.

"Liberty! Hank you have to get Liberty out of there! Liberty is in there!"

My grandfather's heart and soul. Our whole future on this farm. Our business. *Liberty.* I broke down in tears and started screaming.

The fire truck was inching its way down the driveway, following in Hank's truck's tire tracks. We had a fire hydrant on the property but it was buried in the snow.

Hank was running back from the paddock. He managed to save most of the animals but some were unaccounted for. One of the cows was unaccounted for. I could only assume she was inside. I was devastated, watching everything we had worked for, literally burning before our eyes.

Hank looked at me, his eyes wide with fear. I was crushed, screaming hysterically that Liberty was trapped inside.

"I'll get him," Hank said. "Don't worry. I will get him." And he turned to run toward the barn. Just as he made his first step, the roof sparked, a flame shot up, and half of the roof in the front of the barn collapsed onto itself, and a huge ball of fire leapt into the sky.

I fell to my knees, snow squall and ashes whipping around me. I couldn't even yell, I couldn't fight anymore. My heart was in that barn. My best friend. My strength. How would we survive? How would I survive? Liberty saved me, and I couldn't save him. The key to my healing, my escape, the thing I owed everything good to, the last six months of rebuilding, of starting over and taking chances, making choices, all the inspiration for all the beautiful things I was so grateful for, just exploded in horror right before my eyes. And I watched, completely helpless, and couldn't stop it.

***

As dawn broke, the firefighters had gotten most of the flames out, and the storm's winds had died down, which allowed the snow to help extinguish some of the embers. The firefighters were trying to figure out what caused the explosion, whether it was in fact Brody I'd seen by the back of the barn, or if it was some kind of electrical fire or something else.

Pearl and I stood outside, oblivious to the cold, in shock as our entire future, and our past, burned to the ground. The daylight revealed a blackened piled of burned wood, and when we could get near enough to the back part of the barn to see where Liberty's stall was, Hank and I held hands tightly as we approached the wreckage.

My heart was in my throat. I couldn't bear to see my
beloved savior, this magical golden spirit that nuzzled up
to me on the side of that highway, who first alerted Bud
and Joy to my presence there, who walked with me all
those mornings, and listened to my problems, looking into
my eyes with more soul than most humans I'd ever met—I
couldn't bear to see his remains in that fire. I sobbed
uncontrollably as Hank and I, guided by a tall, beefy
firefighter named Chris, navigated the burnt wreckage of
the stalls. We knew we had lost a cow, and one of the
miniature horses. My heart was so heavy for them. But I
could not bear losing Liberty.

Chris held up his hand as we stepped over the fallen roof
trusses. Hank wiped a tear from his face. I squeezed his
hand. I knew Hank had done everything he could to shore
up that roof.

Chris stopped us. "Let me go forward, for a minute," he
said. "I will wave you forward if it's okay." I nodded, and
the tears flowed harder down my face. I looked at Hank,
my eyes pleading for him to somehow wave some magic
wand that this was all just a nightmare.

The grey sky shone through half the missing roof above as
the firefighter carefully stepped on charred boards and
tested the piles of wreckage for how much weight they
could bear. He reached Liberty's stall, and I could see
most of the structure around it was burned. My stomach
turned and my heart tightened.

Chris' reflective yellow jacket moved inside the stall, and his helmet disappeared as he leaned down toward the ground. I buried my head in Hank's chest and sobbed.

Hank held me tight, but for once his strong arms couldn't ease any pain in me. His calm, honest strength could do nothing for the loss I felt.

"Ma'am?" Chris called out. He stood up and took off his helmet, and wiped the soot off his face. My chest felt like it was shot out. I braced myself.

"There's nothing here. *The stall is empty*."

***

"What?" I said. I scrambled over the boards, forgetting about the terrible pain in my side. I tripped and stumbled my way to the stall and looked for myself. There was nothing there. No charred remains of my beloved friend. My inspiration, my spirit. *He escaped*? I put my head down and uncontrollably wept, this time in gratitude. I didn't know where he was, but at least he didn't die in this stall, trapped, wondering why I wasn't coming to save him.

I felt a swell of pride that whatever happened, My Liberty somehow found a way. He wouldn't go out like this. He went out on his terms. On his side of the line.

There was so much wreckage that the firefighter said gently that he might be buried somewhere else, but I knew if he wasn't in that stall, he wasn't anywhere in these ashes.

I looked out at the woods, the leafless tree limbs poking upward from the blurred snowy landscape. As soon as I could, I would go looking for him. I was afraid of what I would find in the freezing temperatures, but I would never leave him out there alone.

I knew I had to call Bud and Joy at some point, but I couldn't. Not until I had real information to give them. And on top of being grief-stricken I was so ashamed. I had lost their boy. My boy. I was shattered seven ways from Sunday. I would put off calling them as long as I could.

Pearl and I spent the rest of the day figuring out temporary shelter for all the animals, and going over insurance papers and whatever finances we had left.

The consensus from the fire investigators was that accelerant was found all over the barn, including on the burnt-out remains of the heaters, which would indicate arson. It had to be Brody, and I let the Sheriff's Deputies know what I saw the night of the fire. The storm blew away any evidence of footprints in the snow, and I couldn't imagine how Brody survived the night in that weather, but it could only have been him. He figured out a way to finally destroy the one last tiny bit I had left of what he thought he killed completely —my spirit. I wondered if Brody lay buried in those ashes somewhere.

The plows came to take care of the driveway. I recovered the Glock from the snow by Pearl's car. The sickening smell of smoke and wet ashes was everywhere, in my nose, my hair, my clothes, my skin. It turned my stomach. I hadn't eaten since before the fire.

Pearl and I sat at the kitchen table in exhausted silence, completely defeated. Hank heated up some chicken noodle soup on the stove.

"You two need to eat this," he said.

"Hank I have to go out and look for Liberty," I said.

"I know you do," Hank said. "We'll go. You need to cinch up that bandage and eat this soup, and we will go. I'd try to stop you, but there would be no point." He poured us all a bowl of soup, and we ate in silence, stunned at the losses we had just suffered, and the uncertain road ahead.

The soup tasted like nothing to me, but it felt good to get something in my body, and I knew I needed some fuel to get out in the woods to look for Liberty. I left Pearl to deal with the insurance and police and fire investigators who were crawling all over the property.

News crews showed up but we kept their trucks at the road, so they couldn't disrupt the responders. "Vultures," I mumbled as I saw their satellite trucks line up along the main road.

But Pearl shook her head. "No, Margaret. They will be very useful to us. You'll see. Let me handle them." I shrugged.

Hank and I bundled up and ventured out to the woods. The snow was a good two feet deep, which was exhausting to trudge through. Every step brought a knife stabbing into my ribs, but I pressed on. I wondered if we would find Brody's frozen body. Or find him alive, and shoot him. And leave him there.

The heavy snowfall and winds wiped away any trace of footprints or tracks that might have been left, so Hank and I started calling for Liberty when we got to the edge of the trees.

I called for him as loudly as I could.

We were outside for hours, and when we got to the fork in the trail, we couldn't go any further.

"This is impassable," Hank said. "We just can't get there. He stood face to face with me, and put his arms around me gently. "We need to turn back right now. But we will figure out a better plan. If he's out there, we will find him."

I collapsed into him and the tears poured down my face. My body trembled from the cold, from fatigue, from pain, from the loss of my friend. Grampa's barn. My future, my past, everything I was counting on, all these gifts I'd been given. Everything that was my responsibility. I let everything and everyone down. I blew it, in every way possible. *Look what I did.*

I slid to the ground, my legs just giving out beneath me.

Hank tried to hold me up but I cried out in pain. The tears wouldn't stop—I couldn't make them stop. My breathing became fast and shallow, and I had no control over my own body.

"Maggie, shhhh. Calm down. Slow your breathing. It's okay, we will find him. We will fix this. We will get through this. Maggie—"

His words had no effect, they just bounced off my ears.

He fumbled in his pocket for his cell phone and called for an ambulance, and I heard him say he thought I was having a panic attack.

Hank scooped me up, and my body melted into all his strength as his long legs carried me through the snow back to the house.

How would I ever recover now? There was no fifty-grand under the seat this time. No kind stranger with coffee. No Bud and Joy. They gave me their most prized possession and I lost and destroyed him. No farm to go home to. I destroyed that too. I brought Brody into this, I brought tragedy, ruin and loss into the whole equation. I had no words in that moment, just tears.

Look what I did.

****

CHAPTER FIFTEEN
Choosing Right

Hank rode with me in the ambulance to the hospital. I'd been in and out of a strange fog since I collapsed in the woods. My breathing was slowing, thanks to some shot they'd given me. I felt for my coat pocket. I looked nervously up at Hank. He smiled. "I gave it to Pearl," he said, knowing I was looking for the Glock.

"Stop worrying," he said emphatically. "We are going to take care of everything," he said. "You need to heal your body, do you understand? They said you're dehydrated for Chrissakes."

I looked up at a saline bag bobbing as the ambulance drove along. It was dripping fluids into an I-V taped onto my hand.

"Margaret," he said sternly. "Stop. I've got this. Take a deep breath for me."

I did as he said, slowly. It helped. The medic took my blood pressure and looked at Hank, with a glance that did not say "good news."

I started to cry again. "I'm sorry, I'm sorry, I don't know why I'm falling apart again, I know everyone is counting on me, and we have so much to take care of—"

Hank put two fingers gently over my lips.

"Shhhh," he said scoldingly. "I said I got this. Stop. Just stop."

He leaned down to whisper in my ear. "Margaret. You are overwhelmed. And it's okay. I'm here. There are all kinds of people who want to help. Let them."

He wiped the tears that were dribbling down the side of my face.

"Hank, I'm so sorry," I whispered. "I'm so sorry I ever dragged you into all of this. Everyone—Bud, Joy, Pearl Liberty—" my heart collapsed on the inside as I started to sob again. "He's gone...he's gone..." I kept repeating.

Hank motioned to the medic to give me another shot and the medic nodded.

"Margaret, I'm going to say this right in front of this guy here," he said. "The past few months have been the best of my adult life. You are so special. *Special to me.* You are true-blue, you are open-hearted, you are a seeker, a soul-searcher, a person who in spite of having the shit kicked out of her got up *one more time*. I love that about you. And all this bullshit happening right now, we're going to handle it. It will be handled. Just like everything else. The people who care about you will help you, if you let them.

And as for me, right now, why would you rob me of this chance to be Your Hero?"

He leaned over and kissed me gently on the lips. I felt my heart slow, finally.

The medic fed something into the I-V, and I started to drift into la-la land. My last thoughts were good ones, before I passed out. They were of Liberty, and he was running…he was charging, hard, glowing like the sun, running forward, toward me in a fury, with snow and light and energy swirling all around him.

***

Pearl was back at the farm, filling out paperwork for the insurance company. She sat at her desk, eyeglasses perched on her nose, carefully notating every single detail with sticky flags and Post-It notes.

She pushed the emotions out of her heart for the time being. She would cry later. I needed to cry now, so Pearl picked up the slack. She figured when I got myself back together in a day or two, she'd let herself feel something.

We had the sense to purchase fire insurance on the barn, and she was figuring out what it would take to get through the police reports and arson charges, to get the actual settlements.

Pearl was an astute businesswoman, when she had skin in the game. But this was also Pearl 2.0, knowing there was so much more at stake here than just an insurance check.

We had begun to build something—a little tribe, a community of misfit volunteers, animals we rescued, a sanctuary. And although our sanctuary had been invaded, Pearl looked at all of it differently than I did. She had a steely determination to right the ship not only to where it was before, but better.

She saw an opportunity, especially in the insurance money, to rebuild stronger and better, and take the lemons and make the best fucking lemonade anybody would ever drink.

The Fire Chief himself had taken a liking to Pearl. Chief Thomas Haloran was a roundish man, sturdy and compact with no right angles anywhere, who could wander onto a fire scene and instinctively understand it—where the fire started, how to put it out. He also could sniff out scam artists, and people who set their high-payment cars on fire on the outskirts of town for the insurance money.

He sat with Pearl and helped her with the investigation information.

"Ms. Pearl this is a pretty cut and dry arson case," he said. "The deaths of the animals and the dollar amount makes it a felony, so the police will talk to the District Attorney and press charges on this Brody fellow, but proving he did it may be tough. No one saw him, he ain't around to confess, no evidence, etc.

"But as for the insurance payouts and all of that, our reports will detail the arson as the cause. The only issue is this. You will have to make sure no one suspects you burned down your own barn."

Pearl was deeply offended. "What the hell—"

"Now Ma'am, I know that's crazy but you wouldn't believe the things folks do for a big insurance check. Hell they murder people," he said. "I don't see no reason to say it's a suspicious fire in the sense that we think it was you. I believe it was this Brody character. But understand that you will be dealing with these County suits in the D.A.'s office, who have no idea who Brody is from a bag of assholes and all they know is a small farm had a fire, and somebody set it. And no one has a motive except you with your big insurance check."

He tapped his fingertips together, his elbows resting on the table. "So I'm not sure I'd hold out so much hope for getting him arrested for this crime is what I'm saying."

Pearl frowned.

"Just do what you can," she said peering sternly over her glasses. "And help me fill out these forms to a 'T'."

Chief Haloran left about an hour later, and the police investigators had a photographer there too, taking pictures and marking crime scene tape off. There had been no sign of Brody, or Liberty, anywhere in the ashes, and no more animals. So far we had officially lost one miniature horse, one cow, four chickens, and one cat was unaccounted for. Pearl was deeply upset about the cat, Gregory. He had been around since Gramma Helen was alive.

Around two o'clock, Pearl made herself a turkey sandwich and turned on the television. She was exhausted. A Deputy was supposed to arrive at five o'clock and stay through the night to watch over her and the house. Pearl watched Judge Judy scold a man who tried to scam a woman with a bad car sale.

"Deadbeat," Pearl said, and dozed off, the television still on.

***

Pearl woke up to the sound of the Deputy knocking on the door. In the blue light of the TV she scrambled to get to her feet. Half-asleep, she shuffled to the front door and opened it without even hesitating.

A blunt whack to the side of her head knocked her to the ground, tipping over the small table that had Cataldo's miniature wooden carving of Liberty on it.

Brody, covered in frozen snow towered over her. He was holding a piece of burnt wood in his hand.

"Pearl." he said. "Where is Maggie?"

"She's not here," Pearl said, her head down and her ears ringing from the blow. "She's at the hospital. You don't need to hurt me, Brody," she said. "I'm not going to fight you. Just tell me what you want, you can have it."

"Okay, I want my fifty thousand dollars." he said. "I want my truck. I see it's parked outside. He closed the door and turned on a light. "Who else is here, Pearl? You know we've never officially met. I'm sure Maggie told you a lot of horrible things about me."

Pearl kept her face to the floor. She tried to hold her hand over the bleeding wound on her cheek. "Ha, well same here, right?" She chuckled meekly.

"Listen." Pearl lifted her head slightly. "Really, you don't need to hurt me. I'm just an old lady. I have no beef with you. I don't know what money you're talking about. But we can find the truck keys, you can have it. Maybe if we can talk for a minute I can help you find the money too? Maggie never told me about any money. She was—she was hurt in the fire. Our barn burned down last night. As you can see. Maybe you're hungry, you look cold, and hungry, Dear. I could make us some food? Let's get you warmed up and fed? You don't need to hurt me."

Brody stood over her, motionless. Pearl lifted her hands off the floor and showed her palms, one bloody, smilingly slightly up at him.

"I am hungry," he said. "Oh, your Deputy is on a call... seems there was a bomb scare at Target. Somebody called it in. He was on his way, but he turned around." He smiled.

Her heart sank. "Eh, we don't really need them around, do we?" Pearl said calmly.

She slowly pulled herself up, wiping more blood from her cheek, and Brody followed her into the kitchen. She heated up soup and made him a sandwich, which Brody inhaled. She watched him closely, like a deer would watch a mountain lion eating another deer. His fingertips looked frostbitten.

She studied his face, and how handsome he was under the scraggly beard. He was tall and strong, like Hank, but Brody's was a wiry, tightly wound force; brittle and ready to pounce. Hank's was a steady, warm strength that would catch you if you fell. Pearl wondered which one of them would win in a fight.

Pearl's eyes fell on the percolator sitting on the stove. "Would you like some hot coffee?" she asked gently. Brody nodded, eating his second sandwich.

Pearl assembled the percolator and put her hands in the pockets of her big sweater as she waited for the coffee to bubble up. Without changing her expression she felt her cell phone in her right pocket. She eyed Brody, taking in his tall build and violent energy. He had a combustible, hair-trigger aura, as if at any moment he would leap from his seat and rip out her jugular.

He didn't look as if he were high. On the contrary, he looked as if he were heading into a downward spiral; on a desperate search for whatever he was previously high on.

She spoke her words softly, in a measured tone. "Are you warming up? Eating enough?"

His dark eyes shot up so fast it scared her. He looked right at her face for a moment. He was terrifying in his intensity. "Yes," he said. "Another sandwich."

"Sure," Pearl said, reaching to pull out more bread and turkey. The percolator bubbled and filled the kitchen with the warm smell of coffee. "Smells good, right? It'll be ready in just a minute," Pearl said with a steady voice.

She made a larger sandwich for him and set it gently in front of him, and turned back to the wall of coffee mugs. She slowly pulled down two mugs. "Do you mind if I have a cup too?"

Brody shrugged. He looked at the clock. "When does Maggie get back?"

"I'm not sure," Pearl said. "Soon I hope…I don't know what we will do for the animals. You can see our barn burned last night…terrible thing. We lost…horses, a cow. Just awful. I know you're angry, Brody, but you don't have to hurt anybody. Really. We can just talk this out. We'll straighten out everything." She held a cold washcloth to her cheek.

"It was a shitty barn anyway," Brody said gruffly through a mouthful of turkey and bread. "Easy to blow up. I poured gasoline all over the heaters, and made a Molotov cocktail, then I just plugged in the heaters and blew it up. It was so easy. That's what you get though, you steal from me, you steal my truck, my money, you think I'm not going to make it right?"

"You burned our barn? Why? I don't know anything about that, Brody," Pearl said. "What money? Brody we could have worked something out—"

He got agitated. "Oh really? My fucking fifty thousand dollars?" he said. "She stole my truck, did she tell you that fucking truck is my truck? That I paid my friend Derrick for that truck? And she just takes it while I'm in jail? Did she tell you that part? Leaves fucking Montana while I'm STUCK IN JAIL, doesn't even bail me out, the night before I am supposed to go on contract work for six months?! Stiffs me for all that rent? Stiffs her job? Just bails? I thought no way would she come here. I went to L.A. looking for her first. But no, she's here. She used to say she hated you. She said all kinds of shit about you. Did you know that? This is the last place I came to look because she hated you that much."

Pearl felt the sting of it being once true, but she knew it wasn't true anymore.

"Hmmm," said Pearl. "What about attacking Maggie the other day, here on the farm? Was that you too?"

"She deserved that! I was just trying to talk to her, but as usual, she wouldn't listen. She made me lose my temper. I was just trying to get her to listen. Who's this guy that's been here? He'll find out what a fucking headcase she is."

"Hank? Oh, I don't think that's serious," Pearl said, turning her back to Brody as she stood at the stove. She lifted the top off the Pyrex percolator carefully. "He fixed the roof on the barn. Lot of good that does us now."

She took a towel and carefully pulled the grounds filter piece out of the percolator pot, and set it on the stove. "Cream and sugar in your coffee?"

"Sure," said Brody.

"Coming right up," Pearl said. She took a deep breath, wrapped her pained fingers with the towel around the handle of the percolator and gripped it as tight as she could. "This will warm you right—"

Pearl whirled around and threw the entire boiling hot pot of percolated coffee in Brody's face. He shrieked in pain and backed over in his chair, falling to the ground. The percolator smashed against the wall and shattered. Pearl scrambled to the front room, hobbling toward the table where the Glock was hidden.

Brody had managed to get to his feet, but he stumbled against the table and chairs for a moment, giving Pearl just enough time to pull the Glock out of the drawer and position it in her hands. She held it up with both hands and pointed it straight at Brody, who was now lurching toward her.

"You fucking BITCH!" he shouted. He held his hands up to his face and stepped forward. She aimed the gun slightly to the right of Brody and squeezed the trigger. The gun fired with a loud "POP" into the wall and Brody froze.

Pearl mustered everything she had to ignore the sting in her wrist and hand from the gun's kickback. She had no idea how many bullets were in the magazine but neither did Brody.

"Help! Send help! Police! To the farm! Our barn just burned!"

"Who the fuck are you talking to?" Brody turned around to look behind him.

"Now you listen to me you son-of-a-bitch," she said, loud and clear, "Get on your knees." Brody didn't move.

"I said GET ON YOUR KNEES or I will shoot you clear through the heart next time. Don't you come after me!" Pearl fired another "POP!" that barely grazed Brody's body and shot clear through the kitchen window. She surprised herself, because she was aiming farther away from him.

Brody finally knelt slowly, one knee at a time, blinking his eyes, holding his hands limp and beginning to whimper.

"Please," he said softly. "You burned me so badly. You really hurt me. I need help. Can you just get me some ice and cold towels? I didn't mean to hurt you before. I'm not here to hurt anyone, I just came for my money. I have nothing, Pearl. She left me. She stole my truck, my money—"

"Shut up with your whining," said Pearl. Her hands were starting to tremble slightly. "Put your head to the floor. DO IT."

Brody lowered his head as the sound of sirens grew louder.

"Do you hear that, Asshole?" Pearl asked him. "Your ride's here."

***

Brody and Pearl were taken to the hospital, Brody for the burns on his face and hands, and Pearl for cuts and bruises. A deputy took a statement from her about the whole event.

I was still in the hospital myself, medicated to stabilize my haywire psyche. It was as though I could see everything clearly from a tiny control room deep inside my brain, but the power had been cut and all systems were being run by random surges of anxiety, sorrow, fear and anger.

Hank had stayed by my side but I asked him to go find Pearl, make sure she was okay and get the whole story from her, which he did. She had dialed 9-1-1 in her sweater pocket, and the operator answered and heard everything from the time Brody sat in the kitchen eating his turkey sandwiches and admitting to burning down the barn, to when Pearl fired a few shots at him in self-defense. Pearl had the presence of mind to identify the farm to the operator without saying the address, which would have tipped Brody off and sent him into a blind rage, but the 9-1-1 operator had figured it all out from the conversation in the kitchen, and sent officers and an ambulance.

Pearl and Hank came back up to my room. She had a bandage on her cheek.

"Jesus, Mom." I sat up gingerly to give her a hug. My cracked rib had become worse from trying to save the animals in the fire.

Pearl leaned down and gently put her arms around my shoulders.

"Margaret," she said, tears welling in her eyes. "I knew he was a terrible person but I had no idea he was...*evil.*"

"Ha," I said quietly. "I had no idea either, Mom. This is not even the Brody I knew. He has…escalated. Maybe drugs or something, I don't know but…he was never physically violent with me. He was scary, and he was awful, but not…volatile. There is something that has snapped in him. Oh Mom, I'm so sorry." I started to cry, and hard. I felt so much guilt for bringing this monster into our world. And he hit my mother. He hurt her. Physically hurt her. He almost killed her. Could have. Would have! If she hadn't been such a badass and been so brave.

"Mom, I can't believe this, if you hadn't had that gun, if you hadn't—"

Pearl stiffened. "Now Margaret! This is not good for you. You are not supposed to get all upset. I am fine. I handled this. Pull yourself together! The things you are worried about did not happen. Don't lose yourself in what-ifs and could-haves. Just breathe deep. I know you are mourning Liberty. We all are. But we will carry on. We have to. Do you hear me? We have to."

She took my face firmly in her hands and looked me straight in my eyes. Her expression was fierce.

"Margaret. We. Have. To." She raised her eyebrows.

Hank looked slightly shocked at her harshness but she wouldn't have it.

"Don't give me that," she said, reading his mind. "This is not the time for crying and collapsing anymore. We have a barn to rebuild. We have to put that piece of garbage behind bars. We have a business to take care of." She turned to me. "So soak up those meds, take a deep breath, comb your fucking hair and get back to the farm."

And with that, she walked out the door.

Hank's stood absolutely motionless, except for his eyes. They followed Pearl out the door, then back to me.

The tears had stopped, and the words were stuck in my throat. I wanted to say a thousand things in my defense, but the words just died, like when they hit the open air they fell apart. *I was shattered! I was wounded! I needed time to recover! I had collapsed for God's sake! My body was not even responding to my own commands— trembling, blood pressure, hyperventilating. I had a cracked rib!*

I lay back on the pillow. Hank stepped closer to me, still not saying anything. He knew better.

Pearl's words ricocheted around my head, competing with my own, but hers got bigger and bigger each time they collided with mine.

"Hank…" I said. He smiled. He knew the tone in my voice. "I need to get out of here." I pressed the call button for the nurse, and when she arrived, I asked her to page the doctor.

"I need a discharge plan," I said. "And I'll keep the anti-depression meds but I want off everything else."

I looked at Hank. "Pearl needs me," I said. "That's what that was all about."

He nodded, because he knew I was half right.

***

When Hank and I arrived back at the farm, the sight of the burned-out remains of the barn swelled fear and panic inside me so badly I wanted to vomit. But Pearl's words were permanently in my head now: *We will carry on. We have to.*

I took a slow breath. Hank carried my bags for me, and I smiled bravely and got out of the truck.

"I can do this," I said. "I know there are parts of me, like my rib, and the part that loved Liberty that need to heal, but I also know that I need to be here. There is so much to do, and Pearl can't do it alone." I searched his face for approval.

"You are doing the right thing," he said. "Just don't be so hard on yourself. It's like you beat yourself because you broke down, and then you beat yourself up when you get back up again because you didn't do it sooner. You're human, Maggie. You've been through a lot in five years. You've been through a lot in five days. Just take one step at a time and realize you aren't made of steel. You're made of flesh and bones and feelings like everybody else."

He sounded slightly annoyed with me, but as he turned to go into the house he winked at me. I understood. I understood Pearl's tough love too. Although I knew some of hers was disguising her own fear and neediness.

Human hearts are really, really complicated. Mine ached for my friend, my soul mate Liberty, and wanted to crawl into a hole and die with him. I took one last look at the ruins of the barn before I walked into the house. *We will carry on. We have to.*

Pearl was cooking a roast in the kitchen. She didn't turn around when I said hello.

"Mom. You were right. Thank you for talking some sense into me. But you also need to understand that I am legitimately wounded, and I have really been through a lot. I still have things I need to heal from. But I am here, and I understand what you meant, okay?"

Pearl never looked away from her roast or her pots and pans and cooking.

"I meant exactly what I said, Margaret," she said. "I meant we have things we have to deal with here. Insurance, rebuilding the barn, fixing the window I shot out. I think I cleaned up all the glass from the percolator but that's another thing—we need a new percolator."

Hank shouted from the other room. "What?" He came running into the kitchen. "The percolator is gone?"

"I told you, I smashed it when I threw the coffee in his face," Pearl said indignantly.

"I guess I didn't really think about it," Hank said. "I will be back." He disappeared out the door and we heard his truck start up.

Pearl and I stared at each other for a minute, and erupted into giggles. He had the greatest gift for levity.

***

The next morning, with coffee percolating in Pearl's new percolator—that was actually exactly like the old one—I sat in Grampa Bill's tattered old robe at the kitchen table. I started making a list of things we needed to do: 1. Get an estimate for rebuilding the barn. 2. Reschedule the Support Group meetings for another location. 3. Follow up with the insurance people. 4. Keep track of all the re-homed animals and make a timeline of when we can bring them back to the farm. I left to Pearl all the fix-its around the house—the window, the bullet holes in the wall.

The house phone rang and Pearl answered it. She had a short conversation and hung up. She turned to me and folded her arms.

"That was the Sheriff's office. Brody has been released from the hospital. He is in the holding center now. They are going to arraign him this afternoon. He will be charged with arson, assault on you, trespassing two counts, assault on me, and other minor charges. He wants me to be charged with assault for the coffee, if you can believe that. The District Attorney is reviewing my case."

My eyes widened. "Do they think there is a case for you to be charged?"

"Well, we'll see. Considering what he did to you, maybe not, since it was all self-defense."

Pearl sat down and put her hand on my hand. "Margaret. I'm going to say something to you. And I want you to just listen, and I want you to think about it before you go off and start yelling about what a bad idea it is."

"Okay," I said, barely opening my mouth.

"I think you should go down to the holding center and talk to him. Get closure. Tell him off, tell him everything you ever wanted to say to him. Now is your chance. Say a proper goodbye to him, like you think you should have. Not because he deserves it. Because you do. You deserve to close this door on him. Margaret, I don't think he is going to live much longer. There is something…self-destructing inside him. I can't explain it exactly but you won't have this chance again to get your closure. To really look him in the eye, and tell him he didn't break you."

I stared at our hands, hers over mine. I thought of all the terrible decisions she'd made in her lifetime. And me in my own. I tried to imagine what good could come out of me confronting Brody like that. Then it hit me: it wasn't about making good out of it. It was about whether it would empower me or not. And that was a no brainer.

"Mom I can't drive yet because of this cracked rib. You'd have to take me."

"Go get dressed," she said.

***

The holding center was depressing, cold, lit with a greenish, sterile bright light that made everything look brittle.

Pearl and I signed in and were escorted to the waiting area. The Deputy said I would be let in to the hall where his cell was. There was no visitors' area.

I thought about the night I walked out on him, when he was drunk, and I still felt some sense of guilt. Hank's voice floated in my head and yelled at me, and I chased the guilt away. I reminded myself that I had spent years being bent to Brody's will. Being shrunk to fit his mold. Being hollowed out to remove my sense of identity because it offended him so much. It was my turn now to give that guilt back to him, reject it once and for all.

Pearl thumbed through a National Geographic magazine and I stared at the public service posters on the wall. Domestic Abuse Hotline. I figured they must do land house business from that poster on the wall in this room.

A Deputy opened the locked door. "Brody Thomas?" I stood up. "You have to leave your purse here, Ma'am," he said. I nodded, handed Pearl my purse and followed him in.

The door clanged behind me. We walked down a flesh-color pink painted corridor to another locked door, and through another flesh-colored corridor. I wondered why, of all colors, did the government always pick this one, or that awful minty-green.

"Here you go, Ma'am. You have fifteen minutes." The Deputy stood behind another door that had a window in it, so he could see me.

I turned and saw Brody through the bars, crumpled in a heap on the bed in a small holding cell. They had shaved his beard and cut his hair, so he looked more like his handsome self, but I could see how much weight he'd lost.

"I came to talk to you," I said flatly.

"Fuck off," he said, keeping his body away from me.

His words stung more than I expected them to. Even after everything he'd done, I still felt sorry for him. And it hurt that he discarded me so completely. Nothing about me, even any nice memories, mattered to him enough to even respect my presence enough to address me. He burned down my fucking barn, murdered my beloved horse. I hated him, and I was still stung by his rejection.

I looked at his shoulders, the back of his neck, his long legs folded up to fit onto the small cot. Why did that ember still burn, even slightly? That mirage: The Masked Good Brody from The Early Days? It was all a lie, but I still wanted to believe somehow that inside his beautiful body, behind his dreamy dark brown eyes, still lived Good Brody. He just needed me to love him enough to wake him up. Heal him. I was stunned at the tenacity of my stupid, long-held fantasy.

I took a sharp deep breath.

"No. I'm not going to fuck off," I said calmly.

"Brody. Where did the fifty thousand dollars come from?"

"Oh you want to ask questions now?"

"Yea, I do. Why not? I would like some answers. I think I am entitled to at least know where that money came from."

"Why because you fucking spent it? On what? A horse?"

He sat up on the bed and faced me. His face was blistered in parts, and covered in some kind of ointment. His freshly shorn, thick black hair fell forward perfectly over his eye like it always did. His hands were wrapped in white bandages.

Inexplicably I wanted to go into the cell and hug him, tell him I was sorry, and for him to say he was sorry, and for us to go back to Los Angeles, all those years ago in those perfect, sweet months, when everything was beautiful. It was so intoxicating, so deep and so soul-satisfying, the best drug ever, that all this time later I still chased that long-lost high of our initial infatuation. *Even though I know it wasn't real.*

I reminded myself instead what he stole from me. And what he slowly destroyed in my soul over all those years, I had to rebuild, painfully, brick by brick.

I repeated my question without emotion. "Where did the fifty thousand dollars come from? What do you care, Brody, it's gone. You won. You destroyed my life. You burned down my barn, killed my horse, beat the shit out of me. Hurt my mother. I know I said I came to talk to you, not to hear you talk to me. Everything you say is a lie anyway. But you won. You got what you wanted. Just tell me."

He laughed. "Oh yea, I'm a big liar. You're the one who ran out on me. You are the one responsible for me being here. I have first and second degree burns on my face and hands." His voice was softening. It almost worked, but I reminded myself that this was his best trick. Playing the victim. "I got what I wanted, huh? I won?…Okay…Okay,

Bitch. I'm going to tell you everything. You know why? Because you deserve the truth," he said, his tone dripping with sarcasm.

He stood up to face me. "About two years ago, I started seeing someone."

He paused, waiting for my reaction. I gave him none, but inside it felt like a gut punch. I was more angry at myself for caring than I was at him for admitting what I knew all along. He was a cheater.

"Her name is Linda. She worked at the Machine Shop. And she is everything you aren't. She's fun, she's spontaneous, sexy as Hell, she's easy going, she is good to go, all the time, anytime."

A *Machine Shop stripper?* I could feel my sympathy for him shriveling up. It felt good. *Keep going*, I thought. I remembered how bad things got around that time too, two years before…Brody really turned up his cruelty around then, especially about my body and if I was tired or ill and turned him down for sex. At the time I thought it was stress from his job.

"So Linda and I are really hitting it off and things are going great for me, you remember I got promoted in the Air Force right then. And Linda breaks her foot skiing, and she can't work for a while, so I started giving her some money for her rent. We spent a lot of time together, I helped her out a lot then. She was really grateful for help, really appreciative. Her foot got better and we started making plans, like future plans. I mean basically, she was in love with me. You and I were miserable, and I was spending more and more time with her. You were so out of it you didn't even notice."

Oh I noticed, I thought. *We fought about it constantly. You told me I was crazy, or I was the one who must be cheating because I was so paranoid. I noticed the money disappearing too, but you told me you were saving it up to buy a house, you lying bastard.*

"Go on," I said.

"I wanted her to work less at that shithole, because she deserved better, so I was giving her more money to live, and then her mother gets sick in Ohio. She needed some money for her mother's medical bills, and I really stepped up. For the right woman, I am the stand-up guy. Not the guy you always said I was, some piece of shit guy. For a woman who knows how to treat a man, I am one hundred percent there. And I helped her a lot. Her mother's medical bills, she wanted new tits, I got her those, I got her a down payment for a car, I paid for her and her girlfriend to go a vacation, it was her dream to go to the Bahamas. I couldn't go because of work and you, and she was living with this dude too, like we were in the same situation with these people we were miserable with. But we were both working on it, talking about getting out."

A smile started to creep up in the corners of my mouth.

"So you were at work one day and this certified letter comes for you, from this lawyer. Some bond matured or something, like some thing your grandmother got you when you were born and it was worth fifty grand now, from her estate, and all I had to do was sign for the letter, forge your name, and deposit the check in our joint account we had, and then pull the money out in cash three days later before you found out. It was so fucking easy. That money was for her. It was for Linda and me. I was going to give it to Linda that night I was leaving, after I left the Machine Shop. She was supposed to meet me there. And I was going to give her the money, and then when I got back we were out of there. But her dude was there and we got I a fight and I got arrested before I could, and I tried calling her but she never answered. Because here was the thing: she was pregnant. *And it was mine.* That's why she needed the money. She told me a few days before. And I tried calling and writing her for weeks and she never answered. And so when I was in Afghanistan I got into some bad shit…it was hard over there. When I came back, Linda was gone, the dude she was living with was gone, no one knew anything about where they were. So I got really into meth and other shit. I was doing meth because of how miserable you made me. And it fucked up my whole life. You fucked up my whole life. I would have been happy with Linda by now, but instead I'm here in a jail cell. And the worst shit is, I found out three weeks ago that she is still with that dude, and they moved to Vegas. They don't have any kids so she must have lost the baby. After that, I just went on a bender and I took off to Vegas to find her, but she wouldn't see me, and I went to L.A. to find you, and then found out you were here. So there's your truth, Mags. You ruined four lives. Most of all mine. But that's what you do, right? You just fuck up things for other people. We were never compatible, because you can't just let things go."

I pressed my lips together and smiled. I couldn't believe what I was hearing.

My truck. My money. My fault?

No. My turn.

I stood up straight. "Brody. I came here to tell you how I feel and all this closure bullshit…But after hearing that…*un-fucking-believable* story…this is all I need to say: I thought that I needed you to recognize all the good things that I did for us, all the bending over backwards and all your bullshit I put up with, and for you to apologize.

But I realize it's not important at all for you to acknowledge what an absolute loser asshole you are. *It's important for me to.*

I needed to see what a worthless cheating piece of shit you are, and *always have been*. Even at the beginning, when you were so amazing for a few months, you were lying the *whole time*, which makes you a piece of shit *even on a good day.*"

I turned to leave, but paused, and faced him again.

"And this one last thing: look how easy it was for you to lie to me. For years. About everything. And we *lived together*. Now, you gave all that money to Linda, right? You sacrificed for her, right? You pretty much threw away your life for her? She gave you all these reasons to, right? She was so wonderful…right?"

He shrugged.

"Well…what makes you think Linda wasn't *lying to you?"*

Brody's eyes flashed wide with terror for a nanosecond. He would rather die than let me see fear in his eyes, so he turned away again. But I knew. That did it.

I won.

"Goodbye Brody. Thanks for the truck. Oh—and the money? I spent it alright. *On myself."*

"Guard?" I knocked on his window. "You can let me out now."

****

CHAPTER SIXTEEN
The Kindness of Strangers, Part Two

Pearl and I drove back to the farm and I felt like a giant weight had been lifted off my shoulders. Now I could face the terrible grief of losing Liberty. I could face rebuilding the farm. I was not wasting energy on managing being abused anymore. It was exhausting, chronically navigating such a mind fuck. All my strength had gone toward managing my feelings for this insane abuser.

As we pulled up to the house, I saw Hank's truck, and he was sitting on the porch steps. My heart jumped when I saw him. I ran to him and hugged him as hard I could with a cracked rib. I looked up at him, and to my surprise he was teary-eyed too.

"I had to wait here for you," he said. "I knew where you were. Pearl called me. I knew you were closing that door, and for some reason I just had to be here to make sure it's slammed shut for good. Because if this—us—is going to go anywhere, that door has to be locked. For good."

"It's boarded shut," I said. "I am facing forward. Line drawn. I am never going back there. For shame or pity or anything else. Ever. I promise."

"Would it be inappropriate to kiss you right now?" he said. "Is that weird?"

"Hell no," I said. For the first time I felt him kissing me without the ghost of Brody hovering over us. I felt we were Hank and "me," not Hank and "some damaged version of me after Brody."

***

Two weeks passed since the barn fire. Pearl and I had a significant shortfall in the insurance money.

When I announced at the next Support Group meeting, which we held at Hank's house, that the barn would not be rebuilt, a lot of groans and mumblings went around the room. I couldn't describe Liberty being gone without crying, and heads hung low as we held a moment of silence for him.

One woman raised her well-manicured hand. "Hello, I'm Maureen if you don't know me. My husband runs three auto dealerships in the County. I know some of us here are pretty well-off. And I don't want to sound vulgar to talk about money. But this group, even in its short life, has really opened my heart and my eyes to so much. I would like to propose a fundraiser to make up for the shortfall to get the barn back up. I want us to hold our meetings there again. I know it's all crazy. But in my life, I have done everything by these unspoken 'rules' and all it's ever gotten me was misery. So if anyone else is with me, what do you say? I feel like we need to rebuild that barn, because if all of us victims let one abuser put us out, then what the fuck."

Every hand went up.

Hank and I looked at each other in shock.

Retired Officer Ted Krandall spoke up. "I'm in, but on one condition. Pearl's coffee has got to be included because no offense Hank but this stuff is shit," he said, as the room broke up in laughter.

***

The fundraiser was held at the Broken Spoke, and Hank got the Bottle Necks to play for free. Pearl had called the local television news stations and they did a story on Brody, and the fire and the whole thing, so we had a huge turnout. I was amazed at Pearl's savvy with the news crews. She had handled them so well the night of the fire, and somehow they treated her like a queen. They even came to the fundraiser and did a story on the whole event.

The crowd was a bizarre mix of old money, new money, and no money, just supporters. The restaurant offered cheap wings and beer specials. We auctioned off a few things, including Gramma Helen's old fur coat, which

Cataldo declined to model for us again, and some of our Support Group members brought in items ranging from autographed hockey sticks to unopened bottles of booze.

It was like a scene from "It's a Wonderful Life" as people filed in, putting cash into a giant basket, or paying the band twenty dollars not to play "Mustang Sally" again, after someone else paid them twenty dollars to play it three times in a row. That went on for a half hour.

The band asked everyone for a moment of silence for Liberty, and Pearl and I both wiped tears from our eyes. Pearl spent the most time on the dance floor, and I noticed her talking an awful lot to the guy who owned the tack shop.

"How much do you need to raise?" Carla the bartender asked me as I bought three more beers for Pearl, Hank and myself.

"Our shortfall was fifteen thousand dollars," I said. "If we can even raise five thousand tonight, we can maybe borrow the rest and at least get the barn back up. We want to call it Liberty Barn."

Carla gave me a sympathetic smile. "You know what, Honey?" she said, "That beautiful boy could be up there, just running free, watching this whole thing and loving it." She grabbed my hand and squeezed it. "I'm so sorry for your loss. Everything. But all this—this is so wonderful. This is community, y'know? I haven't seen this much diversity in this place in I don't know how long. You made something really beautiful out of something really tragic. Some good has to come out of that for you."

"Thank you," I said.

At midnight, Pearl and Retired Officer Ted and an accountant from the County got together and tallied together all the checks, cash, auction bids and band tips for the grand total. The three of them got on the tiny corner stage, and standing among the musicians they held a little piece of paper with the number written on it. Officer Ted held the microphone.

"Ladies and gentlemen, thank you for coming out tonight to this great cause. When one of us in this community is hurting, we all hurt. And we have all come closer together through this terrible tragedy. Let's keep that going, right? We have a total here, for Tree Haven Farms, the raising of what will be Liberty Barn, this fundraiser has been a success!"

Applause and hoots filled the room. "Mr. Drummer, can I have a drum roll please?"

As the drum roll started he handed the paper to Pearl. "Miss Pearl, proprietor of Tree Haven Farm, would you kindly read the grand total of tonight's fundraiser?" Pearl looked at the paper and looked out at the crowd, searching the faces. She found mine and Hank's, and gave us the thumbs up.

"Yes, thank you Officer Ted. Thank you to everyone here. Because of you, Liberty Barn will be rebuilt!!! You are all welcome anytime, come by for my famous coffee!!!"

Applause smattered around the room. "The grand total tonight raised is eighteen thousand, four hundred and twenty-two dollars!"

As the crowd roared, Hank and I stared at each other in disbelief. He kissed my stunned face.

Tree Haven Farm, and Liberty, would rise again, even greater.

****

CHAPTER SEVENTEEN
Out of the Woods

I stepped outside on the first day of February, early in the morning. The crews were already there, hammering and putting up framework. The weather had turned unseasonably mild so we started construction on the barn right away. Pearl and I permanently rehomed the animals; they would be better off transitioning to permanent homes after what they'd been through.

We drew up new plans for a horse sanctuary, with stalls for boarders that would subsidize the rescues. We partnered with a riding school and set up plans to open in the summer.

Our volunteers were all still with us, and they would be arriving in an hour or so. Pearl's cat Gregory had even returned. He was a little worse for wear, but he was okay. He stayed in the house with us now, and he and little kitten Johnny were getting along just fine.

The District Attorney had declined to press any charges against Pearl, and Brody had struck a deal on his. It turned out he had dozens of warrants in Nevada and California too. He was out of my life forever.

I missed my Liberty. My heart was so heavy. I placed the call to Bud and Joy the day after the fundraiser, to tell them of Liberty's loss. They said they had already heard about the fire from Frank, but they were adamant that I should not lose hope. I said I understood, but there was such a deep freeze right after the fire. We would likely find his remains out there, in the woods.

I cried almost every day for him—my spirit guide, my silent counselor. My source of love and understanding that words would never be able to describe.

I decided that I would continue my morning walks in honor of Liberty, and keep talking to him, even if he wasn't there.

I waived at the barn construction crew and headed toward the woods.

It was a beautiful, crisp morning. Hank would be arriving soon too, with some roofing guys.

A few birds tweeted and whistled in the bare tree branches as I stepped along the muddy, cold damp ground. I reached the fork, where the path was too heavy with underbrush to go any further and I sat on a big log.

The tears came as I expected them to. I found myself talking to God. Like I was going over Liberty's head, to the Big Guy.

"Listen," I said. "I never really understood You. I still don't. I know enough to see You at work in my life in the past eight months. And I have expressed my gratitude. But that horse, he was so special to me, to all of us. He was so innocent in all this. And we lost our little horse, our chickens. Our cow. How can You let evil thrive like that? How can You let evil win? I lost my friend. I miss him. I just miss him."

I put my head in my hands and just let it out. I cried for a long time, until I was exhausted.

The birds chirped around me and I heard the faint sounds of construction in the distance, as the barn rose from the ashes, board by board. Finally, I wiped my face, stood up, took a deep, long breath, and looked up at the sky.

"I thank You for Hank, and Pearl, and for the barn, and everything else that is going to Bless me today and tomorrow. I will carry on, *because I have to*." And I headed back.

As I walked out of the woods, I felt so much sadness pulling my heart down, like a weight in my chest, but I kept walking, one foot in front of the other, toward the house and the barn.

I saw Hank coming around from the front of the house, waving, and I waved back.

He started toward me, but suddenly stopped. I was too far away to hear what he was shouting. He started running at me, pointing wildly over my shoulder. I couldn't understand what he was doing, or what he was yelling. I turned around to look behind me.

There was Liberty—tired, worn and thin, but very much alive and golden, walking slowly toward us out of the woods.

****

Acknowledgements

This book would not have been possible without:

+ Everyone at Estep & Fitzgerald—the best team!

+ My father, upon whose insight & counsel I depend daily. I love you, Daddy (and his wife, who doesn't complain about the two-hour phone calls).

+ My mother—my in-house focus group. My personal cheerleader. I love you, Mom.

+ Amy Asbury…my editor, my scribe-sister, my life-saver. You are one of the most special people I've ever met on planet earth. I would never have made this dream come true without your help. Literally. I would still just be scribbling plot ideas on old fast food receipts while driving. I love you, Girl.

+ Amy Borg, my canary in the mine. Love you.

+ Natalie & Taylor at Hair Reformation, thank you for asking about this book <u>every single time I saw you</u>. Love you girls.

+ My friends… I am beyond Blessed to have such wonderful people in my life who encouraged me. THANK YOU.

+ My Lord and Savior Jesus Christ. I respect all religions, including the belief in none, but in Him is where I happen to find my peace, my Blessings, and my strength. Thank You God, for getting me here.

I always write with music; I'm so inspired by it…to see the full playlist I listened to while working on "Taking Liberty," visit AuthorRobbieAnn on www.Spotify.com and follow the "Taking Liberty" playlist.

www.authorRobbieAnn.com

If you are a victim of mental, emotional or physical abuse, domestic violence, or you know someone who is, there is help available.

The National Domestic Violence Hotline website is
http://www.thehotline.org/
or if you are afraid your internet use is being monitored, the phone number is 1–800–799–7233.

My prayers of love and strength to you.

ROBBIE-ANN McPHERSON

ROBBIE-ANN McPHERSON

CPSIA information can be obtained
at www.ICGtesting.com
Printed in the USA
BVHW03s0823181018
530365BV00005B/5/P

9 780998 715155